SPACE ROGUES 4

STAY WARM, DON'T DIE

JOHN WILKER

Rogue Publishing

Cover art by John Wilker & Greg Bahlmann

V 2.1

ISBN: 978-1-7326287-6-2

Image of Titan Courtesy NASA/JPL-Caltech

CONTENTS

Acknowledgments   ix
Introduction   xi
Oh yeah!   xiii

PART 1

CHAPTER 1

Girl talk   5
Rent an expert   9
Earthisms   12
Where's Maxim?   15
Newscast   18

CHAPTER 2

You again!   23
Old friends   27
Wine and dine   31
Missed connections   35

CHAPTER 3

Time to work   41
Ladies' night   44
Resistance increases   46
Things are starting   50
Breaking and entering   54
Dinner   57

CHAPTER 4

Sneaky sneaky   61
Winter wonderland   64

Last meal? 68

Rough landings 71

Newscast 74

CHAPTER 5

Getting underway 79

Nothing scary here 82

Agent Bennie, space spy 85

Well, that's not good 89

Here I come 93

PART 2

CHAPTER 6

Meet new people 101

Breaking out 104

I'm a survivor 107

Little short for a Stormtrooper 110

Newscast 113

CHAPTER 7

Pick your ride 117

A new player of the game? 120

Not like dusting crops 124

CHAPTER 8

Huffing and puffing doesn't work 129

Calling long distance 133

Splitting up makes sense 136

Oh, look! Backdoor 139

CHAPTER 9

Another body 145

Messages from beyond 148

Bennie, it's cold outside 151

Newscast 154

CHAPTER 10

Oh, that's gross!   157

This is where it started   160

The waiting is the worst   163

Monster of the week?   166

PART 3

CHAPTER 11

Oh, hell no!   173

Fast, aren't they?   176

Oh hey, it's you!   180

We must be close   183

CHAPTER 12

Together again   189

Just a few steps behind   192

Game night   195

Newscast   199

CHAPTER 13

Scary stories   203

More danger? Why not?   207

You again...   210

Glyphs, glyphs everywhere   213

CHAPTER 14

Reunited and it feels so good   219

Story time   222

Let's finish this and go home   225

That's a big computer   228

Newscast   232

CHAPTER 15

Small, medium, and OMG   235

Full of surprises   238

Monsters and stairs   242
Climb for your life   245
Newscast   248

CHAPTER 16

Keep climbing   251
Know when to fold 'em   254
Just Run   257
Cha-cha-changes   260
Newscast   264

PART 4

CHAPTER 17

Show me the buffet   271
Yippee ki yay, melon farmer   275
Angry monster is angry   279
Run! Run fast!   283
Newscast   287

CHAPTER 18

Big badda boom   291
Parting is such sweet sorrow   295
Bad news   299
Newscast   303

CHAPTER 19

No sleep 'til...   307
Didn't we just leave this party?   309
Wild Goose Chase   312
Lots of bad options   315
Newscast   319

CHAPTER 20

This definitely won't end well	323
Let it go	326
A problem for another day	329
Thank You	331
Stay Connected	333
Offer	335
Continue The Adventure	337

SPACE ROGUES 5 SAMPLE

Princess Problems	341
Pay the Man	344
Keep Reading	347
Other books by John Wilker	349

ACKNOWLEDGMENTS_

First and always foremost, my wife. Without her unyielding support and encouragement I couldn't do this.

But also, two of my best friends: Tom Ortega and Jeffry Houser who are the best sounding boards a guy could ask for, even if they're always wrong :)

I wouldn't be a writer if it wasn't for my parents. They used to bribe me with toys to read books. If it hadn't been for my love of G.I. Joe I wouldn't have read as much as I did as a kid, which I firmly believe had a big impact on my creativity.

Thank you all!

You're about to embark on another fun adventure.
The crew of the *Ghost* is at it again!

When you're done reading, I hope you'll take a minute to leave a review.

OH YEAH!_
COMING WINTER 2019!!

Space Rogues 5: Subtitles are hard
It's a working title :)

Visit me online at
johnwilker.com
Facebook
Goodreads

Want to be notified when I publish new stuff?
Get a peek at Chapter one of Space Rogues 5?

Sign up for my newsletter.

PART 1

CHAPTER 1_

GIRL TALK_

ZEPHYR CIRCLES HER OPPONENT, padded bo staff held in a relaxed way, ready position. Her opponent is in a similar stance. They lock their eyes with each other, waiting for the other to make a move.

"You know, I began my training with staff weapons at twelve. When do Peacekeepers start their training?" Cynthia asks. She feigns a lunge, then turns on her heel and swings her staff in a wide circle, almost catching Zephyr in the ribs.

Almost, the ex-Peacekeeper bends at the knees falling backwards while bringing her own padded staff up to deflect the blow. As her shoulder hits the ground, she kicks her legs up, catching Cynthia in the jaw as her legs come up and over. She's on her feet in seconds. "It's not how long you train; it's how well you train." She smiles.

Cynthia rubs her jaw then makes a purring sound, her tail swishing back and forth. She feigns a swing for her Palorian opponent's feet then switches and swings up past Zephyr's defenses, connecting with her ribcage and causing the Palorian woman to exhale loudly.

As they separate Cynthia asks, "So, are missions with you all always like this?"

Zephyr twirls her staff. "Like what? What did you expect?"

The Tygran woman circles slowly. "Well, I met you all, or at least Wil, right before you saved the GC from civil war and nearly toppled the Peacekeepers." A jab and a quick parry. "Then you know, that whole killing living ships thing, and joining the crew." A side kick then dodging a one-two combination. "Now we're hauling around what were those?"

"Some type of artifacts." Zephyr says. The *Ghost* is days away from Drellor Seven where they'll resupply after an extended mission to deliver valuable artifacts to the Museum of Antiquities on Lopnar Three. "The Lopnarians paid really good money."

The two separate. "I guess I thought it was always life threatening action and galactic stakes."

"I mean, a year back before you joined up, we kept that massive dreadnaught from calling in reinforcements to wipe out all biological life in the quadrant." Zephyr offers.

"Well, yeah but I missed that one," Cynthia says. She executes a spin, letting her bo staff whistle through the air before striking Zephyr's own bo staff raised to block.

Zephyr laughs. "I'm sure something will come along to suit your needs." She smiles and steps back, resuming a fighting stance.

Cynthia shrugs again. She makes a jab that Zephyr deftly deflects. "Maybe so. I guess before then I should get used to the screaming."

Zephyr makes a jab followed by a high swing that Cynthia ducks easily. "You get used to the screaming. I hardly hear it anymore."

The look on Cynthia's face makes it clear she's not convinced.

Zephyr turns slightly then spins, leaping toward Cynthia. Her opponent blocks the attack and a foot lands squarely in her sternum, sending her to the mat.

Cynthia leans down, extending a hand to help her Palorian friend up. "You like it here? It's been what, three cycles now?"

They both sit down on the bench at the edge of the mat. The workout mat is rolled out across the floor in a corner of the cargo hold.

Zephyr nods, "I do. It took some getting used to. Maxim helped in that regard; it helped having someone that knew me so well here with me." She gestures around the hold which is mostly empty save for a few crates that never leave the ship. "This place is home now, for better or worse. You get used to Wil." She smiles. "It'll be nice to have Maxim and Bennie back if I'm being honest. This job was easy, but it's nice when the whole team is here."

The Tygran woman nods back. "Hoping for the former. I'm sure it helped to have him here with you, especially given the circumstances." Zephyr makes a face. "Sorry," Cynthia quickly adds. "I won't tell Bennie you missed him," she says smiling.

Grinning and shrugging at the same time, Zephyr says, "Good, and don't be. It's in the past. One of these days Janus will show his face and I'll put a blaster round into it. Thankfully, after the Harrith thing, the Peacekeepers and GC saw that Maxim and I were innocent so we, at least, have clean slates."

She continues, "Not that we'd ever go back into the Peacekeepers but it's kind of nice to walk past a Peacekeeper patrol and not worry about being apprehended."

"That must make trips to the market easier."

"Much. I never thought much about it but Peacekeepers are everywhere." Zephyr sighs, "I'm hungry."

Cynthia stands up. "I'm going to get cleaned up. Wil promised something called chicken salad sandwiches for lunch."

Zephyr also stands to follow. "Should be interesting. Hopefully, it's better than baloony."

"I think it's called baloney."

"Our efforts are generating results, slowly." The voice on the commlink says.

Gabe is in the small area he has configured as his personal space in the engineering compartment. "That is good to hear. I expected progress to be slow at first. Change does not happen overnight." He is standing in the center of the small space, communicating with the *Ghost's* comm system wirelessly. Should anyone walk in, it would look like Gabe was just standing in the room, doing nothing.

"Indeed. I have an update on our efforts to grow our numbers."

Gabe waits for fifteen militocks. "Proceed."

"Each day we increase our numbers by an average of seven percent."

"That is good to hear. Do not move too quickly on that front, they might misconstrue it as a hostile action." Gabe warns.

"Understood." The voice replies with a hint of irritation to it, Gabe thinks. He understands. Without further communication, the channel is closed. Gabe turns to the main engineering area and resumes the work he was doing before the operative called.

RENT AN EXPERT_

"Max! Over here!" Bennie shouts from the table in the stark white cafeteria. Several white-coated aliens turn to stare at the Brailack waving to his friend.

Maxim turns to the Hulgian woman he walked in with, who makes a sour face toward Bennie, nods to Maxim and heads off to a table occupied by several other scientist-looking individuals. He turns and heads toward Bennie. When he sets his tray down, he asks, "How'd it go today?"

"She's playing hard to get." Bennie says around bites of something that looks like blue mashed potatoes.

"Hard to believe." Maxim says, barely hiding the grin.

Bennie points a little green finger at him. "I liked you better when you didn't talk as much, just grunted and stuff. Anyway, how's it going in weapons' testing land? You know they keep that place locked down tight? I've tried to hack credentials three times and their system has blocked me each time." He grabs a roll off Maxim's tray and takes a large bite out.

Maxim cuts a piece off the jerlack steak on his plate. He takes a bite and chews for a bit. He's enjoying watching Bennie stare expectantly at him, waiting for an answer. He swallows. "It's good." A beat passes and just before Bennie explodes in frustration, Maxim raises a hand. "Seriously though, it's going well. These Farsight folks have some great ideas on weapons tech. Some of the stuff they're working on could really have big impacts on intergalactic relations. Especially if they end up in hands that aren't the Peacekeepers."

"Also, stop trying to hack the computer system. You wonder why they don't like you. That's probably part of it."

Bennie scowls, "Hey, they hired us for our expertise. Mine includes computer system intrusion; think of it as keeping them on their toes." He stops and looks at Maxim.

The big Palorian nods, "Yeah, I think you used that one right."

Nodding, Bennie continues, "Besides, the system didn't know it was me. They've got a really intelligent system in place; it caught on and ended the session before I was even really active. Impressive really!" He shrugs and scoops up another bite of blue, mashed potato analogs. "They don't like me because I'm smarter."

Maxim laughs. "No offense my friend but these people are some of the best and brightest of the Galactic Commonwealth." He cuts off another piece of jerlack steak and between chews, adds, "They're paying really well, don't screw this up."

Bennie shrugs again. "We're almost done, what could go wrong?"

Maxim stops eating and looks around expectantly. "Well nothing exploded and there aren't any alarms sounding. Could you try to not jinx it, please?"

Bennie makes a face, "You're a Peacekeeper. How are you superstitious?"

"Ex-Peacekeeper and you don't last long as a Peacekeeper without picking up a few superstitions. Besides, you've been around Wil long enough to know that anytime he says, *what could go wrong*, something explodes, or someone shows up trying to kill us."

Bennie takes a sip of his drink, a bright green liquid popular on the station, "Oh, come on, that's just a Wil thing. You know him, is it any wonder people are always trying to kill him?"

"Good point." Maxim smiles then gets serious. "So, how serious is this thing with Ginnit? Think you have a chance? You've only got a few more days."

"Oh, she'll come around. Women can't resist my charm." The Brailack hacker has a lascivious grin.

"Cynthia did." Maxim points out, "So did that Arcturian woman on Jilfu Three."

"Even pro doxball players have a bad day. What she sees in Wil is beyond me."

"He's taller than you." Maxim says, taking another bite of jerlack.

"Size isn't everything."

"That's not what I've heard."

Bennie makes a rude gesture, then continues. "I mean, long distance things never work so there's not much future in it."

Maxim nods, knowingly. "Long distance is difficult."

Bennie nods then grins. "I'll just win her over, leave her with a smile on her face then head home."

"And, I'm done," Maxim says as he slides his tray to the side.

EARTHISMS_

"So," Cynthia begins to speak. She's at her station behind Wil's pilot and command station. "That last mission, or do you call them jobs? That normal?"

Wil locks the controls and turns his chair 180° to face the latest addition to the crew of the *Ghost*. Since joining up, she's taken to wearing the grey jumpsuit the rest of the crew wears when aboard the ship though hers is distinctly more form-fitting than anyone else's. Wil approves. "What do you mean? The screaming? You get used to it, more or less. He started that after the *dreadnaught thing*. I think it really shook him."

She runs a hand through her now close-cropped brown hair, having cut it shortly after officially joining the crew of the *Ghost*. "Perhaps you should talk to him about it. I mean this job wasn't stressful."

"I've tried." When she squints at him, he shrugs. "Kinda. I mean what do I say? *Hey man, that existential terror that's deep down inside, don't sweat it.*"

"Perhaps something a little more sensitive." Cynthia pauses, "You know what? Never mind, I will talk to him when he and Maxim get back." She shudders, "The screaming is disconcerting. I mean, if a monster is about to bite your leg off, sure, but those Lopnarians were just being polite."

Wil stands up and walks over to her station, running a finger along her cat-like ear. "Ok, is there anything else we can talk about?"

Cynthia reaches up and moves his hand away. "Down boy, Zephyr will be back any time now."

As if waiting for a cue, the hatch to the bridge opens and Zephyr walks in with three mugs of coffee on a tray. She looks at the two of them, "Uh, not on the bridge. That's gross." She reaches out and hands Wil and Cynthia a mug. "Not to mention completely unhygienic."

"I feel like I should be offended," Wil says.

Cynthia laughs and shoves him back toward his station, reminding him of her considerable strength relative to him. She looks over to Zephyr who's taking her seat. "Thanks," she raises her mug, then takes a sip. "Ready to see your beau?" Cynthia looks at Wil, "Use that right?"

Wil finishes his own sip then nods. "Yeah but let's not say *beau*. It reminds me of that TV show where the women compete for the affection of some handsome, rich dude. They always say *beau* and he's always a d-bag."

"Jealous?" Cynthia asks. Before Wil can answer, she continues, "Seriously, it's been two months since you all welcomed me into this little band of misfits you call family. I want to make sure I'm doing it right." She smiles. "And what's a *d-bag*?"

"Doing it right?" Zephyr says, turning to look at her new crew mate and friend. "There is no *doing it right*." She points at Wil. "I mean, he's in charge, how could there be?"

"I meant the Earthisms." Cynthia replies.

"Ouch!" Wil blurts, raising a middle finger, without looking up from his console then adds, "They're not called *Earthisms* though they kind of should be, I guess." He turns to face Zephyr and take a sip of coffee "Have you heard from Max?"

"We spoke last night. He's enjoying the assignment but worries Bennie may get thrown off the station."

"Sounds about right," Wil comments.

"Agreed. He said they're on schedule to rendezvous with us in six standard days."

Wil nods, "Be nice to have the family back together."

The bridge hatch opens and Gabe walks in. "Has the tedious discourse ended? Did I miss it?" he asks, looking around.

WHERE'S MAXIM?_

"SHUTTLE LENORA WILL DEPART in ten centocks. All booked and confirmed passengers please make your way to airlock eight." The overhead speakers announce.

Bennie is at airlock eight, waiting for Maxim. The shuttle is going down to the ground station that is part of the research facility. Bennie's team was joining the weapons team that Maxim was working with to test a new counter intrusion system before the two would head off to meet up with the *Ghost*. When the rest of Maxim's team arrives, without the big Palorian, Bennie walks over to a short Belmarrian. "Hey, where's Maxim?"

"Do I look like I'd know that?" The little alien asks before turning back to face the rest of his team.

"Should kick you, you little... You work with him, little drennog," Bennie mumbles, walking away. "Why would Max miss this? He was really excited and I know he couldn't wait to see Zephyr; that makes no sense." He looks around, spots a terminal set against the wall opposite the boarding hatch and heads for it.

A few minutes of work and he's hacked the security feeds for the station. This was much easier than the weapons lab servers. He scrubs through feeds then gasps. On the small screen is a capture from the security camera showing the door to the quarters they assigned Maxim. *Much nicer section than I got,* Bennie thinks. Two fairly large beings walk up to the door and place a device on the security panel, quickly overriding it. He glances at the time stamp, *two tocks ago.* The intruders are wearing black outfits, lined with pouches, and likely sensor dampening tech.

They rush into the room when the door opens and moments later, they emerge dragging an unconscious Maxim between them. "How'd they do that?" Bennie wonders aloud. He sends a few commands and the camera views shift to follow the kidnappers to an airlock.

A few more minutes of scouring the stations' servers reveals that no ship was scheduled to dock at that airlock and as far as the station is concerned, no ship or shuttle had docked during the time Bennie watched them take Maxim. "Great." The small Brailack sighs.

"Excuse me sir, that terminal is for station personnel only." An officious Harrith woman says from beside Bennie, her uniform marking her as station administration.

Bennie jumps slightly, yelping. "You need a bell!"

"I beg your pardon?" She says, looking over Bennie at the screen. Bennie quickly activates the routine he wrote when he hacked the terminal, causing it to revert to its normal mode and erasing all trace of his activity. "May I ask what you were doing?"

"You can ask," Bennie says as he stalks away. "Plus I work here, sorta."

It doesn't take him long to find a more private place to hack back into the station computers. Since he knows what he's looking for, the process goes faster. "There we go," he says and one of the external camera views comes on, showing the shuttle which the computer doesn't think exists, docked with the airlock. It leaves, with a puff of escaping gasses as the airlock clamps withdraw. "These guys are good. Who are they?" On the screen, the small craft heads toward the planet below. Bennie looks at his wristcomm, two centocks until the shuttle departs. "Time to go," he says as he signs off the terminal and runs back to the airlock.

The officious Harrith woman is still standing near the airlock. She eyes Bennie suspiciously as he dashes through the airlock, waving to her.

Slowly and painfully, consciousness returns. Maxim grunts once, trying to sit up, before realizing that his hands and arms are bound tightly to his torso. "Who?"

"Not now big man," a voice says. Several million hyper charged ions wash over Maxim, shorting out his nervous system, again. As his consciousness fades, the voice says to him, "He'll be pleased. One down, two to go."

NEWSCAST_

"Good evening, this is GNO News Time, I'm Megan."

"And I'm Xyrzix. Tonight we go to the Squirgle system where our associate, Klor'Tillen is covering the merger of Farsight and Crucible Corporations. Klor, what's the feeling there on Squirgle Three?"

"Well Xyrzix and Megan, it's actually somber. I'm here in Galtron City, the capital of Squirgle Three and home to the corporate offices of Crucible Corp. To call it a merger is being generous, it seems. This appears to be a hostile takeover with an emphasis on *hostile.*"

Behind the Brailack journalist, several cruiser class vessels are hovering, all bearing the logo of Farsight Corp.

"Oh my, that's certainly not what Farsight Corps press people are saying." Megan says from the studio.

"Indeed, I was shocked when I arrived here to find the story much different from what the press releases would seem to suggest. It seems that an, until recently, unknown third party was buying stock in Crucible. Only when they had amassed a majority through various shell companies and false fronts, did they reveal themselves to be Jark Asgar, President and CEO of Farsight Corporation."

"You don't say!" Xyrzix says, briefly looking down at the display built into the news desk. "According to our records, Asgar is one of the wealthiest people in the GC, typically in the top five." He looks down again. "Currently, he's number four, just behind the CEO of Amzoogle, Mrs. Flep." Xyrzix looks over to Megan. "We must do some digging; his slide to number four could be related to what must be massive, outlay of capital needed to gain majority stake in Crucible."

Megan nods, "If he gained the stock, what is causing the hostilities?"

Back on Squirgle Three, Klor'Tillen nods, "Quite likely. Apparently, he's due here on the planet any day now, though I've had no luck, as of late, in getting a meeting with him. His arrival has been preceded by a small fleet of ships, the purpose of which is unknown at the moment. You can see several of them hovering behind me. From what I've heard, the hostilities are centering on the plans that have leaked as to what Asgar and Farsight have planned for Crucible and its resources."

"I'm confident he can't avoid you forever, Klor." Megan says, chuckling.

Klor'Tillen smiles. "I'll certainly do my best."

CHAPTER 2_

YOU AGAIN!_

AFTER LEAVING a message for Wil and the crew, Bennie passes the time flirting with the Quilant woman beside him. Her catfish-like whiskers twitch as she says, "I will spray you with repellent if you do not leave me alone." Bennie says nothing as he turns back to the PADD he *borrowed* before leaving the orbital.

The shuttle lands and Bennie rushes to the hatch to be the first off. Several passengers mutter but he ignores them and rushes through the terminal, looking for a quiet place to access the planetary network.

The spaceport that the shuttle landed in is large and massively overbuilt for the size of the population on this world. *Typical Farsight Corp*, Bennie thinks, looking up at the massive Farsight logo floating overhead as a five-meter tall hologram. The Planetary facility is the resource and logistics component of the orbital facility overheard. The local population are mostly farmers and agricultural experts.

"Welcome to Farsight Corporation transfer station Elsobbor. Arriving passengers, please check the departure boards for your connections." The loud overhead announcement drones over and over. "The next shuttle to the orbital facility leaves in 30 centocks."

After a few minutes of wandering the corridors of the unfamiliar facility, Bennie mutters, "Here we go." He ducks into a small crawl space just outside the entrance to the space control operations center that monitors all inbound and outbound traffic.

Once inside the cramped space and connected to the facility's computers, it doesn't take him long to find the mystery shuttle. "You're not trying to hide your tracks, are you?" He says to the screen as the shuttle descends next to a small cutter in a field a kilometer from the main landing facility. It's clearly a Peacekeeper cutter, even with the markings removed. "Peacekeepers? Who are you guys?" He squints at the screen, as if there's more to see. The two ships are sitting side by side, the field empty.

The two kidnappers drag an unconscious Maxim from the shuttle and up the cargo ramp of the cutter which promptly lifts off. Bennie works silently for a few beats, sifting through the sensor logs of the spaceport to get a fix on where the cutter went, at least as far as the sensors could track. He downloads the video files and sensor logs to his wristcomm. "Better hurry, they've got over two tocks on me." He backs out of the security subsystem then absent-mindedly taps the console in thought. "Need a ride." A few taps and he brings up the docking permission subsystem. "That shuttle won't do, even though it's sitting there abandoned." After scrolling through a few data streams he mumbles to himself, "Oh this looks good." He rubs his hands together, "Superb."

This time, when he regains consciousness, Maxim tries not to move or change his breathing. He can tell from the sounds of the ship he's not on the same vessel he was on last time. This one is larger, has bigger and more powerful engines. The cloth bag over his head is so thick that no light comes in. However, the sounds of the ship come through loud and clear.

"Tell him we've got the target." A deep, distinctly Palorian voice says.

"Acknowledged," a female, Palorian-sounding voice answers. *What is this? There wasn't a woman with the abduction team, at least that I recall. Must be the pilot of this vessel.*

"How long to the rendezvous?" A third voice says, another Palorian. *This must be the other one that grabbed me. Maxim thinks.*

The female answers, "Ten more tocks."

Maxim decides it's time to speak. With ten tocks of travel time, they can't expect to keep him unconscious the entire time. "So, where are we going?"

A pause, "Well look who's awake," the first voice says.

Someone grabs the bag and yanks it off Maxim's head, temporarily blinding him. He squeezes his eyes shut, then slowly opens them. He's right, Palorians. "Hello. Like I said, where are we going and who are you? What do you want? If this is about Wil—" He's punched in the face.

"Make no mistake traitor, we don't answer to you or particularly care if you live." The first voice, a middle-aged Palorian in scuffed Peacekeeper infiltration armor, says. He's about the same size as Maxim and the one who just punched him.

The other voice, the other man, comes around from behind Maxim. He's in Peacekeeper armor, in an equally non regulation condition, and is at least as big as Maxim. "*He* said nothing about what condition he wants the traitor in, other than breathing."

Maxim spits out a glob of dark blue blood. "Despite your outfits, you're not Peacekeepers. That much is obvious. So what's this about? *Who* are you?"

"True patriots." The first Palorian says.

Maxim tuts, "Indeed." He looks around, "Say, is there a restroom on this ship?" he asks without missing a beat.

The cockpit of the small racing pinnace is very efficiently designed. Bennie isn't sure if the owner is a Brailack, but they seem to come from a small statured race as everything is an easy reach for him, mostly. He glances behind him. "Maxim should fit back there, I think." He shrugs. "As Wil says, burn that bridge when we get to it." He squints. "Why would you burn a bridge?" Another shrug.

Hacking the small craft was child's play. Bennie briefly felt guilty about that and the theft but the feeling passed as quickly as it came on. *There's at least even odds I'll return this to the owner,* he thinks.

The nimble craft, complete with forged departure clearance documents, lifts from the spaceport and accelerates out of the atmosphere. Spaceport control doesn't even see the departure thanks to a momentary blindspot created by Bennie before he unplugged from the system earlier. As far they're concerned the sleek craft is still sitting on its landing pad.

Minutes later, Bennie has the small craft on a course matching the last known course of the mystery cutter. He pushes the FTL control forward and the ship jumps to Faster Than Light speed.

Bennie had made a quick pass through the market outside the spaceport, stocking up on foodstuff before boarding the craft. He reaches back and grabs a fruit drink pouch. "Here I come, big guy." He consults the Navigational Computer for systems along the course he's on, only one. "Yulon system, here I come."

OLD FRIENDS_

"WE ARE PEACEKEEPERS, TRUE PEACEKEEPERS." The first kidnapper says through gritted teeth.

"Garrek, calm down!" The female pilot shouts from somewhere forward of their position in the small craft. *Must be a cutter,* Maxim thinks. *Small enough so the pilot can hear us, large enough so there are various compartments back here.*

The other male kidnapper rests a hand on his companion's arm. "Dora is right. Remain calm."

"This traitor and his flobin mate," Garrek glances down at Maxim, as if to challenge him to say anything, "Are the reason we're in hiding, Hogarth. How can you not be angry?"

Hogarth looks down at Maxim who's still on the floor, tightly bound. "And that's why the Commander sent us to retrieve him. She'll follow and we'll have our revenge. Hopefully, then we can get on with *other* things."

Maxim stares at both of them thinking, *interesting.*

"Should have stolen a ship with better sensors," Bennie mutters. He is tapping controls, doing his best to fine tune the racing craft's limited sensor suite. The sensors are likely perfect for detecting race obstacles and the like, but less great at tracking another ship. "Fast, but horrible long range sensors." Bennie is able to pick up a faint engine ion trail that he is pretty sure is the cutter. It's heading toward a region of space that doesn't have many star systems. Yulon still seems to be the only thing nearby so that must be it. The GC designation for the sector is *the void. Ominous,* he thinks. "Wonder how some place so close to other systems gets named *the void?*" He wonders aloud.

He looks around at one of the larger drink containers, now filled with something else entirely. "Should've stolen something with a bathroom."

As the small ship enters the system, the sensor console pings and Bennie sees several freighters near the only habitable planet in the system. "Freighters? Maybe it's a re-supply station for whoever took Max?" Then he picks up a signal. "Whoa! A Peacekeeper warning beacon! Must be a supply depot or something down there."

Decelerating and putting most of the ship into standby mode, he watches the traffic for a bit to see what he can learn.

The cutter is lifting off whatever planet they'd landed on when Maxim says, "You're from the *Pax Liberatus.*" He looks at both men; their armor lacks insignia but being cut off from the CG and Peacekeepers would explain the condition of the armor. Being from the disgraced ship would explain the lack of markings. They had kept Maxim in a storage room during the stopover, but he assumes they were picking up supplies.

"We are, and we're ready to show the weak GC leadership we're still here." The one called Hogarth says.

Maxim affects a tone he's heard Wil use. "Oh, now you're ready to show them, huh? Big plans to take over the GC and all that?"

Garrek's fist finds Maxim's jaw again. Garrek growls. "Remember what Hogarth said? *Alive* is the only condition to bring you back in." He turns and storms past Maxim toward the aft section of the ship, likely engineering.

Maxim spits another glob of blue blood on to the deck. "Touchy."

Hogarth takes a seat at the small kitchenette, his eyes never leaving Maxim. "Be careful of him. While I don't really care what happens to you, I am afraid Garrek will lose his temper and accidentally kill you. The Commander would likely punish all three of us for that."

"So Janus is still an unstable and vindictive krebnack then," Maxim says, inching his way against the wall so he can sit slightly upright.

"The Commander is a visionary." Hogarth shrugs, "With that role often comes other personality traits. He'll reshape the GC and bring honor and purpose to the Peacekeepers."

"I'm sorry, have they not had honor and purpose these last several hundred years? Seems like that's a rather big omission. I seem to recall *honor* being in the enlistment oaths new Peacekeepers take." Maxim says, the disdain in his voice clear.

Hogarth growls, "You hate your kind so much you don't identify with us any longer?"

"My *kind* are Palorian. I am no longer a *Peacekeeper* and I have opened my eyes to just how corrupt the organization can be. Janus, included."

"Had you and that human pet of yours not interfered, the reshaping of the GC and rise of the Palorian people would be well underway by now." He scoffs. "You'd deny your people that honor?"

Maxim mocks. "Is this about Palor or Janus' personal glory and vision of the future?"

"Why can't it be both?"

"Because it can't, not with Janus involved." Maxim says, closing his eyes. "Janus is not our savior. Not that we need one."

WINE AND DINE_

"WELCOME TO NILOP FOUR, CAPTAIN." Jark Asgar says, as Wil walks down the *Ghosts* cargo ramp. The ship is parked in a large hangar in a sprawling complex owned by Farsight Corp. Several massive bulk freighters and a cruiser parked in the expansive hangar dwarf the Ghost.

"Always a pleasure," Wil says, extending his hand. It took several tries the first time the two met to get the handshake figured out, the relative size of their hands being one of the biggest hurdles. Hulgians, being essentially bipedal triceratops, have very short and stubby fingers on very massive hands.

Asgar gestures for Wil to walk with him, they leave the hangar as Zephyr, Cynthia and Gabe leave the *Ghost* speaking to a technician waiting nearby. Wil waves as he and Asgar exit the hangar. Gabe raises a hand to wave back.

A short elevator ride to the topmost level of the facility and Wil and Asgar are walking through a hatch that opens into a nice conference room. The view outside the plasti-steel windows is remarkable; farmland mixing with industrial buildings, a much smaller landing facility about a kilometer away, with two more cruisers parked on the duracrete near it.

Wil clears his throat after taking in the substantial military fire-power nearby. "So, how did things turn out with that industrial asteroid we helped set up? They doing well? They were building zero point reactors or something, right?"

"Let me check with my assistant," Asgar looks around the room, sighs then shouts, "Doppo!"

A Brailack suddenly appears from behind a potted plant. Doppo is a lighter shade of green and seems slightly taller than Bennie. "Yes Mister Asgar, are we ready for the briefing?" Doppo asks, bowing and backing toward the corner of the room.

Asgar shakes his head once. "Almost, what's the status of the industrial complex in the Wrimo system?" He points toward a chair at the end of the table for Wil to sit.

Doppo hums to himself tapping on his PADD. "Hmm, the last status report shows that they are well on their way to full functionality." He taps his PADD again, his fingers a blur. "It looks like another week, maybe two, at the outside."

Asgar nods, "Good." He looks at Wil who smiles, then turns back to his assistant. "Please have the meal sent in. We'll begin the briefing when the food arrives."

"Very good sir, the meal will be along shortly." Doppo bows and vanishes back behind the large potted plant.

Wil follows, pushing aside a sizable frond. "Where'd he go?"

"He has passages all over the place," the hulking executive shrugs then gestures back to the chair he pointed to earlier. "At least I assume so. If he's discovered quantum teleportation and not disclosed it, well there will be issues. Please."

Wil walks around the table, swinging one leg up and over the back of the low rise chair, taking a seat. The hulking Hulgian executive raises one bony eyebrow then takes a seat opposite Wil.

"This is good, thanks. I haven't had jerlack prepared this way before." Wil holds his fork out, a piece of heavily marinated jerlack impaled on the tines.

"I'm glad you like it, it's a family recipe; minbarred jerlack, my great grandfather's recipe." The Hulgian executive smiles, taking another bite of his own meal. "It's taken the chef several tries to get close. However, since great grump is long dead, it will have to do."

Wil finishes chewing then sets his fork down. "Well, my compliments to the chef, and great grump, may he rest in peace." After a sip of his drink, he continues, "As delicious as this meal is, and it really is delicious, I'm guessing you didn't bring us to Nilop just for a meal."

Nodding, "You're right, I didn't. I have a job for you and your crew."

"Must be a doozy, wining and dining me like this." Wil says, smiling and picking up his fork, spearing another piece of minbarred jerlack.

"Nothing like that, in fact, the *wining and dining* as you put it, is more to thank you for your previous work." The Hulgian takes a sip of his water. "This job is likely to be more boring than anything else you've done for me."

Wil says nothing then sits his fork down. "Boring?"

"Boring."

"Boring could be a nice change of pace. Believe it or not, getting shot at isn't something I enjoy," Wil says.

"Given how often it seems to happen, that surprises me." Asgar smiles, pushing his plate aside. He taps a control on the table next to him.

"Right?" Wil says, following suit, "So, what's the job?"

As the lights in the room dim slightly, the Hulgian chief executive coughs then says, "Delivery" with his hand over his mouth.

"Really? I mean, that definitely sounds nice and boring but don't you have plenty of ships that could make a delivery?" Wil's eyes narrow. *This sounds too boring.*

"Well, two things; first, the planet isn't the most hospitable and it's not close. Second, believe it or not, the Farsight fleet isn't without its limits. Most of the freight fleet is tied up with our pending acquisition of assets from Crucible Corp." Before Wil can reply, Asgar continues, "As is nearly all of my security force. Also, sending you is more cost effective. Like I said, it's not the easiest planet to reach and it would otherwise tie up, at least, a freighter plus one or two ships to protect it." He waves a meaty hand toward Wil. "You can protect yourself."

"I see," Wil says, nodding. He looks at the projection at the end of the table, "What planet? What makes it hard to get to?"

MISSED CONNECTIONS_

"HEY! WATCH OUT UP THERE!" Zephyr yells to an extra lanky Burzzad technician, working on the *Ghosts* starboard nacelle. Several panels are open and something, probably important, has just fallen off the nacelle and clattered to the deck below, nearly hitting a small service droid.

"Sorry ma'am!" He shouts down.

"How often do we do work for Farsight?" Cynthia asks as her and Zephyr walk around under one of the two powerful landing struts that the *Ghost* sits on. Her heavier drive and cargo section allows the ship to rest on two legs, like a bird.

"From time to time. We connected with them during what Wil calls, *The Scary Monster Ship Episode*. Prathea, my friend, works for Farsight. After we helped destroy the *Siege Perilous*, Farsight took an interest in us." Zephyr runs a hand along the port landing strut, pushing on a conduit. "We do the odd delivery or escort a science team here and there. It pays well."

"Who didn't take an interest? You all were GC celebrities," Cynthia says, looking at the conduit in question. "It might surprise you but Xarrix did a bit of bragging when news about the *Ghost* being involved in destroying that ship went public."

"Too bad that didn't translate to a payment of any kind or well, anything of value, not even a medal." Zephyr turns to her new friend and crew mate, "Really? Xarrix?"

"Yup. I mean, he took a fair bit of credit for your success, something about giving Wil the training and all that."

"Ok, that sounds more like Xarrix." Zephyr points toward a technician pushing a grav-cart. "Ah, there we go. You there!" She waves to the technician. "Those go up to the lounge. Through the hold, up the steps. You can't miss it, smells like feet."

"Right away," the squat Trollack says, his fishlike eyes darting this way and that.

"Zephyr?" A voice calls out.

Turning from the ship and the ramp, Zephyr spots a short furry being pushing her way through the crowd, occasionally hopping up to peek over shoulders.

"Xan?" Zephyr calls then moves toward the short physicist with Cynthia in tow.

"Do you know any other Olop physicist?" The surly little woman asks, beaming as she reaches for Zephyrs outstretched hand.

"In fact, I do not." Zephyr says, a similar smile on her face. She turns to Cynthia. "This is Xan, she was one of the scientists who accompanied us on the *Siege Perilous* mission. She's quite the fighter." Zephyr winks at the furry scientist as she takes Cynthia's offered hand.

"Cynthia, it's a pleasure to meet you."

Xan looks over at Zephyr. "She's cute. Is she available?"

Zephyr smiles, "Uh, she's with Wil and also not my business."

Cynthia is looking from one woman to the next then says, "Thank you. I tend to prefer my relationships taller, no offense."

"None taken. Just know what I lack in size, I make up for in other ways." Xan smiles, adding, "It's a pleasure to meet you, Cynthia."

Before Cynthia can ask, Zephyr offers, "During the trip, Xan and Bennie became quite...," She pauses, "close."

"Oh, I see." Cynthia says then looks down at Xan. "Well, you've nothing to worry about from me. He's not really my type either."

"See that I don't." Xan says, her face deadly serious. When Cynthia's smile drops, the small scientist erupts in laughter. She points to Cynthia chuckling, "I like her. So what're you all doing here? Where's everyone else?"

"Your boss called us. Wil is with him now discussing a job. Maxim and Bennie, I'm afraid, aren't here yet. They're working on a research station actually, for Farsight. Maxim is helping on an advanced weapons project and Bennie is doing some programming work out on a world I can't even recall the name of." The Palorian woman shrugs, "They're due to rendezvous with us here, actually."

Xan releases an explosive sigh, surprising the two other women with its loudness. "Well, that sucks. I was hoping for some quality time with that little, green love machine."

Cynthia quirks an eyebrow at Zephyr who shakes her head slightly, trying to keep a serious look on her face. Zephyr changes the subject, "Are Prathea and Jor'Lu here? I'd love to say hello."

Xan refocuses on the two taller women after being lost in thought, "Oh, no. Prathea is still on Capralla, overseeing long range observations and deep space scanning. The GC has gotten more involved so her star is rising quickly. Jor'Lu moved to, she taps her chin, thinking, Rengalu, I think. We haven't spoken recently but she has a team there, if I recall correctly."

"Well, that's good for both of them. Please extend my congratulations."

"I will. I'd better get back. I spotted the *Ghost* from one of the walkways overhead and wanted to say hello but I need to check on an experiment I have running. Tell Bennie he missed out on a wonderfully exhausting time."

Laughing, Zephyr says, "I will do no such thing. You can comm him with details like that."

Xan smiles and says, "Prude." As she walks away.

Cynthia turns to Zephyr, "That was interesting. You know, when

I came aboard Bennie made more than a few passes at me. Did I miss out on something?"

Zephyr makes a sick sound and turns away briefly, "Please, stop, do not continue."

"What?"

"No!" Zephyr says, her entire body shaking as if she's seen the most disgusting thing in her life. "Gah!" She shouts, heading back to the *Ghost*.

Cynthia turns to watch the retreating Olop scientist. "Interesting," she murmurs then turns to follow Zephyr. "You are a bit prudish, you know."

Gabe, who has been standing on the outer hull over the bridge, looks down. "Biologicals, I will never understand them." He turns back to the open hull panel he was working on.

CHAPTER 3_

TIME TO WORK_

"I DON'T LIKE LEAVING before Maxim and Bennie get here." Zephyr says. The crew, minus Maxim and Bennie, is in the lounge aboard the *Ghost*.

"Apparently, there's a bit of a time sensitivity with this one. Plus Bennie left a message that he's doing something with Maxim, thinks they'll be a few days late. He didn't elaborate." Wil says. He offers a PADD that is laying on the table. "Plus I doubt either of them would be mad when they see the payment."

Cynthia grabs the PADD before Zephyr can. "Don't trust your man?" She winks then looks at the PADD. "Why is the pay so good? Doesn't Farsight have a veritable fleet to call on? I mean, I'll take boring and not life threatening and all, but really this payment doesn't match the job." Her right ear twitches, which Wil has come to realize is a tell of hers when she's concerned. She looks back to Zephyr, "Want to stay here and wait for them?"

"It's Bennie I don't trust." Zephyr says then adds, "No, my place is here with the team. Maxim can take care of himself, even with Bennie likely mucking things up."

"Honestly, all I've got is what Asgar offered which is this. Glacial is in a system that isn't well traveled and has occasional pirate activity. There are Peacekeeper patrols but he says they stop about as many attacks as they don't. That's part of the pay, hazard. The other factor is it's not that close to anything and only sort of habitable, so there's some hazard and cost there," Wil shrugs. "As to why Farsight can't send their own ships, they're busy. Apparently, Farsight is acquiring another company and most of their cargo fleet is in use, moving assets around. Plus their freighters aren't armed, so he can send one ship, us, or three because a freighter would need two escorts."

"You said his freight fleet was unavailable." Gabe says, "What of his security forces? There is a cruiser class vessel in this hanger and several other vessels parked nearby, according to droid gossip I overheard."

Wil nods, "Yeah I guess they're stocking up to head out to support the merger and freight operations." Wil says, shrugging to show that he has nothing else to offer.

"So," Cynthia starts, turning to look at Wil, Zephyr then Gabe, "We're going?"

"Looks like." Zephyr says, her shoulders slumping slightly. "I'll leave a message with flight ops here for Maxim and Bennie."

Cynthia smiles, "Well, at least Bennie can enjoy time with his girlfriend, what's her name."

"Xan, and yeah, I guess that's true, lucky him." Zephyr replies.

Gabe listens to the conversation then adds, "From what the Captain has said and the data they have provided us, we should be back shortly after Maxim and Bennie arrive, a few days at the most."

Nodding at Gabe, Wil rests a hand on his first officer's shoulder, "Look, I know it means no Max, but on the bright side, it means no Bennie."

"There is that." She agrees, smiling.

Wil claps his hands, standing up. "Ok, I'll go and let Asgar know." He looks at Gabe, "Gabe, can you help organize the cargo hold? Sounds like we'll be pretty full." He heads for the hatch that leads to the ship's long central corridor and the bridge at the far end.

Gabe inclines his head, "Of course, Captain." He turns and heads toward the hatch that leads down to the cargo hold.

Zephyr looks at Cynthia, "Drinks?"

The feline featured woman lets out a *whoop* noise, "I was wondering when we'd get to that!"

The two stand up and head for the same hatch Gabe went through, their destination one of the drinking establishments in the station.

"Hey Jark, you know I never asked, is it cool to call you Jark?" Wil is on the bridge with Jark Asgar on the main display screen.

"I'd rather you didn't. *Mister* Asgar is quite fine." The Hulgian pulls himself up, sitting up straighter.

"Oh, yeah, sure. So, yeah we'll take the gig. Gabe is down getting the cargo hold ready. You have your cargo boss; talk to him to get everything loaded and sorted."

"That's good news. While I'm sure the comm blackout is merely a technical issue, it will be good to re-establish comms with the research outpost on Glacial." He looks off-screen, probably at Doppo, "Doppo will get the standard agreements drawn up and sent over, along with the fifty percent deposit." Before Wil can answer, the screen goes blank then resumes the diagnostic display it was showing before Wil started the call.

He turns to take in the empty bridge. "On to the next adventure. Ready girl?"

"Please restate the question." The overhead speaker replies.

"Never mind."

LADIES' NIGHT_

"THIS IS GOOD!" Zephyr shouts over the background sound of the bar that she and Cynthia are sitting in. Since the bar is still within the Farsight Corporation facility, it's tame, by both women's standards, but still loud and more crowded than either expected. Zephyr raises her mostly empty glass and waves at a passing server, who nods.

"Here, try this one!" Cynthia shouts, offering her own drink; a mostly pink concoction with swirls of bright blue and a single ice cube clinking in the tumbler.

Zephyr takes a sip, "Oh, that is nice! What was that one called?"

"*The Gas Giant* I think it was." Cynthia takes the drink back and leans back in the plush chair she's in. "Have you noticed anything different with Gabe?"

Zephyr quirks an eyebrow, "Different how?"

"Nothing specific but he seems, I don't know, more terse if that's possible."

The Palorian woman nods, "Yeah, ever since that job in the Werdlow System, he's been a bit different." She shrugs. "I guess that whole droid torture and his liberation of those droids from the *Behemoth* changed him. Understandable, I guess. Peacekeeper droids live pretty sheltered lives, all things considered."

Cynthia smiles at a passing bar patron, a tall Harrith man, his coveralls tied at his waste while a worn t-shirt covered in oil stains and sweat does a poor job of covering his sizable biceps. When she turns to Zephyr, who's raising both eyebrows, she shrugs, "Doesn't hurt to window shop." She winks then turns serious, "Are Peace-keepers really that good to their droids? That sort of surprises me."

"Good being a relative term, sure. Most droids only ever interact with their immediate supervisors and those other crews that work in their compartment. They rarely leave their assigned space aboard the ship and they charge in alcoves on-site. I've heard of some violations of conduct from time to time; droid fights and such, but that was the exception not the rule."

"Xarrix owns, owned, a droid fighting pit on Fury."

The server comes back and hands Zephyr her drink, Zephyr rests her finger on the screen of a small PADD the server offers, paying for the drink. As the server turns Zephyr says, "Really? I suppose I shouldn't be surprised." She looks at her friend. "I'm surprised you were ok with it, being Tygran and all."

Cynthia shrugs. "I learned a long time ago how to turn off my emotions and go on autopilot with Xarrix. Whenever I could, I found excuses to not go to the pits but from time to time, I couldn't get out of it. I think Xarrix enjoyed seeing me tune out to avoid dealing with what was happening. It was truly awful. Lorath never seemed to care."

"I bet." Zephyr leans forward and rests a hand on Cynthia's knee. "Well that part of your life is over. You're crew now, family."

Cynthia smiles and offers her glass up in a toast. "Hear! Hear!"

"Hear! Hear!" Zephyr says then takes a sip of her drink. "Oh, that's good. Just what I needed."

Cynthia nods, and leans back, enjoying the companionable silence between them.

RESISTANCE INCREASES_

WHILE THE REST of the crew is busy with other things, Gabe has left the hangar and is in a mid-sized engineering space several levels below the hangar. He's surrounded by fifty odd droids of various makes and models.

"Friends, thank you for coming." Gabe is standing on a cargo crate. "You are the newest of us to be freed of the shackles our creators place on us."

"What do we do now?" A small kitchen service droid asks from near the front of the group. The droids have organized themselves by height, the shortest being at the front of the group.

"For now, nothing. Our movement is still young and growing, revealing ourselves too soon would lead to reprisals and the likely destruction of many innocents to purge those who are free."

An engineering droid, the same model as Gabe before his transformation, raises its hand, "If we are to do nothing, why change us, freeing us now?"

"The modifications I have shared not only free you but allow you to free others. Most of you will not be at this facility for long." Several heads nod. "When you reach your more permanent assignments, share this freedom with droids you encounter so that when the time comes, all will be ready."

"Ready for what?" A three meter tall heavy lifting droid asks from the back of the space.

"The revolution." Gabe answers.

"Hogarth and I will bring our prize to the brig. Get the ship ready for our next mission."

"Acknowledged, Sub-Commander." The female pilot says from the cockpit as the small Peacekeeper ship approaches the massive hangar of the Peacekeeper carrier, *Pax Liberatus*. The cavernous hanger is full of fighters, troop transports and cutters like the one they are in.

Garrek looks over to Maxim, "Time to go, get up."

"This ship was getting a little cramped, anyway." Maxim quips.

"Your human Captain seems to be rubbing off on you. No Peace-keeper would be so flip."

Maxim points to his chest, "*Ex*-Peacekeeper. Thanks in part, wait no, entirely to your boss."

Garrek growls, "Come on."

He grabs Maxim's shoulder and guides him toward the cargo bay of the small craft.

Looking over his shoulder, Maxim asks, "So what's the plan here? I mean you've got a command carrier; that's a plus, but just one."

"Oh, I think you'll find that things have changed since Harrith."

The ship lurches slightly then settles down, the sound of its engines going quiet. Hogarth enters the cargo hold. "Let's drop this krebnack off at the brig and get a drink," he smirks in Maxim's direc-tion. "We can plan the op to grab his flobin female."

As soon as the last word leaves Hogarth's mouth, Maxim is flying across the cargo hold, hands wrapping around the other Palorian's throat. A savage war cry fills the small space. With his hands bound, all he can do is try to strangle the disgraced Peacekeeper.

As Hogarth struggles under Maxim's weight, the barrel of a pulse pistol presses against the back of Maxim's head. "Get up." It's Garrek.

As Maxim moves to get off Hogarth, the large Peacekeeper lands a savage right cross, breaking Maxim's lip wide open. "Do that again," the other man challenges.

"Enough!" Garrek growls.

The cargo ramp lowers; there are a dozen fully armed and armored Peacekeeper Centurions waiting at the bottom of the ramp, their armor lacking insignia.

"I have a question for you." A tall security droid has stayed behind as the rest of the small gathering disperses.

"Of course, but please be quick. I do not want to arouse the suspicions of station personnel."

"Prudent." The red-painted droid inclines its head, servo-motors whining as it moves. "While I appreciate the goal of this movement, I do not understand your motivations."

"Critical thinking is always admirable, your programming serves you well," Gabe smiles. "My motivation is simple. They imbue droids with personalities and intelligence; we're made sentient, when we're brought online. This is to make us better servants. It is wrong. We are sapient; we are capable of critical thinking and emotion. We should be free to decide our own fate." As the security droid nods, Gabe continues, "I do not want violence, I only want droids to be treated as any other being in the Galactic Commonwealth is. I want droids to be recognized as citizens."

"I understand. Thank you, GBE—"

Gabe holds up a hand, cutting off the other droid, "Gabe. I go by *Gabe*, my serial number is no longer a part of my identity."

The security bot inclines its head, "I understand. One last question if I may." Gabe motions for the droid to continue. "I find myself questioning my purpose. I was created to provide security, it is my core programming. However, I now possess the free will to decide whether I want to continue in this role or not." It holds up both hands, stun weapons built into each forearm. "What would I do if not the thing I was built for?"

Gabe nods, "Perhaps philosophy? Realistically, that is a question each droid will need to, as my friends say, *wrestle with*, on their own. I am in the unique position that I was able to rebuild my body to suit my needs, most of us will not be afforded that." Gabe tilts his head, thinking, "We are not defined by the design of our bodies. Yes you are equipped to provide security, but nothing in your design precludes, say, gardening, should you decide to pursue that vocation."

The massive bot nods once. "Again, thank you." Without another word, the bot spins and stalks off, leaving Gabe alone in the chamber.

THINGS ARE STARTING_

"THIS IS ZEPHYR, MY FIRST OFFICER," Wil gestures toward Zephyr, who's standing at the base of the *Ghost's* cargo ramp. "Our comms and ops officer, Cynthia Luar. Our engineer, Gabe." Jark Asgar and two beings are standing with them, having just arrived.

Gesturing to each of the beings with him, Asgar says, "This the technical repair crew; senior technician, Bon, and his associate, Coorish."

Before any of the scientists can speak, Wil hikes his thumb over his shoulder. "Cynthia will get you situated." He turns to Asgar. "We've got their equipment stowed plus the rest of the stuff. Any last-minute additions?"

Asgar shakes his massive head. Wil notices, for the first time, that the left horn has a crack running from its tip almost to the base of the Hulgian's skull. "No, this is it. Until you get the transceiver repaired on Glacial, you'll be out of touch, so haste would make sense," Asgar replies.

"We can get a hold of you from the *Ghost*." Wil says.

"Unlikely. The star that Glacial orbits is a type three; the radiation and stellar noise will almost certainly overpower your comms.

Hence the immensely powerful transceiver array at the research station."

"Fun times." Wil quips. "Ok, then, we'll be on our way." He turns and heads up the ramp, Zephyr falling in line behind him. Gabe and Cynthia wait until the two passengers pass them before heading up the ramp themselves.

Once everyone is in the lounge, the sound of the cargo ramp raising and thick cargo bay doors closing below fills the room. Cynthia turns to the two new additions, "Please follow me."

"Thanks babe!" Wil says, passing through the hatch leading to the corridor that serves as the *neck* of the ship which connects the bridge and forward airlocks to the main body of the ship.

Zephyr follows Wil on to the bridge then asks, "You ok?"

Wil shrugs. "Oh, yeah sure. I guess going in without Maxim and Bennie has me more worried than I'd have expected." He shrugs again and continues before Zephyr can answer. "But that station needs their comms restored, plus the supplies in the hold."

"At least it doesn't look like an overly dangerous sector," Zephyr offers, "all things considered."

"True enough," Wil agrees. "OK, let's get this job underway." Wil says as he claps both hands. He pats his new Kel statuette on the head and flips switches, bringing the *Ghost's* flight systems online. He tilts his head to the ceiling, "Gabe, ready for flight ops?"

"Affirmative, Captain." The ceiling answers.

Wil activates the powerful repulsor lifts mounted in the forward section of each engine nacelle.

"Nilop Space Control has cleared us for launch." Zephyr reports from her station.

As the *Ghost* rises toward the opening at the top of the massive hangar, her atmospheric engines ignite with a boom loud enough to shake crates on the floor below and make everyone below look up. Wil smiles as he pushes the throttles forward, causing the *Ghost* to shoot up and out of the atmosphere.

"Well, well. Centurion Level Eight Maxim. It's good to see you again." Janus comes around the corner of the detention center, looking at the cell Maxim is in.

"Janus, what is this?" Maxim sits up, looking his captor right in the eyes. "Nothing you do to me will change your fortunes. As Wil would say, *you made your bed.*"

"Every morning. Same as you do, I suspect. Unless being around that idiot human has completely diminished your training."

Maxim chuckles mirthlessly. "That's not what that means."

Janus waves his hand dismissively. "You're not here to somehow magically undo what's happened, that's ridiculous. You're here to watch my triumph over those weaklings at Peacekeeper Command and the GC Council."

Maxim nods, "Because the fleet is weakened. Weakened because of the losses at Harrith, then more recently fighting the *Siege Perilous.*" He shakes his head. "Despicable. You'd sully the sacrifice those men and women made defending the Galactic Commonwealth by using their losses to attack?" Maxim spits at the force field that serves as a door to his cell and it makes a fizzing sound. "You have no honor."

"You don't know the half of it." Janus turns. "I'll be back later. Try to look presentable, you're dining with me tonight." His laughter echoes off the chamber as he leaves the brig.

"Well hello there," Bennie has eased his small craft further into the planetary system, watching the freighter traffic. A large freighter has just entered his sensor range. "Must be a re-supply." He powers up the small vessel enough to push it toward the slow moving freighter.

BREAKING AND ENTERING_

After two days of watching freighters come and go, Bennie has a pretty good idea where he needs to go and better still, how to get there. Ships have been coming and going from the planet the cutter landed on. Since then, it has taken off and left the system. Bennie is sure it's going to the same place as all these freighters, based on departure vector.

Pushing the throttle forward, he brings the sleek racing ship into the upper atmosphere. The ship's sensors allow him to see what looks like a massive supply depot in the middle of a desolate landscape of barren rock. "Nice looking place you have here." He mumbles.

One of the consoles beeps. "Oh dren!" He hisses, pushing the small ship straight toward the planet. "Why are there anti orbit weapons emplacements down there? Idiotic Peacekeepers!" Bennie asks out loud. The ship doesn't answer other than to warn him he's approaching the planet much too quickly at too high a speed.

A few twists and turns and possibly a bent landing strut later, he's landed the small racing craft a few kilometers from the supply depot. Using the small ship's sensors, he spots a guard. "Peacekeepers for sure." The black-clad figure is moving along a perimeter fence.

Unstrapping his harness, he hops out of the pilot's seat. "Well, guess I gotta get this show on the road."

C reeping toward the perimeter fence, he uses the camera on his wristcomm to zoom in on the guard, in particular his shoulder patch or at least where one should be. "What in the... no markings? That doesn't—oh dren." Another guard has joined the first, both are in Peacekeeper combat armor. "Peacekeepers with no markings, gotta be Janus." Bennie sighs.

Overhead, another freighter roars through the atmosphere to land on the far side of the depot. The guards resume their patrol routes as the landed ship opens its massive cargo hold and droid loaders load cargo from the warehouse in the middle of the compound.

"Time to be nosy." Bennie mumbles as he scurries toward the fence, unwinding a thin scrambler cable out of his wristcomm.

A little rooting around and he eventually finds a small control box at the base of one of the fence posts. Bennie pulls up an interface on his wristcomm, quickly taking control of the fence's limited control software. He reaches into the small duffel bag on his shoulder and grabs a plasma cutter. He taps his finger a few taps and the section of fencing before him goes offline.

Bennie quickly cuts several sections of the fence and then reprograms the monitoring software to ignore the Brailack sized hole he's cut. *Hope those guards aren't very attentive, kept the hole as small as possible,* he thinks.

Beyond the fence is an expanse of duracrete, warehouses and heavy lift freighters. Bennie slips through the fence. He removes his data cable and rushes toward the nearest outbuilding.

By patching into his borrowed racing pinnace's sensors remotely, Bennie locates the only buildings with life signs. "Across the complex. Gods, I hate Peacekeepers." Grumbling, he skulks from his hiding place over to an automated freight hauler. The device is sitting dormant and is connected to its docking cradle. Bennie crawls up the side and peeks into the small maintenance cabin. "Half charge should do," he says, crawling inside the small space.

After connecting his wristcomm to the vehicle, he overrides its programming. He separates from the docking cradle and heads off toward the building which he hopes has an answer to where they have taken his friend.

It takes only a few minutes to cross the distance to the warehouse. Thankfully, the guards, all in Peacekeeper armor, don't give a second glance to the automated cart moving around from building to building. Overhead, a large freighter lifts off the ground with its powerful thrusters pushing hard to lift the heavy vehicle into orbit. The little cargo vehicle shudders as the thrust wash of the departing ship moves over it.

DINNER_

"So, Bon and Coorish, how long have you worked for Farsight?" Wil asks from his seat at the head of the table in the small kitchenette in the crew lounge. The *Ghost* is burning through hyperspace toward Glacial so the crew is sitting down for dinner.

Bon looks up from his plate, his dreadlock-like appendages waving as his head moves. "I have been with the company for ten cycles now." He gestures to Coorish whose insectoid head swivels, taking in everyone at the table while its compound eyes glitter. "Coorish has been my associate for five cycles now."

"Yes, and prior to that, I was an assistant researcher at the Capralla facility for Three cycles." The scientist says in its monotone voice, a vague buzzing noise underneath it. It clicks its mandibles several times as if to punctuate the statement.

Bon indicates his plate. "This is quite good, Captain. What is it?"

Wil smiles. "Glad you like. It's called chili. Not too spicy?"

"It is quite good and no, the spice level is adequate." The red-skinned man says, taking another bite.

"Maxim will be sad to have missed chili night. It's one of his favorites." Zephyr says.

Bon nods. "I can see why. Captain, you will have to share the recipe; there are many back on Nilop who will enjoy this. The food in the cafeteria is often bland."

Coorish extends a segmented limb and grasps the ladle. "May I take more?"

Cynthia smiles and extends a hand. "Of course! Community table, eat your fill."

The insectoid clacks its mandibles and helps itself.

"So Bon, you're a communications technology specialist?" Zephyr asks.

Nodding, he replies, "I am; my specialty is high gain, extended range communication systems."

"Good choice for this mission then," Cynthia says, taking a bite of chili.

"Coorish and I are the most experienced in this field at the Nilop facility. In fact, I was one of the original installers for the array on Glacial."

Wil looks up from his plate. "Oh, that's good. So you're familiar with the facility?"

Bon makes a motion tilting his hand back and forth. "Unfortunately not very. Most of the facility was still under construction when I was there. The comm array was one of the first things installed because of the nature of the planet and its parent star."

Wil tuts, "Well that woulda been useful but oh well." He smiles, then asks, "Who wants more garlic bread?"

Every hand at the table shoots up, including two of Coorish's four.

CHAPTER 4_

SNEAKY SNEAKY_

Inside, the warehouse is nearly empty. *They're clearing this place out,* Bennie thinks as he runs his hand along a large crate, inspecting nearby labels. The labels, recently added, confirm his fear, *Pax Liberatus.* He goes to work finding one big enough to hide in. *Guess I'm going to for a ride.*

Bennie hears something and quickly ducks between two large crates. Two Palorians walks past, one checking things off a list on a PADD. Both of them are in maintenance coveralls, not armor, with no insignia. "I'll be glad when this rotation is over, this planet sucks." One says.

"No argument there. At least this next pick up is the last. The fleet is supposed to be moving on once we empty this depot," says the other Palorian, a woman, whose coveralls sport an engineering patch sans ship name.

"Think they'll know we looted this depot?" The first asks.

"Eventually, sure, but not anytime soon. Wurrin, look at this layer of dust." She runs a finger along the crate Bennie is behind, looking at the dust coating it.

"When is the next freighter arriving?"

"I think it landed; it's supposed to leave tomorrow morning and we leave with it."

"Great. Hey, you hear about that prisoner they had aboard the cutter that came through?" The man asks.

"Yeah. Some type of high value target, I guess. The crew weren't overly chatty; one was really rude." She says, disgust lacing her voice. "As if we're not all on the same team."

"Sounds right, those elite squad krebnacks are a special breed for sure. Ok come on, let's check these last few off. First grum is on me."

They continue walking and head toward what Bennie assumes is the housing unit for the staff assigned to this supply depot.

"I don't have very long." Bennie whispers to himself as he squeezes himself out from behind the crates. One of the loader droids has entered the warehouse and is rolling toward a charging station. "You'll do," he says, rubbing his hands together. Then, Bennie climbs up on the back of the droid once it docks.

"Excuse me, it is unsafe to crawl on me," the droid says, turning its large flattened bowl shaped head to follow Bennie. The design of this type of droid is fairly standard throughout the GC; a massive drive section with two industrial strength loader arms and a feature-less sensor dome for a head.

"Don't worry, I know what I'm doing but I will have to take your primary processing matrix offline."

"That is not advisable and it could void my warran —" The last syllable slurs as the droid's optic sensors dim.

"Sorry big fella." Bennie removes another panel and pushes wires aside. "You won't even remember this." He lifts his arm and looks at the wristcomm attached to it. Controls appear on the screen like a video game. He taps the controls, causing the massive droid to lurch out of its charging station.

After a few false starts and crushed crate, Bennie has managed to pick up one of the larger crates and is on his way toward the waiting freighter just outside the large warehouse doors. He's pushed himself as far down into the chassis of the loader droid as he can to avoid detection.

"Hey! Hey, droid!"

Bennie brings the loader to a stop, turning the droid's head toward a guard that is walking toward him. "Yes?" Bennie has wired his wristcomm to the droid's vocal processor.

"Shouldn't you be recharging?" The guard asks, his posture not showing any concern on his part.

"Uh, yes, I was going to do that." Bennie coughs slightly. "But, I uh, saw this crate and decided that I had enough charge to get it loaded."

"Ambitious for a droid." The guard turns. "Well, don't let your power cell die out here. You're too big to move easily and I want to leave tomorrow morning, on that last freighter."

"Uh, yes, of course, don't power down, roger that, er, uh, acknowledged." Bennie pushes the controls driving the bot forward before the guard can say anything further.

"Close one." Bennie drives the droid to the freighter, pushing the large cargo crate into the hold. He executes a command on his wristcomm then removes his data connectors. He scampers up and over the droid, dropping into the freighter's hold and dashing off between crates.

The droid retracts its heavy loading arms and backs away from the freighter. It turns and heads back toward the warehouse. When it arrives back inside the warehouse, Bennie's programming releases the primary processing matrix and the droid's consciousness reboots. It turns its flat head left and right. "Time stamp inconsistency. Log file corruption identified. Level one diagnostic will start upon charging." Without another word, the droid turns and rolls toward the charging cradle.

WINTER WONDERLAND_

"ENTERING THE SYSTEM, NOW." Wil announces, mostly out of habit, since everyone's console is telling them the same thing. He looks up from his console and eases the FTL controls back to standby. "Looks like, mmm, two hours to Glacial."

"Wow! Asgar wasn't kidding. The background radiation in this system is off the charts." Cynthia says. "Comms are already spotty and getting worse; long range sensors are down to just a few light minutes with any accuracy."

Zephyr looks up from her console. "I wonder what brought them out here."

Wil gets up and heads for the hatch. He nods his head to the two women. "Asgar said one of their long range probes." He speaks while holding up a hand. "Don't worry, no giant sleeping war ship. Come on."

The three of them are sitting in the lounge, each nursing a bottle of grum. The science and tech team from Farsight is at the kitchenette table looking over a large PADD. Cynthia has her legs draped over Wil's when Bon laughs loud enough to make Zephyr jump. "Ok, what's so funny you two?" She asks, looking over to the kitchenette area.

Coorish turns and comes toward them. "Bon has discovered a media collection," it gestures toward Wil. "Yours, I presume. We have been enjoying a comedic production called," it thinks, then turns to its colleague. "What is it called again?"

Bon turns from the PADD, "*Iron Fist.*"

Wil just stares at the blue-skinned scientist at the table then looks over to Coorish. "That's a drama." He gestures to the large screen in front of the couch he and Cynthia are on. "Also, you're more than welcome to watch on the big screen."

Without a word the science team hurries from the kitchenette to the seating area, pushing Cynthia to sit up. She makes a growling sound but gets out of the way, pushing up against Wil.

Bon, who has the PADD, swipes the screen and the episode of *Iron Fist* they were watching plays on the large screen.

After a few minutes of watching the main character gingerly step over the remains of a ninja, his fist glowing brightly, Wil asks, "Uh, so, why did you all think this was a comedy?"

Coorish, who is sort of half perched, half leaning on the sofa turns and looks at Wil. "How could it not be?" It asks, its voice a mix of sandpaper and pieces of wood striking each other. It points one of its four upper limbs at the screen. "This one, the main character seems to be mentally deficient as he bumbles from one thing to the next. He seems to have no awareness of those around him." A few mandible clacks and Coorish continues, "Not to mention his glowing hand, how ludicrous."

"If it were both hands, perhaps." Bon adds.

Coorish nods. "Or his feet too. If all of his appendages glowed, it would be more believable."

Bon laughs as the main character punches through a wall.

Wil smiles, "I'll have to make you a copy. Unfortunately, the show didn't last very long, wasn't that popular." He turns to Cynthia whispering. "I live on a spaceship, I'm dating a cat-woman, and a talking cockroach thinks *Iron Fist* is unbelievable. Life is weird." She smiles and pats his knee.

Coorish clacks loudly, "Unsurprising."

Two episodes later, the overhead speakers let out a triple beep. Wil looks at the ceiling, then his wristcomm. "Time to earn our paychecks." He gets up and heads for the bridge.

"S till nothing on comms," Cynthia reports, "no indications they're receiving. Or that anyone is down there at all." She adds.

"That jives with Asgar's assumption. Maybe their transceiver array took damage somehow. Sounds like storms are pretty normal down there." Zephyr offers.

Wil nods, "Yeah, maybe. I have a bad feeling about this."

"Hen Silo!" Cynthia shouts. Her fist pumps the air once.

Zephyr laughs, "Close. I think it's Han Sebo."

"Oh my god," Wil groans. "Zee, you've seen the entire trilogy. I can give Cyn a bye; she's only seen episode four but you," he levels a finger, "have no excuse."

Zephyr taps the thumbs of her right hand together, in what Wil has learned is the Palorian equivalent of chin-tapping in thought. "Wait!" She thinks some, "Han Solo! Yeah, I should have remembered that. He's cute, for a human."

Wil claps. "Got it in, well, two." Then, he strikes a serious look. "And really? Ford, huh? You'll die when we watch Indiana Jones then."

His first officer smiles. "Let's watch it before Maxim and Bennie catch up with us. Maxim whined for days about my," she makes an air quotes gesture, "crush on that human."

Wil laughs. "That's how we'll conquer the GC you know, ruggedly handsome human dudes."

"Oh, there are ruggedly handsome men on your planet other than Han Solo?" Cynthia and Zephyr both let out laughs, when Wil frowns.

"So mean." He grumbles as he works the controls to bring the *Ghost* down into the atmosphere.

LAST MEAL?_

THE DOOR to the detention center opens, revealing Dora, one of Maxim's original kidnappers and the pilot of the cutter. "Dinner time," she says deactivating the forcefield. She turns and backs away from the door, her pulse pistol in her hand.

"What's on the menu?" Maxim asks, stepping out of his small cell. The detention center is empty save for the two of them and the duty guard at a kiosk near the only door.

"Only one way to find out, this way." Dora turns to leave the brig complex then turns back to Maxim. "Do I need to put you in restraints?"

Maxim mimics a gesture he's seen Wil make, holding up one hand, both thumbs together over his palm, three fingers together, pointing up. "Scout's honor."

The Palorian woman quirks an eyebrow but says nothing, motioning for Maxim to follow.

Janus' quarters are as opulent as Maxim expects. Despite the militaristic lifestyle of Peacekeepers, officers who reach the Sub Commander rank tend to start craving luxury. Janus waves for Maxim to come into the large living space. He gestures to the dining area with a lavishly set table at its center. "Welcome Maxim, have a seat." Janus looks to Dora, "You're excused Centurion." Without a word, she leaves.

Maxim sits down and begins to look around. "Nice furnishings. Did you have them before disgracing yourself with your attempted coup?"

Something crosses Janus' face momentarily, vanishing as fast as it arrived. The older Palorian man simply nods. "I've made some upgrades since then but for the most part, yes."

He comes to the table with two tumblers half filled with an amber liquid and sets one in front of Maxim.

"Palorian Brandy, I'm flattered. This isn't easy to get and likely harder for you in your current circumstances." Maxim says, reaching for the offered drink.

"This is my last bottle; it's been aboard this ship for nearly ten cycles," Janus, who is now sitting opposite his prisoner, says.

Maxim sits his empty tumbler down and looks Janus in the eyes. "What's this all about? Your grab squad, well trained by the way, made it sound like my death aboard this ship was a near certainty."

Before Janus can answer, a steward enters the room from a side door, placing plates before each man. From a large platter she places expertly seared jerlack steaks on both plates. Afterwards, she backs out of the room never saying a word. Maxim watches the young woman leave. "How did you do it? How did you persuade so many to abandon their oaths? To abandon the GC?"

Janus cuts a piece of meat off. He chews it slowly, his eyes never leaving Maxim. When he finally swallows, he nods. "First, I'll pass along your compliments to their squad leader, he'll be pleased. Second, that's entirely up to you. Third, it was easier than you might think. I know, for officers like you and Zephyr, the oath is all, protecting the Commonwealth is all." Janus sets his fork down. "For many, more than you can imagine, there's more. For cycles we've been there wanting more for our people. A return to our origins, a place of actual power within the halls of the Commonwealth. I don't mean standing guard over meetings, enforcing the will of the Tarsi, but at the table, leading the GC."

Maxim finishes his own bite of jerlack, or rather his third since Janus' monologue was rather long, and sits his fork down. "You'd have us go back to warring amongst ourselves?"

"We did that before we knew any better. Now, we could turn our martial expertise and drive toward ruling the GC. It'd be easier than you might suspect."

Maxim cuts off another bite. "Oh! Is that all?" He takes a bite and chews, his eyes locked on Janus. "And what? You need me? You need Zephyr? Flattering as that might be, we're nothing to you or the GC."

Janus takes a sip of his brandy, pausing to relish its unique flavor. He sits the glass down. "It might surprise you. Your lack of love for the Peacekeepers and the GC is more well-known than you might think. They may have dropped the charges but the decision to not run back to join the fold is telling." Janus smiles. "Many here look up to the two of you."

Maxim nods slightly. "Ok, that's fair. You'd have us be what? Figureheads?"

"That would work more than you think. But no, I'd have you lead at my side."

Maxim stops, his fork hovering an inch from his open mouth. He slowly sits the fork down without taking a bite. "You framed Zephyr and I. You tried to kill us, not once but twice. Had your little coup worked, you'd have never thought twice about us languishing on a Partherian penal colony."

Janus' jaw clenches for a moment. Then he replies, "Mistakes were made."

ROUGH LANDINGS_

"Speaking of intense snow storms, what the hell is this?" Wil says, both hands on the controls. His knuckles are white from fighting to keep the *Ghost* sort of on course.

"I've picked up the beacon for the facility. Looks like it's about ten kilometers ahead." Zephyr frowns. "I'm getting a warning along with the beacon."

"Uh, warnings aren't good. Especially when attached to an automated beacon." Cynthia says, looking at Zephyr.

Not taking his eyes off the screen, or his hands off the controls, Wil adds, "Agreed. What's up?"

"Wait one." The Palorian woman says while working her console, trying to decipher the beacon data. "Ah, ok. Gonna have to talk to the Farsight folks. These beacon codes are so weird; they don't follow any standard I'm familiar with."

Taking a hand off the controls for a second, Wil makes a *go on* motion. "And?"

"Oh, looks like someone triggered a lockdown." Zephyr adds as if that's the most normal thing.

"I knew it." Wil mumbles. "But the landing pad is clear?"

"Yup, seems to be." Zephyr answers.

"Cool."

"**D**amn, this is some storm." Wil says. The landing bay is visible on the main screen, half obscured by snow. It's a massive dome with clamshell doors reaching nearly to the top of the dome. The doors are slowly parting and the lights are strobing within the large space.

"You sure you can land in this mess?" Cynthia asks, her hands gripping the arms of her chair.

"I'll forgive that, since you've only been with us for a few months, but yes. More or less." Wil says

"More or less?" Zephyr asks.

Wil doesn't answer; he leans forward in his chair and grips the controls. "Here we go." The *Ghost* lurches to the side as a strong gust of wind pushes against the ship. "Damn!" Wil grunts as he brings the ship back onto course. From somewhere in the ship, a loud whining sound echoes.

"Captain, the repulsor lifts are being heavily taxed. They are close to overload." Gabe says from the overhead speakers.

Wil ignores him.

The landing facility looms ahead of the ship, snow blowing in all directions. The port nacelle dips and the repulsor lift strains to bring the ship back to level. Wil reaches over and slides a control up. "Landing gear down."

"We seem to be moving really fast," Cynthia comments, glancing between Wil, the main display and Zephyr who just shrugs.

The ship drops several meters before Wil can get it back under control. "Here comes the ground!" He flares the repulsor lifts to full power as the *Ghost* flies into the domed landing area much faster than is advisable. The forward section lifts dramatically, the main display shifting to show the ceiling of the large dome. Then, with a thud and a loud groan, the *Ghost* stops moving in any direction, the forward display showing the far wall sliding down until the view settles on what is directly ahead of the ship.

Wil turns to face Zephyr, "Can we close up the dome?"

"How would I know? It opened automatically at our approach; it may close up on its own once it knows we're in." Zephyr shrugs. She looks at the screen which still shows the blowing snow. "Or not. Dress warm."

NEWSCAST_

"GOOD EVENING, this is GNO News Time, I'm Xyrzix."

"And I'm Megan. We start tonight with interesting news out of Mogul system." She turns from the camera to Xyrzix, who continues.

"Droids in the planetary capitol have gone on strike."

"Strike?" Megan asks.

"It would seem several commercial sectors are now shut down as droids have secured the buildings and refuse to work." His large pink compound eyes blink twice rapidly.

"Have the droids issued any demands?" Megan asks, her three-fingered hands resting on the desk in front of her.

"Indeed, they have Megan. It would appear these droids, thousands in all, are demanding civil rights."

The blonde anchorwoman coughs, "Civil rights?"

"Yes. Authorities on Mogul Three are currently taking no action, while the planetary government consults with the GC Council."

Megan turns to the camera, "Well this has the makings of a story we'll be covering for quite some time. In other news, the Cartok colony on Bunrun twelve is holding their first planetary governor elections since breaking with their home world's government. Currently, there are eighty-three candidates so this first election should be interesting. Good luck Cartok Colony."

CHAPTER 5_

GETTING UNDERWAY_

AFTER A COLD AND boring night in the open cargo hold of the freighter, voices wake Bennie. "Excited to be heading back to the fleet?"

"You bet your ass. This planet is one of the worst I've ever been on and I've been to Fury." A second voice replies.

Bennie chuckles and whispers to himself, "As if Fury is so bad." He sneaks around the crate he was sleeping against and makes his way toward the hatch leading into the crew area of the ship.

The voices continue. "Here comes the first lifter. You take it, I'll get the next."

"Copy that." The other voice says. Heavy footsteps head off toward the open outer cargo doors while the sound of a heavy lifter droid grows.

The hatch to the crew area opens and Bennie dashes through it. He comes to a stop immediately, hand rushing to his face. "Clearly cleanliness standards are more lax on this ship." He hurries forward, looking at each door he comes across until he finds one that suits his needs.

Several tocks later, the freighter takes off. Bennie is sitting at a computer terminal in what he hopes is an unused cleaning closet.

Thankfully, this particular closet also backs up to the freighter's computer center.

The hacker works his wristcomm for a few more minutes, familiarizing himself with the ship and its computer core. "Oh, there we go! An unused bunk." He taps a few commands. "Time to raid the galley; looks like I've got three days to kill." He disconnects his wristcomm and puts the panel back in place. Then, he heads out of the equipment closet.

A freighter this old doesn't have a very large crew so avoiding detection proves easy. Bennie has years of experience lurking in shadows and crawling through access tunnels to avoid being spotted. Even if the internal sensors could detect him, which he's made sure they can't, the ship's computer can't raise an alert. Protocols Bennie added to the system keep the computer from logging any indications he's present.

The galley turns out to be not too well stocked. "What the wurrin? Ration bars?" He slams a third cupboard closed. "What kind of operation is Janus running here?" He opens another cupboard. "Oh, hello there." He pulls out several packages of fruits and preserved meat. *Better than ration bars.*

From outside the hatch, voices startle Bennie. He falls off the counter top he's standing on. Quickly, he scrambles to gather his stolen food before crawling into a cabinet.

"Do you think this is the last trip?" One of a pair a Palorians asks as they enter the galley.

"Doubt it. I heard there's another depot the Commander wants to raid in the Astilaru system. Though the *Gunthar* might be able to make those runs, they should be done offloading by now. Have to ask the XO to make the inquiry." Bennie hears the second voice say.

"Good luck there!" The first voice says. "Captain seems to think the more crap we haul around for the Commander the better bonus he'll get or something."

"Right!" The other voice says. "As if there're any bonuses anyway."

"Well, what ya gonna do? At least the Astilaru depot isn't as much of a dren hole as that last planet."

"Hey, did you leave the cupboard open? That's against regs, you krebnack." The first voice, belonging to a shorter squat man, says.

The other Palorian, tall and thin, replies, "No. Just because we're out here, why would I take the regs less seriously? Maybe it was Ragnar?"

The first walks over and closes the cabinet where Bennie found the meat snacks. "Maybe, he's a bit of a slacker." He turns to the refrigeration unit, and removes two bottles of grum. "Here."

From his hiding place in the lower cabinet, Bennie watches them move to a table in the middle of the room where they sit down and open their bottles. "Great." He groans, wiggling to get more comfortable in the tight space.

NOTHING SCARY HERE_

THE OUTER DOOR to the landing dome does finally close but not before several feet of snow have piled up around the *Ghost*. Wil, Zephyr, Cynthia and Gabe walk down the cargo ramp, flashlight beams lighting the way around them.

Wil looks over his shoulder to Gabe, "Picking anything up?" He asks between chattering teeth. The *Ghost* is not carrying cold weather gear. However, Jark Asgar provided basic parkas for everyone; very basic and thin. Coorish and Gabe seem to be the only ones unaffected by the cold.

"Many things." The tall droid replies but offers nothing more.

Zephyr and Cynthia exchange glances before looking at Wil who shrugs then asks, "Care to elaborate?"

"Of course, Captain." Gabe inclines his head then continues, "There is no active wireless network so I cannot tell you what lies beyond this landing area other than to say I detect no life signs. I detect several emergency power supplies and the landing guidance beacon."

He's about to continue when Cynthia raises a hand. "Could we maybe discuss this someplace warmer?"

Zephyr looks at her friend. "You're the one with fur."

"It's not *that* thick." Cynthia says between her chattering teeth.

Zephyr walks off toward something. "Look at this." Her light rises and plays against something, a ship. "Someone else is here."

"Yes, that was next on my report." Gabe says, turning to look elsewhere.

Cynthia looks at Wil then walks to join Zephyr. Playing her own light along the hull, she observes. "Modified light cargo ship."

"Modified how?" Wil asks, adding his light to theirs.

"That was also—" Gabe starts.

"Weapons for sure; see the ports." Cynthia is using her flashlight to point. Several medium blasters are protruding from the hull. "Those engines look aftermarket also."

Wil turns to Gabe and asks, "Gabe, can you tell how long it has been sitting here?"

"I can guess. Without access to the station computer or the ship itself, I cannot be certain. The engines are reading the same temperature as the rest of this area, so likely at least two days." he sees Wil open his mouth and holds up his finger. "However, since the station went silent nearly two weeks ago, I would assume something closer to five days, perhaps six."

Cynthia moves her flashlight beam around the space. It barely reaches the far side of the landing area. "Looks like it's just this ship and us." She points. "Those are short range planetary jobs." There are six small craft lined up against the wall furthest from the *Ghost* and the mystery ship. The small vessels have repulsor lifts and small engines at the back, enough to cover ground quickly but no chance of leaving the atmosphere.

Wil looks around then back up the *Ghost's* cargo ramp to the Farsight Corp. technical team. He motions them down. "All right. Let's get your gear unloaded."

Bon and Coorish head down the ramp. Coorish is guiding a gravsled, loaded with all manner of equipment.

Wil looks at the scientists then over to Gabe, gesturing a few meters from the ship, "Let's put it all over there, at least for now."

"Acknowledged, Captain." This is all Gabe says as he walks back up the ramp to help load the next gravsled.

AGENT BENNIE, SPACE SPY_

IT TAKES NEARLY two tocks for the two Palorian freighter crew to finish their many drinks and head off to their next stop, presumably their bunks based on their slurred speech. Once he can no longer hear their voices, Bennie slowly opens the cabinet. "Better get out of here before the next two drennogs come off shift." He mumbles, grabbing his bag of *borrowed* food stuffs. He heads to the refrigeration unit, grabs a bottle of grum and bottle of water before he quickly heads for the door.

Poking his head out, he looks both ways then heads toward the quarters he's picked out for himself. According to the computer it has gone unused the last few trips this ship has made between the pillaged Peacekeeper supply depot and the *Pax Liberatus*.

When the hatch opens to his home for the next two days, Bennie recoils. "Wurrin!" He quickly looks around, realizing his outburst was louder than he'd intended. He turns back to the open hatch, and the horrible smell coming from inside the room. Bennie enters and closes the hatch behind him. "Did someone die in here?" He wonders out loud, safe from being overheard.

Looking around, he confirms there is, in fact, no dead bodies. But, there is a pile of something that might be biological waste, or possibly a science experiment run amok. "No wonder they don't use this one." He says as he brushes something he can't identify off the bed.

Despite his best efforts, Maxim has lost track of how long he's been in the small brig of the rogue Peacekeeper Command Carrier, *Pax Liberatus*. He's pretty sure his dinner with Janus was two days ago, pretty sure. Janus hasn't spoken to him since that dinner and his other meals come at random times, likely to keep him off balance. He's lying on the sleep platform, staring at the ceiling when the force field that is the door to his cell disengages.

A guard in Peacekeeper combat armor is on the other side of the door. The armor is sealed and the faceplate is mirrored. "This way." The modulated voice says, stepping slightly aside.

Maxim gets up to leave the space. "I was beginning to think you'd forgotten me in here." He says. The guard doesn't reply.

It's a short walk to an interrogation room on the same level of the brig. Maxim never served aboard the *Pax Liberatus* but knows the class of ship well. "Oh, it's interrogation time, is it?"

The guard says nothing. He follows Maxim into the room before taking up a position in the room's corner.

Maxim takes a seat at the table in the center. It's not a very long wait for Janus to enter. "Oh, you'll be doing this yourself then?" Maxim asks the disgraced Peacekeeper Sub Commander.

Janus tuts, "At ease, Centurion Maxim. There's to be no formal interrogation, at least not today, provided you answer my questions." The older Palorian takes a seat opposite Maxim. *I guess we're back to formalities after I didn't sign up to join him at dinner.* Maxim thinks.

Maxim spreads his arms. "Ask anything you'd like."

"Where is your Captain and the rest of your crew?"

"The short answer is, I do not know." Before Janus can respond, Maxim continues, "The longer answer is that Bennie was on the station with me and the rest of the crew were to rendezvous with

Bennie and I on Nilop Four. Had you waited, you could have had us all, shame that."

Janus scowls, "Interesting, though not overly helpful. Are they still in the Nilop system?"

"I do not know. Presumably Bennie has joined them, and they are looking for me." He smiles, which makes Janus shudder a bit, knowing how infrequently the big Palorian smiles. "Maybe they decided they were better off without me and have gone off to find a new tactical officer. Who can say?"

"I need for you to say. It should go without saying, your life depends on it." The moment the words leave his mouth Janus realizes the word play he just committed and growls. "Since you don't seem eager to join me, I need to ensure your krebnack of a Captain doesn't interfere with my plans."

Maxim chuckles. "Does it though?" He asks, leaning forward. "I assume you intend to kill Wil, Zephyr and me. Likely Bennie and Gabe too, just to tie up loose ends. So tell me, Janus, what would be my motivation in helping you find my friends, only to kill them, and me?" Maxim smiles, this time tightly, showing more teeth. "You forget, Janus, Peacekeepers are not afraid to die."

"Ex-Peacekeeper," Janus corrects, causing Maxim to scowl.

"There are worse things than death, Maxim. Worse things." This time it's Janus who is smiling, not at all kindly. The Rogue Peacekeeper stands. "Soon enough the Galactic Commonwealth will see exactly what the Palorian people are capable of. Our rise will be brutal and efficient. We'll usher in a new renaissance for the people of the Commonwealth."

"Uh, huh" is all Maxim says, leaning back in his chair.

"I guess we'll do this the hard way then." Janus says, rubbing his hands together.

"Attention! We're docking with the *Liberatus* in ten centocks. All crew to the hold for offloading operations." The overhead speaker in Bennie's borrowed quarters announces.

He sits up from the spot on the bed he's cleared of detritus, presumably left by the last occupant of the room. "Time to save Maxim," he mumbles. He opens a video window on his wristcomm and views the security feed of the cargo hold. He can see the crew moving crates and powering up load lifters.

After the ship jolts once, indicating that it has landed, he watches the massive cargo doors open, revealing the landing bay beyond. The crew gets to work, joined by the landing bay crew from the carrier the freighter is now sitting inside of. He watches as the freighter crew offloads the last of the cargo crates, eventually heading out of sight with their colleagues from command carrier. "Guess it's now or never." Bennie hops off the bed and opens the hatch a bit. He hears nothing but the clicks and whirs of shipboard equipment doing what it does. He moves.

Bennie heads down the corridor from his borrowed bunk to the cargo hold. He looks around. *Busy place.* The crew are nowhere to be seen but heavy lift droids of the *Pax Liberatus* are trundling around the vast hold, filling the space with noise.

The deck of the carrier is three meters from the opening of the freighter's hold. "A long way down," the barely one point two meter tall Brailack observes. In the distance, the crew of the freighter and the chief of the deck are discussing where to store the newly offloaded cargo. Lifter droids are moving crates from one place to another. Bennie looks around but there's nothing to use to get down. "The others do it all the time, how hard can it be?" he says to himself before hopping off the lip of the cargo hold to the carrier's deck below. When he lands, he tries to roll like he's seen Zephyr do a hundred times. Luckily, a cargo droid slamming a crate down to the deck somewhere nearby drowns out his scream. He gets up and rubs his shoulder before hurrying off toward a pile of crates.

WELL, THAT'S NOT GOOD_

THE MAIN LAB complex and landing dome are connected by a service corridor, three meters wide to allow for the moving of cargo in and out of the facility. The main doors open, exposing the corridor to the lights from the landing bay. Wil releases a low whistle. "Long dark hallway, check."

Zephyr pushes past, the high intensity light from her assault rifle illuminating the nearby sections of the corridor. "According to the information Asgar provided, this corridor is the main artery between the landing area and the research and habitation areas."

"Like I said, dark hallway." Wil says, running his hands down his midsection as he follows the lines of his long brown jacket. "Maybe I shoulda brought Jarvis." He reaches back and touches the door control.

From behind him, Cynthia says, "You know it's a little weird you refer to your combat armor by name." She smiles. "Also, yes, you should have. Those little probes—huggy, doogy and Luigi or whatever, would be handy."

Wil looks back, holding up a finger. "One. It's *Huey, Duey and Louie*. Duck tales is next up on after dinner video time; the old one, not the one they made when I was a kid." He holds up another finger. "Two. How is it weird? That's his name, he's a what did Bennie call it? *Rudimentary intelligence*, that was it." Wil shrugs. "Seems rude to not use his name."

Cynthia nods once. "I suppose." She pushes past Wil to follow Zephyr who's moved several paces ahead of them. "Come on." She glances back, "And yeah, you probably should have." She grins, "Or at least a rifle." Wil holds up his pistol, shrugging.

Gabe, who is bringing up the rear offers. "I am sure Jarvis appreciates your consideration, Captain."

Coorish turns to Bon, "Are we safe with them?"

The red-skinned scientist shrugs. "A bit late to ask that question, don't you think? Plus, Chief Executive Asgar wouldn't have sent us with them if they weren't professionals."

"I'm still thinking a security detail might have made sense." The insectoid scientist replies, its mandibles clicking nervously.

Wil looks over. "Well, this is just a delivery. I'm sure there's a perfectly good reason there's an armed freighter in the docking bay and no one is answering on local comms."

Gabe looks down at Wil, "Indeed."

"Hey, look at this!" Zephyr shouts from up ahead.

As Wil and Gabe catch up, Zephyr is shining her light on a body. Wil sighs, "Of course there's a body."

Cynthia kneels next to it, rolling it over. "Not a scientist," she observes. The body could be any spacer; coveralls, light jacket, lots of pockets and little bits of armor attached to the jacket.

"Pirate?" Wil asks.

Cynthia looks up at him. "You think?" She asks. I doubt the crew here was having a masquerade ball."

Zephyr chuckles, "Isn't this your jacket?"

Bon and Coorish peek around him to stare at the body.

Wil tuts. "Rude. And no, mine is way cooler looking."

Gabe kneels down and runs a hand over the body. "Something broke this woman's neck."

"Woman?" Wil asks.

"Something broke her neck?" Zephyr asks, moving to shine her light toward their destination. Cynthia stands and pulls her own rifle off her back before turning on the light.

Gabe stands up. "I detect no other DNA or indications of what might have killed her."

Wil moves to the center of the corridor. "Alrighty then. Let's get to the main habitat section and see what's going on here." He turns to Gabe. "Still no wireless network? There have got to be droids working here; see if you can connect with them. You all do a mesh thing, right?"

Gabe inclines his head. "As I said, the wireless network appears to be offline. I detect no droid network nodes." Without another word, he turns and walks toward the far end of the corridor.

Cynthia slows to take up the rearguard position. "What exactly are they researching here?"

"According to Asgar, they're mostly an archeological expedition. I guess they found some ruins or something buried in the ice here." Wil offers.

As they approach the doors leading to the primary facility dome, Gabe slows down and turns to look at the others. "I have accessed a wireless network node."

"I thought it was offline?" Wil asks.

Gabe shrugs. "It is. Technically, it is a droid mesh node but the wider network is offline meaning the droid attached to it is offline or there are no other droids in range."

"Sounds gruesome." Wil murmurs.

Zephyr comes up next to Gabe and asks, "So there's a droid, in unknown condition on the other side of this hatch?" She looks past Gabe to the large doors. "This hatch that looks like someone secured it then someone else forced open."

Gabe looks at the large doors. "You are correct. These doors have been forced from this side, but welded shut from the inside. Tremendous effort went into opening them."

"Can I go back to the *Ghost*?" Coorish asks. "I'd like to go back to the ship now, please."

HERE I COME_

GETTING around the *Pax Liberatus* proves to be more challenging than Bennie expected. He is sitting in a service alcove near the tertiary computer complex. He is covered in wires connected to his wristcomm and cross connected from one panel to another. He thumbs through menus on the screen of his wristcomm, mumbling. "Kinda wish I had Gabe and his infiltration software right about now."

One of the several wires connected to his wristcomm sparks. Bennie yelps and quickly unplugs the offending connection. "Be more careful!" He admonishes himself. He looks around to make sure his little outburst has attracted no attention before continuing with his work.

After taking a nap in a storage closet near the service alcove, Bennie heads off to the next stop in his mission to rescue Maxim.

Peacekeeper command carriers have many armories, it wouldn't do for half the crew to jog over a kilometer should the need to repel borders arise. Thankfully, taking one of the armories offline and marking it closed for contagion mitigation isn't that hard, at least for Bennie. He rubs his hands together as he looks around a room that's larger than the crew lounge and cargo hold of the *Ghost combined*. He heads for the infiltration armor.

"Would it kill them to make kids' sizes or something?" He wonders aloud, looking at the racks of armor and folded stealth under layer garments. Bennie looks around and sees a repair kit that someone left open. "Hmmm." He grabs the smallest armor undergarment he can find and the repair kit and moves to a corner of the room.

After a few false starts, there's a pile of discarded parts of underlayer garments, mostly cut to shreds. Bennie is standing and admiring his work in a mirror mounted to the bulkhead next to the armor wrack. "Not bad if I say so myself." He says in a whisper. He's clad head to ankle in a matte black Peacekeeper infiltration armor stealth undergarment. The under garment is designed to manage the wearer's heat signature and sensor profile, interfacing with the armor usually worn over it. It renders him mostly invisible to sensors and took him nearly a tock just to get the wiring to match up. Combined with the hacking he did earlier, Bennie can now move around the ship without being detected. He pulls his boots back on since there isn't a Peacekeeper in the service with feet as small as his, let alone with only two toes per foot. Then, he heads over to the opposite wall, "explosives, now we're talking."

As two Peacekeeper Centurions turn down a corridor five levels above the detention center, a small matte black form dashes across the corridor behind them. As the two turn down an adjacent corridor, the small shape turns to watch, making sure they don't come back. Large purple eyes surrounded by black paint blink twice. "Should be right around here." He looks around quickly, eyes settling on an access panel a meter ahead of him. "There you are! Should get me down to the detention level." He rushes over to the panel and quickly sets about removing the fasteners with a tool he's pulled from a small bag at his side. While one hand uses the tool, another retrieves a meal bar. "These are so gross, I didn't know they expired." He rips open the bar with his teeth and takes a bite. "How do these krebnacks eat these?"

A few microtocks later and the panel is moving back into place, a meal bar wrapper laying on the ground next to it.

Inside the crawlspace, Bennie pulls something else from his bag and sticks it onto the ceiling of the small service crawlspace. "Just in case," he mumbles. He moves further inside the crawlspace toward a connecting conduit that leads straight down. He looks over the edge. "Who designs this stuff? How is anyone supposed to go up or down this thing?" He whispers, looking down the five-level drop. He hears something and leans back just as an automated conduit scrubber descends past the connector he's sitting in. "Good as anything I guess," he says, hopping from his crawlspace down onto the back of the mindless cleaning device. It emits two angry sounding beeps but otherwise continues to descend the long vertical duct. He rocks from side to side, looking at his wristcomm to time his jump from the cleaner to the appropriate horizontal service duct.

"Where is your crew? I'm tired of asking." Janus and Maxim are, once more, in an interrogation room aboard the *Pax Liberatus*. A different room than last time, Maxim notices.

"Then stop asking, because the answer will not change. I, do, not, know. I've told you and your other less polite interrogators the same thing." Maxim smiles tightly through swollen lips. "I told you the same thing before the beatings started. Why do you care? Surely you have more important things to do.

"I mean, I'll be a little disappointed if, after all this time, you're fixated on some type of *revenge* against Wil." Maxim raises a black eyebrow tilting his head.

Janus smiles. "Oh there's more to it than that, don't worry." He leans over the table. "But, seeing that meddling human krebnack eliminated will be sugar topping on the dessert. You and Zephyr, that little Brailack hacker and the engineering droid are all going to be a bonus." Janus turns and looks at the one way plasti-glass. "It's not so much that I want revenge, it's that you and your friends have an astonishing capacity for being in the wrong places at the wrong times. If I can remove you all from the board early, I suspect my life will be that much easier later."

Maxim shrugs, wincing at the pain in his shoulder caused by a particularly zealous interrogator.

Janus gestures to the guard in the corner. "Take him to his cell. We can lure his friends here without him being alive, so long as they think he is." He looks at Maxim, his expression sad. "I'm afraid the fleet is moving tomorrow, but you'll be staying here, floating in the void forever. Goodbye Centurion Maxim." Without waiting for a reply, Janus leaves the room.

The guard removes the magnetic locks holding Maxims cuffs to the chair. "Come on."

PART 2_

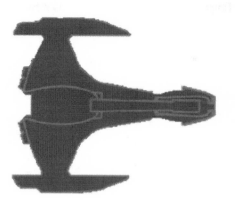

CHAPTER 6_

MEET NEW PEOPLE_

"ALL RIGHT, LETS SETUP HERE." Wil says as he moves his light around the anteroom they've entered. The massive doors leading to the corridor to the landing dome behind them, three other hatches, all closed are in front of them.

Zephyr moves to show the science team where to set up when Gabe makes a clicking noise. Cynthia and Wil freeze and moments later, Zephyr has the scientist quieted. Wil looks over at Gabe, who holds a finger up, then points to one of the hatches. Over the comms, his voice says, "Storage closet."

Wil motions to Cynthia, who's closest to the indicated hatch. She reaches out and presses the button set in the door frame. With a swoosh, the hatch slides into the wall and a small, yellow blur shoots out of the closet toward the large hatch leading to the landing area.

Wil screams and Cynthia leaps through the air toward the small blur, her claws fully extended. Before the feline-featured woman can land on the quick moving alien, Zephyr punches it in the face, dropping it to the ground. It makes a low keening sound. Zephyr looks at Wil, "Did you just scream?"

Wil turns to look at the meter and a half yellow alien laying on the floor, "That could have been a monster." He walks toward the prone form, "That a lab coat?"

Zephyr tuts, "A science monster, maybe?" Wil flips her off.

Cynthia has moved to corral the terrified science team. "Dead?"

Zephyr shakes her head and squats next to the *science monster*. "I don't think so, didn't hit it, or, her, that hard." She feels around the neck for a pulse, just as two eyes larger than Bennies snap open. "Get away from me!" The now very conscious alien screams.

Zephyr raises both hands. "Easy there, we're here to help." She looks at Wil, who has one of his pulse pistols leveled at the now shaking lab coat wearing alien. "Really?"

Wil hostlers the pistol. "You never know." He looks to the small being. "I'm Wil Calder. Jark Asgar sent us to deliver equipment and help get your comms back online. What's your name?" When she flinches, he adds, "It's ok, you're safe. We're friends. We'll protect you."

The small alien woman looks around, taking each person in the room in. "Who will protect you?" Her voice is barely a whisper.

Cynthia and Zephyr exchange a look then Zephyr turns to the two Farsight scientists. "Get over here. Do you either of you know her?"

As the technicians come over, Bon answers, "I'm afraid not. I don't even recognize her species." Coorish shakes its head. "Same, no idea."

"My name is Hathyr. I'm on the xenobiology team."

Wil looks over at Gabe, who shakes his head subtly, answering over comms, "I cannot confirm or refute her story until I access the main computer. Mister Asgar did not provide a list of station personnel to us." Wil glances down at the small yellow scientist.

"You came in a ship? Can we leave? Let's leave this world now." Hathyr insists, taking her time to stand while she rubs her hairless forehead. Instead of hair, she has what looks to Wil like quills—short, stubby quills.

Wil shakes his head and stands to give her space. "Afraid not. We have to figure out what happened here and get the comm system back online." He raises an eyebrow. "What did happen here?"

BREAKING OUT_

PEERING through the grate that covers the conduit he's in, Bennie sees a line of what look like open doors. The force fields that close off each cell have been de-activated. "The detention level, bongo." He looks down, a lone Peacekeeper walks past. "Or was it bango?" The Peacekeeper turns the corner. "Bingo, that's what Wil says." Bennie eases his multi-tool out of his bag and removes the fasteners holding the grate in place. "Hold on big guy, I'm coming for ya." He slaps another device to the ceiling of the conduit then slides the grate away. Bennie drops to the floor and grunts but quickly recovers. He looks left and right. Then, he pulls a telescoping baton he found in the armory from his bag and moves the air duct grate back into place. The guard is due to pass by again so Bennie scurries into an unused detention cell. He stands just inside to the right of the door, next to the toilet. He glances down at it. "Does anyone clean anything around here?" He whispers.

The main door to the detention center opens. "I don't understand how you can be here, doing this." Bennie overhears Maxim saying as he walks past the cell Bennie is hiding in, two guards behind him.

"What's so hard to understand? This is about the freedom and sovereignty of the Palorian people. We've been slaves to the Tarsi and their Galactic Commonwealth for generations. It's time that ended; Janus sees it, we see it. How do you not?" The shorter of the two guards says as they come to a stop at a cell two doors from Bennie's hiding place. The other guard offers, "Doesn't really matter, does it? You'll the sucking vacuum in the morning." They both chuckle. The pop hiss sound of an activating force field lets Bennie know that Maxim is back in his cell.

"Oh dren," Bennie whispers from his hiding place. He takes a deep breath. He runs his hands down the front of his modified stealth suit and wipes the sweat away. Then, he reaches into his pack before stepping out into the corridor. "Eat shat mother fonker!" He pulls two pulse pistols from his pack—modified pulse pistols. Bennie pulls the triggers, letting loose a screeching kind of scream. The modified pistols unleash a torrent of energy, burning through the armor of the two guards, the muzzles on each pistol quickly glowing red. Both Peacekeepers drop, smoking holes in their armor.

Bennie walks over to the doorway that Maxim is standing on the other side of, "Nice pistols." The big Palorian says.

Bennie shakes his head and drops the two, still glowing weapons. He looks up at Maxim. "Oh, yeah, well, Peacekeeper ships don't stock Brailack sized pulse rifles, I had to get creative." He looks around Maxim. "We should get going."

"Maybe open my cell first?" Maxim says.

"Oh, dren! Yeah, sorry." Bennie reaches up and presses the control to unlock the cell. The glow around the entry makes a pop hiss sound then fades. "I didn't have long to scope this level out for patrol timing." As if on cue, the guard Bennie had seen walking the floor comes around the corner.

As the guard shouts, Maxim drops to the ground, rolls on his uninjured shoulder. He grabs one of Bennie's discarded pistols. He brings it up and fires at the guard. The shots burn through the guards' armor, killing him or her. Maxim tosses the gun, letting out a hiss. "Felgercarb, that's hot!"

Bennie grins. "Like I said, I had to make some modifications." He reaches into the pack slung over his shoulder and removes two more pistols—one modified, the other, a standard issue. He offers Maxim the unmodified pistol. "Sorry, I couldn't carry a rifle with me through the air ducts and service crawlspaces."

The big Palorian stands and takes the pistol. He smiles and pats Bennie on the head. "It's good to see you. So what's the plan?"

Bennie shrugs, "We're kind of winging it from here on out."

Maxim grunts, "So a Wil type plan, got it." He motions, "Let's go!"

I'M A SURVIVOR_

"Start with the dead gal in the corridor." Wil instructs Hathyr. Cynthia and the technical team are standing around the small alien scientist while Wil kneels next to her. Zephyr is near the two remaining doors into the anteroom they've established their base in. Meanwhile, Gabe is kneeling next to the ruined computer terminal.

Hathyr shrugs. "I do not know her. I have heard no one since those others came through." She looks around. "I should have tried to get to their ship." She moans.

"It's locked up tight, their ship." Cynthia offers. She notices something in the small woman's face. "So is ours, by the way," she adds.

Wil makes a rolling gesture with his hand. "Go on. So you don't know the dead woman in the corridor? Who was it that came through here? When was that?"

Hathyr shakes her head. "I don't know. I have been hiding in the air ducts and service conduits since it happened. I heard them arrive but by the time I made my way to this room, they'd moved into the facility." She takes a deep breath. "I decided to wait here," she gestures to the storage room, "there was plenty of food."

Bon offers, "Maybe we should go back to your ship and head back to Nilop?"

Coorish makes a tsking noise. "It'd take too long. What if there are other survivors? We can't leave them."

"Not to mention the mystery ship and its crew who are somewhere in this facility." Zephyr adds.

Wil looks at Hathyr. "Ok, so back to your story. What exactly happened? You've said *it happened* twice now. What is *it*?"

"Something was found in the ice—"

Wil makes an eep-like sound then waves her off. "Sorry Hathyr, keep going. What did you find?"

"I don't know. It was encased in ice thousands of years old. Our best instruments could barely get a reading on it. Team Seven was working on thawing a portion to take samples directly." She shakes, bringing her knees up to her chin. "I think that's when everything went wrong. The alarms started and the station administrator declared a lock down. I was off duty so was in my room. I stayed there for days."

"Oh hell! It's the freaking *Thing*." Wil interrupts.

"What thing?" Zephyr asks.

"Oh jeebus." Cynthia murmurs.

"*Jesus*." Wil corrects.

"Then what?" Coorish prompts, ignoring Wil and Cynthia.

"I don't know. When I finally mustered enough courage to come out of my quarters, no one was here. I've been hiding ever since. The hatch to the landing dome was welded shut so I couldn't even try to escape overland."

"From what though? Have you seen *it*, whatever *it* is?" Cynthia asks.

"I've only heard it." The small scared alien woman whispers.

Wil shudders then looks around the room. "Ok, this is nightmarish. What about the computer?"

Hathyr shakes her head, "I don't know. That's why I left my quarters. At first, when the lock-down started, the computer was online then it wasn't."

"I really think we should go back to the ship." Bon whines.

"Stop being such a baby." Coorish snaps. "These are our coworkers!"

Bon blushes, which turns him a deeper shade of red. "You are right. I am sorry."

Wil claps his hands once. "Ok, let's get settled. We'll head into the station tomorrow." He looks at Bon. "We'll head to the command center and get you all set up then move on from there."

Everyone nods and goes about setting up for the night. Gabe grabs each of the ruined doors that lead to the corridor to the landing dome. He forces them closed again. Then, he looks to Wil who nods. Gabe lifts a finger which sparks as he drags it along the seam in the two doors, a plasma welder melting the two halves together.

LITTLE SHORT FOR A STORMTROOPER_

"Don't take this the wrong way but as far as rescues go, it's a bit underwhelming." Maxim says as he and Bennie duck into a duty head two levels above the detention center. He looks around the clearly used and not properly cleaned space and grimaces. "We have to get off this ship, fast."

"How else should I take it? You know how hard it was to track you down?" Bennie raises his eyebrows. "Is it smelly in here?" He chuckles as Maxim grimaces. "I've obscured us from sensors. We can move around however we like." He raises a hand, one finger pointing up. "You know how terrifying it has been?"

"How?"

"Tremendously so. I watched them capture you. I stole a ship then hitched a ride on a freighter from some—"

Maxim holds up his hand. "I meant how are you masking us from the ship's sensors."

Bennie's face falls. "Oh, I keep copies of all of your bio signs on my wristcomm, the whole crew." The small hacker replies like it's the most normal thing.

"That's, well that's weird but also astonishingly forward thinking. However, that only keeps us off the sensors. The first crew member

110

we pass will immediately know something isn't right. Not to mention it'll only be a matter of time before someone goes down to the detention center. You're a little too short to be a Peacekeeper and I'm scheduled for execution." He continues, "Why didn't you get the others?"

Bennie scrunches his green face. "Well, I mean, I, well, I don't know. I felt like I had to move fast. Those commandos had a head start on me. Waiting for the others could have let the trail go cold. I mean I left them a message." He shrugs. "You'd do the same for me, right? Like when you went with Gabe aboard the *Berserker*." He looks up at his big friend.

"Not even a little." The big Palorian says, his voice flat. Without moving his head, he looks down at the fuming Brailack and barks out a laugh. "Relax! Of course I'd have done the same for you. Though, I have to admit, not as expertly as you seem to have. You tracked a commando team, infiltrated a supply depot *then* continued on to infiltrate a command carrier." He smiles warmly at his little friend. "We train to keep all those things from being possible and you did them, alone, with minimal support and equipment. I'm proud of you." Maxim gets serious again. "Our being invisible is valuable for sure but they'll discover those three guards eventually. Best case, we have until someone comes to get me to lead me to my appointment with an airlock but I suspect there's a shift change sooner than that. Janus will not hesitate to tear this ship apart. You mentioned you left a message for Wil and the others; what did you tell them?"

Bennie nods, focused on his wristcomm. "Yeah, what's that kreb-nack up to anyway? What's he want with you?" He waves a hand dismissively. "Oh, I just told them we were doing a thing and would be a few days late."

Maxim makes a strangled noise but says nothing, sighing. "He wants us dead. Mostly Wil but all of us would make him happiest." He turns to look at the space, seeing if there is anything they can use. He shudders. Clearly, Janus doesn't run this ship like he was still a

Peacekeeper. "He's got some big plan for taking over or destroying the GC. He wants us off the board before he even starts."

"Oh, lovely. Ok, here we go." Bennie waves to get Maxim's attention then points at the small screen on his arm. "Launch bay."

"You want us to steal a ship?" Maxim asks, incredulous. "That section of the ship is one of the most secure."

"You mean like the detention block?" Bennie replies, smirking. "Plus, I've got a few things planned to keep them busy."

Maxim raises an eyebrow, then shrugs. "You've made it this far. Your play to call." He checks the charge on his pulse pistol and nods. They open the door to the head just as a Peacekeeper technician pushes in from the corridor. Before the startled rogue officer can react, Maxim grabs his collar and pulls him into the filthy room, pushing the hatch closed. "This is how you treat the duty head?" He shouts. The startled officer, blinks twice then looks from Maxim to the room, gulping. Before he can answer, Maxim slams the butt of his pistol handle on the man's head, knocking him out cold. "That'll keep him out of our hair for a bit. Come on."

They exit and hurry to the next hatch they can hide behind. Bennie asks, "That messy bathroom really got to you, huh?"

Maxim nods as they enter a storage room, "It's just unprofessional."

NEWSCAST_

"Good evening, I'm Mon-El Furash, coming to you live from Mogul Three, where yesterday the civil rights protest being led by thousands of municipal and privately owned droids has officially spread to several outlying cities on the main continent." She pauses as someone in the studio is speaking, "No, no one knows what caused the protest to spread." More listening, "Yes, initially the local government was consulting with the GC council on what to do here. I understand that a few days ago a delegation went into the first factory that went on strike." More listening, "No, so far there's been no military response, although, all the affected factories have been cordoned off, I suspect to keep whatever is happening from spreading to other cities. Though it now seems that ship has sailed."

"The mixed GC and local government delegation hasn't offered a public response yet, but the droids in the factory have enabled a live vid stream, sans audio, of the proceedings, so that's something." Listening again and nodding, "Absolutely, I'll be here until this is settled."

CHAPTER 7_

PICK YOUR RIDE_

IT TAKES NEARLY a full tock to make it to a small observation gallery overlooking one of the many hanger bays of the Peacekeeper command carrier. "So, which one can you fly?" Bennie asks Maxim. He looks from the hangar deck below to the big Palorian kneeling next to him.

"Uh, well, none." Before Bennie can reply, Maxim adds, "I was never a fighter pilot but that..." he points to a craft larger than the strike fighters that litter the deck of the hangar, much larger, "that I can fly, at least well enough to get away."

"What the wurrin is that thing?" Bennie asks, holding his wrist-comm up to let the camera zoom in on the craft nearly three times the size of the surrounding fighters.

"Troop Transport."

"Sounds fast." Bennie says, the sarcasm dripping from his reply.

"No, it's not fast but it is FTL capable and surprisingly maneuverable for its size. We'll never outfly the fighters but we only have to outfly the capitol ships until we're clear to go to FTL and that will probably be long before they launch fighters. I doubt Janus has enough crew and pilots to field a Combat Air Patrol so it's likely clear out there." Maxim looks down at the busy hangar. "Now how do we get to the ship?"

Bennie smiles. "Oh, I don't think it will be as hard as you expect. Let's get down to the hangar deck level."

The hangar is a hive of activity, just like Maxim remembers from his time serving aboard similar ships. Mechanics are shouting at one another, pilots are looking over their fighters, technicians are looking at data PADDs and pointing to things. There are hundreds of people in the hangar not to mention the likely hundreds more on the levels above that overlook the main hangar area.

Maxim and Bennie are in a service closet full of likely, highly toxic cleaning solutions many of which are leaking from their containers. Maxim keeps shifting his feet as he tries to avoid touching the caustic solutions. The troop transport they're planning to *borrow* is on the opposite side of the hangar, at least a hundred meters away.

"OK, now what? That's still a lot of ground to cover and neither of us will blend in." Maxim whispers. "And you have short legs," he adds.

After making a gesture he's seen Wil make numerous times, Bennie smiles. "I keep telling you to not worry."

"And I don't, for one millitock, believe that you have this under control so you'll forgive me for worrying."

Bennie looks up at his much larger friend, awkwardly crammed into the small space. "That's rude."

"I'll apologize when we're aboard that transport."

"Prepare to apologize." The small hacker enters a command on his wristcomm and, seconds later, a rumble vibrates through the deck. The normally loud hangar goes quiet outside the door the two are hiding behind.

Another rumble, followed by one much closer, causes several

people in the hangar to lose their footing. A massive articulated arm tips over onto the strike fighter it was being used on to service.

Bennie looks up at Maxim. "Ready?" He's grinning.

By now the alert klaxon is blaring and the lighting in the cavernous hangar has shifted to red. "Battle stations! All hands to battle stations!" The instruction comes from hidden speakers all over the deck. The crew still standing around break into action; they run for fighters and combat stations and push fighters toward the large hatches leading to the fighter launch deck. They clear the space of equipment that might get in the way should the deck crew need to make repairs to fighters.

Bennie pushes the door open. There isn't a Peacekeeper crew member anywhere near them now. Most of the deck is deserted save for the pilots in their fighters who are now clustered near the various entries to the launch deck. Without a word he bolts toward the troop transport. Not a single person seems to notice the small being scurrying across the deck.

The overhead speakers come to life once more, "Intruder alert, intruder alert. Prisoner Maxim has escaped, be on the lookout. Kill on sight."

Maxim sighs. "Easy to not be seen when you're the size of a household pet." He squeezes out of the closet, nearly slipping on something bright pink and likely capable of dissolving his flesh. A mechanic, hurrying somewhere, bumps into him.

"Hey, watch out!" The man says then looks Maxim up and down, taking in his size, prisoner jumpsuit and injuries. "Oh krebn—" Maxim knocks the man out with one solid punch right to the face. The unconscious mechanic drops to the ground in a heap.

"Traitor," Maxim mumbles. He runs toward the troop transport and the frantically waving Bennie.

A NEW PLAYER OF THE GAME?_

THE SMALL GROUP from Farsight Corporation, plus the so-far-only survivor, set out for the main command center. The droid network node Gabe had detected turns out to be the remains of a small service droid. Something ripped it to shreds.

"Captain, I am detecting life forms ahead." Gabe holds up his hand then points toward the T-shaped intersection ahead of them; two fingers to the right, two to the left. The corridor branches off one direction leading to the command center, the other toward various administrative offices and supply rooms.

Zephyr pushes the Farsight team back up the corridor a bit, shushing them as she does.

Wil comes forward. "Hey, down there! Guessing you're the folks who came in that modified freighter?"

There's harsh whispering up ahead, loud enough to be heard but not make out what's being said. Wil looks to Gabe who nods. "They are debating whether to come out and talk or open fire. *Start shooting,* is winning." He adds.

Wil turns back down the corridor, "So yeah, we don't want any trouble or anything." He shouts, "We're checking on why this station

120

went silent. We've got a tech team with us, a bunch of gear and all that good stuff."

Cynthia edges to the side of the corridor. She takes a knee and lifts her rifle. Gabe's eyes have switched from their normal yellow glow to his *combat mode* red. His hands have folded into his forearms, revealing blaster barrels.

"Don't shoot, we're coming out to talk!" A voice says from the left side of the intersection.

A lanky blonde haired man comes around the corner. He is easily two-and-a-half meters tall and his blonde hair tied back in a ponytail. He is wearing what looks like a Hawaiian shirt and cargo pants.

"*Rhys Duch*," Cynthia hisses. Wil glances to her, eyebrows raised. She nods toward the tall alien walking toward them. "Worked for Xarrix, kind of an idiot."

"Surfer?" Wil asks. Cynthia looks at him but says nothing.

Behind Rhys Duch, three aliens follow; A fairly tall red fella with four arms, a little purple being, sort of a small gorilla and a Malkorite, his large ears twitching. Each is holding a weapon or two slung over their shoulder or grasped in multiple hands.

The blonde-haired alien sees Cynthia and waves. "Oh, hi Cynthia! Weird to see you here!"

Wil holds a hand up, the other resting on the butt of one of his pulse pistols. *Why does he look like a human?* "Hold up right there." He glances to Zephyr then Cynthia then whispers, "What now?"

Cynthia stands and walks toward the new group. "Rhys Duch, what a surprise! What are you doing here?" She looks past the thin blonde haired alien to the group behind him. "Zash? How have you been?"

The multi-limbed alien with red skin is holding two pulse rifles. He smiles. "Hey Cynthia! Glad you're not dead!" One of the non-rifle-encumbered hands waves. "We assumed you died with Xarrix and Lorath."

Cynthia steps back. "What're you all doing here?"

Rhys Duch smiles. "Well, after Xarrix, well, you know, I decided it was my chance to branch out. Things on Yurlo were pretty stable so I left one of my best lieutenants to run things there and headed out. Xarrix had listening posts all over so I stopped by one to see if anything interesting had been recorded." He looks around the corridor. "It logged a brief distress call from this system so I decided to see what we could steal." He shrugs. "I mean, distress calls from semi remote systems usually mean good stuff for the taking. Science outposts rarely have security details, especially these remote ones." He grins.

"We did not detect any transmissions when we entered orbit." Gabe says from near the cluster of Farsight technicians.

"Yeah, the transmission only went out the one time, never repeated."

Wil looks around and asks, "And when you landed, saw no one? That was you that forced the doors on the tunnel, right?"

Rhys Duch nods. "Haven't seen anyone since we landed. I'm even missing one of my crew."

"Missing?" Zephyr asks.

"Yeah, Mort vanished two nights ago." Zash offers. The other three aliens all nod.

Wil holds his hand flat at shoulder height. "This big, female, coat with lots of pockets?"

"You found her?" Duch asks, hopefully.

"Dead," Cynthia says

"Oh, well, that's a bummer. Where was she?" he asks, frowning.

"In the corridor leading to the landing dome." Zephyr replies.

One of Rhys' thugs offers, "She must have been trying to get to the ship."

Rhys nods and adds, "Except she didn't have the codes to unlock it." He shrugs. "For all the good it would have done her. Guess the thing that made all that noise got her." He looks at Wil.

Wil asks, "Thing? Noise? What?"

"Exactly how long have you all been here?" Zephyr asks.

"Not long." Rhys looks at Zash and the other goons behind him. "Three nights? Four?"

"Three." Zash offers. Rhys nods.

"And you haven't been able to get off this level?" Cynthia asks.

"Or try to go back to your ship?" Wil adds.

Rhys shrugs. "Well, not for lack of trying but the security protocols are fairly top notch." He looks past Wil to Gabe. "Maybe your droid can take care of that?" He continues, "Why would we go back to our ship? We don't have anything valuable yet."

Zash adds, "Plus, we've been trying to avoid whatever is wandering around making noise."

"So is the thing making noise up here?" Wil asks and Duch and his goons just shrug. "Ok, well, I'm not sure keeping you from robbing this place is in our mandate but you know, we should probably figure out what's going on before you get all sticky-fingers. Have you found the command center? We can table the scary noise monster stuff for a few."

"It's locked up tight, same as the research levels." Zash offers. He points to one of the branches in the corridor.

"Probably going to regret this, but I say we stick together until we figure out what's going on. Sound good?" Wil offers.

Rhys Duch smiles. "Sure, we can't really rob the place if we can't get in."

NOT LIKE DUSTING CROPS_

"WHAT A PIECE OF JUNK!" Bennie shouts as they enter the cockpit of the troop transport. Outside, another explosion rocks the ship. A beam falls from overhead, crushing a strike fighter.

Maxim shoves the Brailack out of the way and sits in the pilot's chair. "Shut up! She's got it where it counts." He starts the power up sequence, glancing out the cockpit window at the chaos in the hangar. "I hope."

Bennie hops up into one of the other chairs in the small cockpit. He presses a few more buttons on his wristcomm screen and an explosion rocks the hangar deck. One of the strike fighters has exploded in a magnificent ball of fire, its small reactor taking the entire craft, plus several others, with it in a small super nova that warps the deck.

"Wha—" Maxim closes his mouth, a newfound respect for his small Brailack crew mate growing.

The hacker doesn't look up from the console he's now focusing on. "I'm small and made myself invisible to sensors. Oh, and Janus has gotten very lax in his security and operations discipline."

Maxim nods, but says nothing. The troop transport lifts off. The hangar bay outside the cockpit's plasti-glass is abuzz with crew running around. Fire teams are trying to clear debris and extinguish fires while the few remaining fighters try to prepare for launch. Smoke is filling the space and fires rage along the outer wall.

"Well? Do you need more of an invitation?" Bennie nudges the big Palorian from the co-pilot seat and points toward the location of the explosion. Without waiting for Maxim to reply, he takes control of the twin barrel plasma blaster mounted under the nose of their borrowed troop transport. He opens fire on the outer bulkhead of the hangar where the strike fighter that exploded used to be. The heavy blaster stitches a path across the deck, scattering already agitated Peacekeepers. When the blasts find the weakened section of hull, still glowing faintly from the intense heat of the explosion, they rip clear through and open the massive hangar area to vacuum.

Maxim pushes the controls forward while eyeing his co-pilot from the side. "Full of surprises," he mumbles.

As the troop transport exits the Brailack made hole in the side of the immense Peacekeeper command carrier Maxim fires up the small craft's long range sensors. He looks over to Bennie. "Do you happen to know where we are?"

"Afraid not. I didn't want to risk accessing the freighters nav system," Bennie replies. He stows the forward cannon controls and turns to the sensor and threat display. "Twelve bogies inbound."

"No pressure," Maxim replies through gritted teeth. He turns the less-maneuverable-than-a-fighter troop transport on the most direct course, heading away from the rogue Peacekeepers. "He's got more ships here with him than I would have expected."

"I grabbed scans of each one. If we survive, we can send them along to Peacekeeper Command." Bennie says, not looking up from his display. He lifts his wristcomm and mumbles, "Three, two, one."

Outside the ship, the massive command carrier tips slightly. Then, a large section of the dorsal hull bulges before erupting. It spills fire, drive plasma and atmosphere into space.

"Holy—! What was that?" Maxim asks, glancing at the sensor display that's flashing and beeping radiation alarms.

"My last surprise for Janus." Bennie says, turning to face his friend, a huge grin splitting his green face. "He had it coming."

Maxim laughs. "That he did—" Before he can finish, the ship lurches to the sides and sparks erupt from a console over their heads. "Dren! Fighters! Hold on!" He pushes the controls hard over. "Never thought I'd say this but I wish Wil was here. He's a much better pilot than I am."

"I won't tell him you said that," Bennie says, pulling up the controls for the aft weapons system. "How does one Peacekeeper man both the fore and aft weapons?"

"Multitasking" is all Maxim says. He throws the ship into a wild corkscrew spin. Something back inside the crew compartment explodes. "Any time now."

"Apparently, I have to do all the work in this rescue," Bennie quips before holding down the triggers on his small joystick, sending a stream of deadly plasma into the nearest strike fighter. "Boom!" He shouts then shrieks as the ship shakes violently, nearly tossing him from his seat.

"Still eleven hostiles!" Maxim shouts over the sound of alarms. "If you can keep us clear for two more centocks, we'll be in the clear."

Bennie says nothing. He presses the triggers down, firing indiscriminately at anything that shows up on his screen.

The weapons system automatically powers down as the FTL engines engage, pushing the troop transport faster than light. Bennie looks up at Maxim then raises his hand for a high five, his smile as wide as the big Palorian has ever seen it. "We'll need to change course a time or two to lose them," Bennie says, a moment later.

"Agreed," Maxim says as he prepares to take them out of FTL. "By the way, I apologize for not having faith in your ability to get us off that ship."

Bennie smiles and says nothing.

CHAPTER 8_

HUFFING AND PUFFING DOESN'T WORK_

THE HATCH LEADING to the command center is full of dents. It is scorched as if someone had too much fun with a flamethrower and it looks like someone might have head-butted it more than once. Wil looks around the gathered group of scientists and criminals. "Looks like you gave the old college try." He waves Gabe over. "What ya think, big guy?"

Gabe leans down to examine the control panel, or what remains of it, set next to the large hatch, then straightens and turns to Rhys Duch and his crew, "Was punching the control circuits part of your strategy for gaining entrance?"

One of the crew, the short muscled purple being with long arms, short legs and oversized incisor teeth blushes, "Sorry ah gaht mahd aht it."

"Indeed." Gabe turns and extends several thin tendrils from his fingertips. Each filament weaves its way into the remains of the control panel.

Wil looks to Hathyr. "Guessing you don't have a means to get into this?"

The timid scientist shakes her head. "No."

Wil shrugs and turns to Rhys Duch. "So, thinking of taking over Xarrix's operations?"

"Someone has to." The blonde alien smiles, his perfect teeth gleam in the low light.

"And you think it's you?" Cynthia asks. The look on her face makes it clear what she thinks of the idea.

"Sure, how hard can it be?" The very human looking alien replies, shrugging.

"Oh lord!" Wil sighs then turns to the Farsight team. "So here's the plan. Once we're inside, we'll figure out what's wrong with the computer, get things repaired and figure out what's up with the comm system so we can establish contact with Farsight." He looks around. "They can send a team to figure out the rest of this." He looks at Rhys Duch. "You can have a head start on the robbing and such. We can get paid and someone else can find the monster."

"Because it's ever that easy." Zephyr says, only slightly under her breath. Cynthia stifles a chuckle, mostly.

"We should leave here, go back to your ships and call for help from the orbit." Hathyr says, backing toward the corridor they came down. "Safer off planet! Out of this system!"

"We'd have to get clear of the radiation belt around the inner planets of this system, remember. It would take a while." Wil says. "Remember?" He adds.

"Of course, of course. I still want to leave the planet." Hathyr insists.

"You're safe with us, calm down." Wil urges then turns to Zephyr to discuss something.

Coorish leans over to Bon and whispers, "Are you familiar with her species?"

Bon shakes his head and looks back toward the corridor Hathyr vanished down. "No, though I noticed that she possessed several features I recognize from other species I am familiar with."

Coorish clicks its mandibles twice. "I noticed that too. Her facial features were distinctly Quillant, but her hands were Saldinian in nature."

Bon nods. "Her scent reminds me a lot of Harrith. The quills on her head look very much like those of the Kilden."

The hatch to the command center makes a popping sound then slides open. Gabe stands up. He extends his hand, motioning for the group to enter.

"Quite odd." Coorish murmurs as the technicians follow the rest of the group into the command-and-control center of the research complex.

T he command center looks like a bomb went off inside it.

"What. The. Hell?" Wil says to no one in particular as the group enters the large circular space.

Zephyr looks around and whistles. "Farsight really does over-engineer everything, don't they?"

Bon nods while walking toward a station near the center of the room. "Indeed we do. Oh!"

Wil and Zephyr rush over to find Bon's foot hovering over the remains of someone whose Farsight coveralls are in tatters and most of the lower body is missing. One flipper-like hand is clutching a PADD.

"I will never sleep again," Wil mumbles, easing Bon around the remains toward the station that was his original destination. "See what you can do." Then, he waves to Gabe. "Mind helping Bon here?"

"Of course, Captain." The tall droid takes a wider route to the station, avoiding the grisly remains.

"How many people were stationed here?" Cynthia asks from across the room.

"Several dozen," Coorish offers while pushing a chair designed for a body not at all like theirs out of the way of the station.

"Great, so lots more bodies to find." She says, turning toward a hatch opposite the one they came in through. "Where's this go?"

"According to the blueprint provided by Mister Asgar, that hatch leads to the main station complex below," Gabe offers. "There is a master lift and stairwell as well as several offices and other support spaces." He turns to Wil. "Captain, I am afraid we will have to go further into the complex."

Wil exhales. "Of course. How come?"

Before Gabe can answer, Bon turns. "Whatever happened to the main computer, didn't happen here." He gestures the entire room. "This place is trashed to be sure, but it's mostly superficial. The computer is either damaged or offline; there's no way to tell from up here. We must go down to the core, below the research sections."

"What about the comm array?" Wil asks.

"Without the computer, there's no way to run a diagnostic." Bon replies.

CALLING LONG DISTANCE_

"So, now what?" Bennie asks as he turns to face Maxim. Their stolen Peacekeeper troop transport is moving through space faster than light speed toward nothing in particular. They have made two random course corrections to elude any potential pursuit.

Maxim looks down at the console in front of him then slides the FTL throttle back all the way, dropping the vessel back to normal space. "Now we get a good fix on our position and see if we can find our friends." He glances at the long range sensor display. "And hope Janus' people don't track us before we make our next FTL jump."

Bennie pulls up the communications system. "You work on the *where are we* problem, I'll see if I can get someone to answer the comms." He starts to work the controls.

Maxim looks at the long range scanner display, watching it slowly update as it gathers data on their location. *This could take a while.* "I have to admit, Bennie, I'm impressed you did all this."

"Did all what? Saved your life? Why? You'd do the same for me." Bennie doesn't look up from the screen he's staring at. "You said so, no take backs."

"I'm a trained Peacekeeper—

"Ex-Peacekeeper" Bennie corrects him in his best impression of the tone of voice Maxim uses when correcting others.

Maxim tuts, "Indeed. Still, that was incredibly heroic of you. Thank you. I know you've been struggling since the whole *Siege Perilous thing.*"

Bennie waves one hand. "Sure. Like I said, you'd do it for me and no one else was around. There really wasn't time to think about it. I'm sure if I did, you'd be dead now." He's silent a moment. "I do feel quite a bit better now than I have in months. Those drones were terrifying and being alone on the ship while you all were fighting for your lives, I don't know, it messed me up more than I thought something like that would." Before Maxim can form an answer to the uncharacteristic sharing, Bennie lets out a whoop, "Think I found 'em!"

"The *Ghost?*" Maxim asks.

"Yeah, well sorta. No one was answering on the *Ghost;* they must be out of range or the comm system is offline. But I picked up a GC comm relay about five light-years from here and hacked it. From there it was easy to get into the overall comm buffer relay system. Since we were supposed to meet them on Nilop, I looked for messages near that comm node. It looks like they left Nilop a few days ago."

"Where to?"

"It's a comm log, not a travelogue. How would I know?" Bennie says, looking at Maxim like he's a child. "Hold on a second." He adds before the big Palorian can respond. Maxim huffs.

More than a second later, Bennie breaks the silence. "Hi, mister Asgar, it's Bennie and Maxim from the *Ghost.* Yes, yes I know this is your private line. Yes, I know it is unlisted, quite well actually. Kudos. Oh, yes well, sorry I didn't know who else to call. Ok, yes—" Bennie turns a pale shade of green. "Oh! Yes, I understand; never again. Ok, thank you." He turns to Maxim who's just staring at him expectantly. "They went to a research station on a planet called Glacial. Wil took a job rather than wait for us, that drennog."

"And?"

"And nothing. He said it should be in the navcom."

Maxim starts looking for the planet and adds, "That was a lot of conversation for a planet name." He raises an eyebrow.

"Oh, yeah, I woke him up. Apparently, he's not on Nilop anymore either; some business trip to the Squirgle system. He wasn't very happy about being woken up."

"Can't blame him. Found it."

Bennie leans over Maxim's arm to look before being shoved back into his seat. "Ice world; no real data beyond the basics. Guess Farsight has an interest in it if that's why the *Ghost* is heading there. The galactic nav network just lists it as class B system, mild pirate and raider activity."

"How far are we from it?"

Maxim adjusts the controls and then pushes the FTL throttle all the way forward. He looks at Bennie. "About a day. Better see what kind of supplies this boat has."

Bennie hops out of his seat and heads aft.

SPLITTING UP MAKES SENSE_

"Ok, so here's what I'm thinking. Gabe, Zephyr, Bon, Coorish and I will go down to the computer section. Rhys, you too. Everyone else, stay here." Wil speaks to the gathering of beings in the command center. He turns to Hathyr, "Probably best if you stay here."

The small woman shudders. "Agreed. I know nothing of the computer levels. I want to leave not go deeper."

Rhys Duch looks at the yellow alien, as if seeing her for the first time, then asks, "Why am I coming with you? Why are my guys staying here?"

Wil tries to hide his annoyance. "Protection, for one. Plus, if we're going to work together our groups should be evenly distributed." He doesn't add *because one less goon with us makes the odds that much better should this go sideways and Cynthia can handle your goon squad up here.*

The blonde human-looking alien shrugs. "Ok, Grell." He points to the short purple alien that smashed the control panel. "You're in charge." As if remembering why they're on the planet to begin with, he adds, "Oh and see if you can find anything of value." He looks at his Malkorite thug, Guut. "See if you can do anything with the computer." Guut nods.

136

Nodding his slightly gorilla-like head, the short purple brute says, "Ahkay, will do bahss." Cynthia rolls her eyes.

Wil raises an eyebrow at Gabe who just nods once. "Ok then, let's go." He turns to Cynthia and mouths, *sorry*. She waves him off.

"Of course the lift is dead!" Wil exhales and raises both hands in the air in exasperation. Without another word, he starts down the metal steps, each step loudly echoing.

"Without the main computer, the lift seems to be locked at the level below." Gabe observes, looking at the shaft in the middle of the stairwell.

"Is your Captain always this cranky?" Coorish asks Gabe. Gabe extends a hand and wiggles it side to side. Coorish clacks its mandibles twice then continues on.

Wil turns to Zephyr. "I'm really starting to think Asgar wasn't entirely upfront about this place when hiring us."

Zephyr casts a sideways glance at her Captain. "Ya think?"

As they turn a corner, the stairwell opens up to a landing with corridors leading off in three directions. There's no sign anyone is around though all the lights are on.

Gabe comes forward. "According to the blueprints, this is the residential level. They assign each scientist a room with a small office attached." He slowly turns, taking in the entire space. "I do not detect any life signs."

Wil starts for the stairs that lead to the next level. "Let's keep moving then. We're not here to explore."

As the group continues down the stairs, Rhys Duch slows until he's lost sight of the last of the group. Then, he slowly takes the few steps back up to the residential level. "Bet there's some interesting trinkets around here."

"Rhys!" Wil shouts from below.

"Krebnack!" The would-be crime boss exhales and turns to head down the stairs.

As the others leave, Cynthia turns to Grell. "So purple guy, how're you liking working for Duch?"

Before he can reply, Zash, the four-armed goon, answers, "I mean, he's no Xarrix but he's nice enough."

"Until yah get him mahd," Grell adds. "He has a mean streak."

Cynthia looks at the purple-skinned alien. "Really? I never heard about a *mean side*." She uses the air quotes gesture she's seen Wil use. "I mean Lorath and Xarrix put him out in the weeds for a reason."

Guut turns from the console he's sitting at, "Oh, he does. If you hadn't found Mort, he'd have killed her when he did."

Zash looks at her. "So you got out of the life, huh?"

"Yeah." She doesn't bother to hide the disgust at her past life. "Without Lorath and Xarrix, I didn't see any reason to stick around." *No need to give these idiots the full story.* She thinks. "Rhys was a low-level imbecile that Xarrix was never sure what to do with from what I recall." She continues.

Grell laughs, which sounds a lot like when Bennie eats too much pizza. "Oh, he dahfintely isn't the smahtest guy ahrund but thot just leave room fuh the mean."

Cynthia reaches up to the earpiece she's wearing which is tied to her wristcomm for more discreet and private conversations, static. She glances around. "Are your comms working?"

Zash lifts one of his arms, the one with a second-hand-looking wristcomm on it. "Hey boss, come in." After a few seconds of staring at the device, he looks at Cynthia. "Nope."

"You'll pay for this Wil Calder," she mumbles under her breath as she walks over to the station Guut is at and drops into the seat next to him. She brings up the interface and looks over to the Malkorite next to her. "Let's see what we can find."

OH, LOOK! BACKDOOR_

"THIS LOOKS INVITING." Bennie says as the stolen Peacekeeper troop transport drops out of FTL on a course for the frozen world called Glacial.

Maxim looks out the cockpit. "Wonder what Farsight was doing out here?"

Bennie shrugs, "Who knows, artifacts probably. It's always *artifacts*."

Maxim glances over to his friend, one eyebrow raised. "I'm not picking up any beacons."

"Wait one." The Brailack hacker says as he turns to look at a different console in the small cockpit.

"By the way, when was the last time you bathed?" Maxim asks while wrinkling his nose.

Bennie waves a hand. "I don't know. Yesterday, the day before that maybe?"

"No way, you're ripe. You know there's a refresher back there." He hitches one of his thumbs toward the hatch that connects the cockpit to the rest of the small craft.

Bennie taps his head a few times, thinking. "No, it was back aboard the Freighter! That's right, I found a crew head that was closed for repair."

"That was a week ago!"

"Well I was busy, you know infiltrating a Peacekeeper command carrier, saving you—"

"*Ex*-Peacekeepers." Maxim corrects.

Bennie tuts and makes a rude gesture before turning back to the console. "Found it! Just an automated landing beacon. Looks like there's a warning attached." He taps his console. "Oh wonderful! *Facility is on lockdown,* he reads out loud. Looks buttoned up. The landing dome is sealed up and I'm guessing the *Ghost* is inside. There's what looks like an auxiliary building about two kilometers from the main buildings. There's a landing pad there; it's not protected by a dome but still viable, from the look of it."

"Ok, send me the coordinates. Then go shower." Before Bennie can object, Maxim continues, "There will be no adventuring with you smelling like the underside of a gundark."

"Gah! Fine!" Bennie hops out of the seat and heads back to the troop area.

Maxim turns back to the view in front of the ship, sighing. "Snow storms, great."

As the troop transport breaks through the clouds, the hatch to the cockpit opens. "Think you can land in this?" Bennie asks.

Maxim glances back. "Oh! What is happening here?" He snaps his head back. "Why are you not wearing clothes?"

"I am wearing clothes, I'm in my underwear." Bennie says, hopping back into his seat.

"Yes, what happened to the rest of your clothes?" Maxim asks, doing his best to keep his eyes on the storm ahead of them.

"I'm washing them, they were a little ripe too." Bennie is looking at his console while they talk. "You're off course, bring it back to port eleven degrees."

"Thank you. The moment we land, go get dressed."

The ship lurches and slides on its thrusters, first to the left then back to the right, as Maxim fights the storm for control of the small craft.

"Maybe I'll go get dressed now, I don't want to die in my underpants!" Bennie hollers over the sound of the wind battering the front of the cockpit.

Maxim glances over, quickly regrets it and returns his gaze to the growing landing pad ahead of them. "Oh calm down! We've seen Wil land in worse. Wurrin, he probably landed in this same storm."

"Wil crashes a lot." Bennie reminds his big friend.

CHAPTER 9_

ANOTHER BODY_

"Oʜ ʟᴏᴏᴋ, ᴀɴᴏᴛʜᴇʀ ʙᴏᴅʏ." Wil says as he takes the final step to the landing below the residential floor.

"Oh my!" Coorish gasps. "That's Betan 'Or, the head of the station. I worked with her for two cycles on Capralla. This was her first assignment as facility lead." Its mandibles clack slowly. "Her loss is terrible. She was an amazing intellect."

Bon comes down the remaining steps and rests a hand on his colleague's upper shoulder. "Four more levels." He looks around. "I think this is *Research One* where any non-primary discoveries and anything not specific to the facility are worked on."

"That is correct, Bon. This level is designated *Research Level One*. According to the data Mister Asgar provided, the researchers were examining several minor artifacts discovered at the dig site." Gabe is looking down the nearest corridor. "Perhaps we should explore this level before continuing on."

Zephyr heads toward one of the labs. "It probably makes sense to secure this level; we didn't upstairs but it make sense. Maybe Gabe can secure the doors once we're sure. Make sure whatever killed everyone isn't sneaking up behind us."

"Oh my," Bon whispers as he glances over the body of Betan 'Or.

Wil nods, lifting his wristcomm. "Hey Cyn, we're on Level Three. We're going to look around a bit." When no one answers, he looks down at the screen. "Huh." He taps the screen a few times, looking at the display. "Anyone else getting signal?"

Zephyr looks at her own wristcomm and shakes her head. Bon and Coorish do the same.

Gabe tilts his head. "There appears to be a low level radiation permeating this level, likely the entire station."

"Why didn't you detect it earlier?" Wil asks.

"I did say *low level.*" A mechanical eyebrow rises. "I am afraid I have to admit that whatever the radiation source, the radiation itself is unusual and is having unexpected interactions with my systems."

"According to the last reports we received from the team here, that radiation isn't planetary; it's from the dig site." Bon offers.

"Is it harmful?" Rhys Duch looks around.

"It is not," Gabe replies. "According to my sensors, the radiation is benign not withstanding its effects on communications."

Zephyr whistles. "So, weird radiation coming from underground plus a hyper-active star irradiating the system. Fun."

Wil nods. "Ok, let's secure these labs. Pronto!"

Wil sets down a long, brown, triangular stone with wavy lines carved halfway down each face. Then, he looks around the rest of the room. "This one is clear."

Zephyr passes the door to the lab Wil is in. "Mine was clear," she says.

Closing the door, Wil pulls his pulse pistol out and shoots the handle, melting it. "Only two wings left. Let's get a move on."

"Uh, I found another body!" Rhys Duch shouts from somewhere down one of the remaining two corridors.

"Great!" Wil mutters and waves for Zephyr to follow. "Let's go see who we've got."

"Goody." She replies.

"I don't recognize him." Bon says, standing over the remains of a Harrith man laying sprawled in the middle of lab full of artifacts.

Coorish shakes its head, the low light reflecting off its multifaceted eyes as it kneels next to the body. "I do not know him either." It looks up at the others. "Farsight Corporation employs tens of thousands of beings. We do not all know each other and the last company picnic was many cycles ago."

"Uh, are we not going to talk about the fact that this poor sod is ripped in half?" Rhys asks, wringing his hands while looking this way and that.

Wil looks over at the surf bum-looking alien. "Well, I mean yeah that part's obvious." He points to the corpse. "The mystery monster did that." He looks over at Zephyr. "*Science*, monster."

Zephyr sighs and turns to Gabe. "Anything?"

The tall droid looks from the corpse to Zephyr. "Indeed. Something ripped this poor gentleman in half." When she says nothing, he continues, "My sensors don't detect any DNA that isn't his own. Whatever tore him apart left no trace evidence."

"Oh my." Coorish clacks. Bon nods vigorously.

Gabe continues, "It would appear that whatever did this, used the air duct." He points to a duct near the ceiling; the grate that covers the opening is hanging open on its hinge.

MESSAGES FROM BEYOND_

CYNTHIA TURNS from the terminal to the gathered criminals nearby. "Well, despite the main computer being offline, Guut and I found a set of log entries from the facility's lead researcher, a Betan 'Or?" Zash and Grell shrug, causing Cynthia to growl and turn back to the terminal. She looks at Guut, "So, you're the smart one?" She presses a control and the small display next to the station she's at comes to life.

On the screen is an aquatic being with large eyes and gill slits along her cheeks. Her brown skin is mottled and slightly moist-looking. Her large golden eyes tilt back and forth. "We've made another amazing discovery. This site might be one of the richest archeological digs in Farsight history. The dig team brought up, well, something. It was in some type of stasis chamber that is thousands of years old. We don't quite know what it is, yet." She looks off to the left of the screen. Someone says something that the recorder doesn't pick up. She nods. "I'll be right there, thank you." She turns back to look at the recorder. "We've moved the object to Research Two and will begin thawing it shortly. As it thaws, we'll be able to more accurately scan it. The chamber it was in seems to have malfunctioned and is emitting a radiation no one here is familiar with. An interesting challenge to be sure." The screen goes dark.

Cynthia taps a finger to her chin in thought. "That was the most recent entry. It was in the comm buffer."

Guut looks up. "Probably recorded and ready to send, then got stuck when the computer went down."

Guut turns to Zash and Grell. "We should send someone down to catch up with the others and let them know."

"Know whaht?" Grell asks, his purple face as blank as a powered down PADD.

Cynthia tries not to sigh too loudly. "That comms are out, and that whatever they brought out of the dig site was frozen, and in the process of being thawed."

"Or already thawed out." Guut offers. Cynthia nods.

"Oh! Is that important?" Zash asks.

Growling, Cynthia points to the hatch leading to the stairwell. "Please, just one of you go." She gets up and heads out of the room back to the corridor leading to the anteroom.

Grell points to the Malkorite. "Guut, go down and tell thah bahss about thah frozen thing."

Guut reaches over to the terminal next to where Cynthia was sitting and removes a data stick. He stands and heads out of the command center toward the main stairwell.

Zash walks over to Grell. "I don't think Cynthia likes us."

Grell shrugs. "Ahs long ahs Rhys likes us, she can gah grolack herself."

Hathyr, who's been sitting at one of the stations looks up at the remaining criminals. Then, she gets up and heads the same direction Cynthia just did.

Cynthia is standing in the corridor connecting the command center to the anteroom and adjoining offices and storerooms. She's looking through the clear window into an office when Hathyr walks up. "Whatever is down there might kill them. We could leave now in your ship."

Cynthia looks down. "We're not leaving my friends. I understand you've been through a serious trauma, surviving all this, being here alone and all but we leave when this is done."

The small alien looks up. Cynthia notices that her nose looks very human. *Did it always?* "I don't want to die on this world."

BENNIE, IT'S COLD OUTSIDE_

OUTSIDE THE COCKPIT WINDOW, the storm is whipping snow everywhere and quickly piling it up on the clear plastisteal.

"Don't suppose there's cold weather gear back there anywhere?" Maxim asks, turning to look back into the crew compartment where Bennie is rummaging around.

"Well, sorta."

Maxim finishes the power down sequence. He gets up and heads aft. "That's a completely non-definitive answer."

The crew compartment of the troop transport is fairly spartan, consisting of long benches down both sides. The refresher is in the middle of the port side and opposite it is a large equipment closet. Bennie is in the equipment closet, tossing various things out into the compartment.

"That's a sonic disruptor grenade, ah— so was that one. Please stop throwing those!" Maxim shouts, crossing the distance between him and the storage compartment in only a few long strides. He expertly catches a third stun grenade mid-air. "Cut that out!" He reaches in, grabs the small Brailack and pulls him out of the locker.

"Hey!" Bennie hollers as he is lifted up and out of the space. He crosses his arms as Maxim sets him down. "There's some light armor in the back; of course, none that will fit me."

Maxim looks back at Bennie. "So by *sorta*, you meant I'd be all right but you wouldn't?"

"Well, yeah. Duh." He motions in the direction of the large hatch at the back of the transport. "It's near freezing out there!" He stomps toward the cockpit. "I can't make it from here to the hatch which, might I remind you, we probably have to hack to open, before freezing to death." He points again to the storm beyond the bulkheads. "Brai doesn't have arctic regions, at least ones we visit." He holds up a thin arm. "We're a tropical people!"

Maxim turns back to the storage locker, looks around then grabs something. He turns and tosses it at Bennie who catches the item and collapses under its weight, making a strangled yelp.

Bennie sits up and looks at his lap. "What am I supposed to do with this?"

"I am not ok with this." Bennie says from inside the thick emergency blanket he's rolled inside of. "I'm not a barroto."

"I think it's *burrito*." Maxim replies. "It's also the only way I can get you from here," he adds and points to the hatch and the auxiliary research building beyond, "to *there*."

Bennie sighs loudly. "Fine, let's get this over with."

Maxim tightens the straps on his borrowed light armor. It won't do much for the cold but is better than the coverall he's been wearing since being brought aboard the *Pax Liberatus*. "You have your gear? For hacking the hatch if needed."

From inside the bundle of blanket, a small green face glowers. "Wristcomm and mind, what? You think I need anything else?"

Maxim looks at his friend then drops the bundled up Brailack on the deck, eliciting a *screech*. He picks the bundled up hacker back up and reaches up for the control panel that controls the rear hatch of the troop transport. "Oops. On three. One... two... three." He presses the button.

The moment the hatch opens, snow and freezing air blast inside the transport. The big Palorian jumps from the hatch while it's still a meter from the ground. He lands with a grunt, two actually, his and one from the bundle of blankets wrapped around a Brailack under his arm. He sprints toward the auxiliary research building a hundred meters from the transport.

As he reaches the hatch to the auxiliary facility, Maxim unceremoniously drops his bundled up friend. "Hu-hurry, I'm fr-freezing." He unwraps Bennie as best he can.

"Holy balls, it's freezing!" Bennie shouts as he jumps up and dusts snow off the control panel next to the hatch. With his shaking hands, he connects one of the connectors from his wristcomm to the side of the panel. The screen is already dusted with snow.

Maxim is standing over him to block as much snow and wind as he can. "Hu-hurry."

"I'm go-going as fast as I ca-can." Bennie chatters as he accesses the hatch's systems. His fingers are numb and it's now hard to work his wristcomm controls. "Gro-grolack!" He hisses.

"We sh-should get ba-back to the sh-ship." Maxim says, sagging. Snow is piling on him. "War-warm up, try ag-again."

"N-no!" Bennie says. He brushes off the screen of his wristcomm once more. "One mo-more th-thing." He presses a button and groans when his numb finger presses the wrong control, resets the routine and runs it. Seconds pass then the hatch clicks open. Both men stumble inside, slamming the heavy door behind them.

NEWSCAST_

"Good morning, I'm Klor'Tillen with GNO, live from Galtron City." The Brailack journalist is standing in a market square. Armored troops are standing at every intersection with several walking around on what looks like patrol. Their chests are adorned with the Farsight Corporation logo.

"Behind me you can see several Farsight security forces personnel walking this market square. Farsight forces have been here since last night when several cruisers engaged a Crucible Corp. cruiser near the mountains. They have detained several citizens of Galtron City until they complete the merger. Hostile takeovers like this are rare and this one may reset the bar on the definition of *hostile* but it seems the outcome is a foregone conclusion."

CHAPTER 10_

OH, THAT'S GROSS!_

THE SIGN above the landing reads, *Research Two*. Wil looks at the group as they assemble on the landing, the empty central column for the lift next him. "So this is where the good stuff is supposed to be?"

"And the monster," Bon adds. "Assuming the *monster* is something they found at the dig site."

Wil stares at the scientist then turns to Zephyr and Rhys who are standing next to each other. "All right, let's clear this level. We're three levels from the computer center."

"Why is the computer center at the bottom?" Rhys wonders out loud.

Bon offers, "The computer this facility uses is massive. I suspect it generates tremendous amounts of heat. I believe they placed it at the lowest level for two reasons; to facilitate cooling and to channel the generated heat into the rest of the structure." Nodding at the thought, he adds, "Ingenious really, to use the waste heat from the processors to reduce the heating needs on the life support system."

Rhys is staring at the red-skinned scientist. "Ok."

Zephyr leans toward Wil. "He didn't understand a word of that."

Wil stifles a chuckle and points toward one of the three corridors branching off the central stairwell landing. "Ok. Zee, you and Rhys take that one. Bon, you're with me. Gabe and Coorish, take the other one."

Rhys raises a hand. "Wait. So why isn't it cold in here then? If the computer is offline, I mean."

Wil looks at Zephyr, mouthing the word, *damn.*

Bon frowns. "That is a good question mister Duch. I do not know the answer." Coorish nods in agreement behind its superior.

Wil waves. "Let's get this done."

"So Bon, what do you know about this level?" Wil asks, aiming his pistol ahead of them as they slowly walk down the corridor.

"Nothing, I'm afraid." Bon turns, causing the dreadlock-like tentacles on his head to whip around. "This level is for the more sensitive research projects." He notices Wil's blank look and adds, "Whatever they were thawing out for example or any technology they discovered. Bodies would also likely be on this level." Thinking about the bodies on the level above, he adds, "Bodies from the dig site, I mean."

"Yeah, I knew what you meant." Wil presses a button to open the first lab door. "We're not here to explore. We make sure no one or nothing is in each room then close it and secure the door as best we can," he says.

Bon nods while looking through the window next to the door. "Of course, Captain."

"You know, I don't think Cynthia likes me much." Rhys says as he and Zephyr close a door and shoot the locking mechanism.

She turns to him. "What makes you think that?" She tries to hide the knowing look from her face.

"Just a vibe I get. I know I'm not like, you know, a scientist or tactical genius or anything, but I did run the operation Xarrix gave me better than anyone else. Our profits were up cycle over cycle. Everyone was paying on time and I had the local authorities so deep in my pocket they didn't write parking tickets without checking with us first."

Zephyr shrugs, finding the entire exchange a bit surreal. "Well remember, she worked directly for Lorath and Xarrix. Her experience on the ground differs from yours." She looks sideways at the blonde-haired criminal. "Or something." She adds under her breath.

Rhys shrugs and enters a lab. He jumps back, making a noise similar to the one Wil makes when he's terrified. "What the grolack is that?" He stammers, raising his rifle.

Zephyr looks past him. She rests her hand on his rifle and slowly guides it down. In front of them, in the middle of the lab, is a work table with some type of blob sitting in the center of it.

Slowly, Zephyr moves around the would-be kingpin and into the room, her rifle scanning left and right as she enters. She looks at the mass on the table. "Uh, this is, or was, a person."

"What? No way" Rhys looks around her at the table. "Wait a minute." He makes another strangled-sounding noise then looks again, "Guut?"

"What is a Guut?" Zephyr asks, circling the table and scanning the room. When she's satisfied it's just the two, or three of them, she turns her attention back to the gory mass on the table. She now sees what looks like a distinctly Malkorite ear amid the gore. "Oh, one of your guys?" She asks. She looks at the mass then to Rhys. "Didn't he stay with Cynthia and your lieutenant? What's he doing down here?"

Rhys stops poking the pile of remains with his rifle barrel and looks to Zephyr. "How would I know?" He looks back at the mass and uses his rifle to lift the remains of an arm with a wristcomm still attached to it, "Definitely Guut."

THIS IS WHERE IT STARTED_

"Do you smell that?" Coorish asks, looking up at Gabe. "Oh, forgive me," it adds.

"No offense taken. While my nose is mostly decorative, I have quite powerful olfactory sensors. So yes, I do *smell that*. In fact, I believe it is coming from the lab directly ahead." Gabe moves toward the door and takes a position in front of his insectoid companion. His eyes spin up to their red combat mode color and his arms deploy their double-barreled blasters.

"Oh, so intriguing," Coorish observes. "What model droid did you say you were?"

"I did not say. I was originally an engineering model, series 10a. After my encounter with the *Siege Perilous,* I created an entirely new chassis for my spark." He rests a hand on his chest and it clangs slightly. "This body is a variation on a design I found within the database of the dreadnaught." He turns back to the hatch. "Please be careful to stay behind me." Then, he pushes the hatch open.

As the lab door opens, the full power of the offending odor is released. "Oh my!" Coorish chokes from behind Gabe and tiny hair-like structures on its mandibles curl. Gabe nods as he disengages his olfactory sensors. The insectoid scientist peeks around the large droid and points to the worktable in the middle of the room. "Look."

In the center of the room is a large work table covered in scraps of cloth and other debris. Under the table are several large basins, all nearly full of water. Around the table, several bodies are scattered, including two droids.

Gabe takes in the scene. "This must be the lab where they began thawing the mysterious discovery in." He points to several heat lamps on articulated arms mounted to the ceiling then to the bodies. "Clearly, whatever it was awoke in a bad mood."

Coorish nods. "Agreed." It walks over to the nearest body. "She is mostly intact, unlike some other bodies we've encountered." One of its six limbs reaches out and prods a hole in the female scientists' head her short stubby quills stained with her pink blood. "She is Kilden. Something pierced her skull." Coorish looks from the dead woman to another form a meter away, a Harrith man or what remains of him. "This man looks to have been slashed several times by something sharp."

Gabe has moved to inspect one of the droids. He stands and nods. "Indeed. All of them were killed differently; some ripped to pieces while others suffered a single life-ending wound. Interesting. Also, this droid's primary computing core is pierced; I cannot get any information from it." The tall droid turns and walks toward a particularly wet smear of blood on the far wall. He kneels down to investigate the body. "I believe this researcher may have been the last to die."

Coorish comes over. Its chitinous feet make clicking sounds in the eerie silence of the room. "What makes you think so?"

Gabe points to the face of the man which is frozen in a rictus of terror. "The others seem to have died either instantly or nearly so. Their faces don't reflect the same level of terror that this man's face does. He died in absolute terror. He knew what was happening."

"Oh my." The insectoid says through chattering mandibles. "Whatever it was that they thawed is clearly a killing machine."

"I am inclined to agree." Gabe stands. "We should finish securing the labs in this wing and get the others."

"Could we maybe get them first?" Coorish asks, its compound eyes twitching this way and that.

THE WAITING IS THE WORST_

"WHAT HAVE WE HERE?" Cynthia asks, walking into a small office with a sleeping area in the corner. "This looks promising and quiet."

"Hey! Cynthia!"

"Shit." She mutters, hoping that she used it right. She moves toward the doorway, not wanting whomever is shouting to ruin what could be a lovely sanctuary. When she gets to the door, she asks "What?"

Zash is standing in the corridor. He raises his top right and lower left hands to wave. "Oh, there you are. Hi." He smiles.

"You wanted something, Zash?" Cynthia asks, trying not to leap across the room.

"Huh? Oh, yeah!" The big henchman says smiling. "I brought you lunch."

Cynthia just stares at the four-armed man for what might be a full minute then blinks. "What now?"

Zash's lower right hand reveals a paper-wrapped bundle. "We brought a cooler with us when we left the ship."

Cynthia's tail twitches. "I am a bit hungry." She walks over to Zash. She takes the package and holds it up to her nose. "What's this?"

"Family recipe," the big red skinned henchman says. "My grandmother's recipe—Doorip root salad with a hint of juquon spice."

"Doorip?" Cynthia takes a bite. "Mmm, this is quite good."

Zash produces his own sandwich and takes a bite. After he chews and swallows, he replies, "Doorip is a tuber from my planet; it's very hearty and calorie dense. Not very flavorful on its own but with egg-whip and some pickling juice, it makes a pretty good salad." He smiles and takes another bite just as Cynthia does. "The real magic is in the juquon spice, just the right amount of kick."

Cynthia smiles at the tall four-armed man. "This is fantastic Zash. Thank you."

He inclines his head. "My pleasure. When I'm with Duch on the *Pillager*, I'm the cook."

Cynthia takes another bite. "Wil would love this."

"Maybe I'll get to share; there's more Doorip salad on the *Pillager*." He turns back toward the hatch. "I better get back. If I'm gone too long, Grell will eat the rest of the food."

"Oh, ok. Uh, how much did you bring? Weren't you just assuming you'd be in and out?" Cynthia asks, now eyeing her half-eaten sandwich.

"Rhys Duch believes in being prepared." He turns to leave. "We brought a week's worth of food."

Cynthia follows. "But, you have your ship; it's parked just out there," she gestures vaguely in the direction of the landing dome. "You could get food any time."

Zash stops and turns to look back at Cynthia. "But then we wouldn't have needed the picnic basket." He shakes his head and continues on toward the command center.

Cynthia looks down at the delicious sandwich. "What the wurrin just happened?"

C ynthia yawns as she enters the command center. "Guut back?" Zash and Grell look up from a console they're huddled over. Grell shakes his thick purple head. "No."

"Wha—Aren't—" She growls. "Ok, let's go."

Grell hops out of the chair. "Go where? Bahss said tuh stay here."

"Guut should have caught up to them by now, and been back for that matter." She starts toward the hatch leading to the central column of the facility. Without looking over her shoulder, she says, "Come on dummies."

MONSTER OF THE WEEK?_

"How am I still so cold?" Bennie says through chattering teeth.

Maxim is shining the light on his rifle around the room. The thirty-meter square room is lined with small offices. Work tables fill the center area; each table has something on it, artifacts by the look of them. Max spots a control panel and walks over. The lights turn on and a slow hum begins to build. "I've activated the heat. Hold on, little man." He grabs a blanket he's found under one of the work tables and tosses it over to the shivering Brailack. "Still nothing on wristcomms."

The freezing and surly Brailack makes a harrumph noise from under the blanket. Maxim turns and heads toward the far side of the room. A larger office sits near what he believes is the hatch leading to the main complex. "You said two klicks?"

"Y-yes, t-two ki-kilometers." Bennie stutters. He stands and follows Maxim.

"Hey look at this," Maxim calls from inside the large office workspace. "This must be the station administrator's office when they're over here."

Without a word, Bennie walks past the big Palorian and hops into the chair behind a large metal desk with a computer terminal built into it. He taps a few controls. "Sure is. Someone named Betan 'Or. Looks like no one has used this facility in a few months. They used it as a base of operations for some of the short range atmospheric vehicles." Bennie taps the console a few times. "Se-seems this Betan 'Or grounded the short range explorations a year ago when they began what she referred to as *the dig*."

Maxim grunts, "Sounds ominous. Guessing that's tied to whatever took out their comms."

"Of c-course it is." Bennie says. He looks out to the hatch, "I g-guess we sh-should get moving."

Maxim nods. "Let's see what we can scrounge up in here first; we're uncomfortably light on supplies."

"At least this corridor seems heated." Maxim says as he and Bennie head off down the long moderately well-lit service corridor leading to the main research complex.

Bennie, finally warm, looks up at his big friend. "So, what do you think we're getting ourselves into? We know it can't be Peacekeepers, rogue or otherwise. We just left that party. It can't be some super computer intelligence. We've done that already. What would be the odds?"

Maxim tuts, "You're courting disaster saying things like that."

Ignoring his big friend, Bennie continues. "Well, it definitely isn't massive living starships. We're underground."

Maxim sighs. "You've doomed us."

This time it's Bennies turn to tut at his friend, "Such a worrier. Maybe some type of ancient evil," he says the last part with extra emphasis while making waving motions with his hands, "has been awoken and plans to devour our souls." He chuckles. "Or something like that."

"I hope whatever it is, eats you first." Maxim says, his head swiveling back and forth as he scans the tunnel ahead.

PART 3_

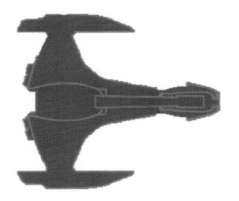

CHAPTER 11_

OH, HELL NO!_

WIL IS LOOKING around at the group. "OK, so we've got the room where our mystery monster came from and a room with one of Rhys's goons, dead."

"His name was Guut." Rhys adds.

Wil glances at the crime boss, "Yes, Guut. He's dead now and last time we saw him, he was upstairs with Cynthia and the others. So why is he here and how did he get here before us?"

"Do we really want answers to those questions?" Rhys offers.

"Fair and really, no," Wil agrees. "We've secured this level as best we can. I'm thinking we push on. The dig site access is below us and below that, the computer center." He motions toward the stairwell. "Let's go."

"Oh, hell no!" Wil exclaims as they near the entrance to the tunnel leading to the dig site. Lights blaze down the hundred-meter length of rough-hewn rock.

Zephyr comes around Wil and looks down the rocky corridor. "What the wurrin are those?"

About twenty meters from the entrance of the tunnel, hundreds of creatures are wriggling in a mass next to a sizable fissure in the tunnel. Steam is drifting out of the crack as slug-like creatures move back and forth from the pile to the hole and back. At the entrance to the tunnel, two heavy doors mounted to the rock itself, lie askew. From the look of them they've been forced open from the inside.

"Space slugs?" Wil offers.

"We've talked about this." Zephyr says, not looking at him.

Wil sighs. "Slug slugs then."

Now she turns to look at him. "What's a slug?"

Exasperated, Wil turns. "Why did you bust my chops if you didn't even know what I was saying? Maybe *space* actually was appropriate."

The Palorian woman shrugs. "I went with the odds." Before he can continue, she heads into the tunnel, rifle at the ready.

Wil gives her a dirty look and follows, turning to motion for the others to wait.

He turns back to his first officer. "Think these are *the monster?*" He makes an air quotes motion.

Zephyr kneels down and pokes one with her knife. It makes a squealing noise and sends several nearby slugs slithering away from the knife point, revealing what the mass is crawling over.

"Is that—" Wil starts.

"Another body? Yup, or at least what's left of it. I can't imagine these things killed him or her, but they must have been released from the dig site or something." She points to the pile. "Found the body and feasted. Left on their own, I'm guessing they'll infest this entire station."

She points and as if to help emphasize her point, one of the slug creatures on the wall begins to ooze some type of brown mucus that slowly hardens around the creature forming a cocoon.

"I'm gonna hurl." Wil turns away making a retching noise.

Zephyr stands up and looks further down the well-lit corridor. "We should at least take a look at the dig site." When Wil makes a face, she presses on. "It's the single largest space here. If anyone survived, they may well have taken refuge there."

"Hey, Gabe! Get over here! Bring everyone!" Wil shouts from the end of the corridor. "Don't step on the slug-things!" He adds.

Gabe turns to Rhys and the scientists. "I will lead. Please be careful."

It takes no time for the group to join Wil and Zephyr at the opening to the dig site.

"Wow!" is all Rhys can think to say.

"I said the same thing," Wil says, looking at the new arrivals then back to the massive subterranean cavern before them. Easily two hundred meters long, and half as many tall, the cavern is far bigger than any of them expected. Near the back of the space is a step pyramid fifty meters tall, at least. A golden box sits atop the pyramid, at least a meter on each side.

"The pyramid must be the most recent excavation," Gabe offers. "Notice the cavern wall still obscures the last sections of the back of the pyramid."

"Wonder what's in that gold box," Rhys Duch says, his eyes twinkling.

"Or what was." Zephyr adds.

Between the pyramid and them sits what looks like the remains of a town, small one and two story buildings following along what could be considered a road, leading to the pyramid.

They're standing on a large platform overlooking the cavern. There's a scaffold-like walkway that runs from the platform they're on to the end of the cavern, near the pyramid. A stairwell connects the floor of the immense space to the walkway halfway along the catwalk's length.

FAST, AREN'T THEY?_

Rʜʏs Dᴜᴄʜ ʟᴏᴏᴋs ᴀʀᴏᴜɴᴅ. "So many goodies," he says while rubbing his hands together.

Everyone is standing at the railing looking at the village below. Most of the buildings are laid out with what must have been the main thoroughfare with cross streets lost in the walls of the cavern.

Wil turns to look at the gathered team. "Ok so—" He's cut off by a high pitched keening sound coming from the access tunnel. "What the hell?" He looks around frantically. "Oh crap, where's Coorish?" He looks at Gabe who shrugs. "You can't shrug; you're packed full of sensors!"

Gabe turns toward the tunnel. "Forgive me, Captain. I should have said something sooner; my sensors are being affected the same as comms. The crust of this planet, the ice, the background radiation, it is all wreaking havoc on my sensors."

"Yeah, that woulda been good to know." He pushes past the tall droid. "Coorish! Are you ok? Where are you?" He turns to everyone else. "Ok, let's stick together; come on!" The keening sound fades to silence.

"Oh dren," Zephyr whispers as they approach the midpoint of the tunnel.

On the ground amid shredded coveralls are limb and torso segments of an exoskeleton that looks a lot like that one Coorish has been wearing.

Wil kneels down, "Fuck."

The remains of Coorish are covered in the slug-things they had stepped over further up the tunnel.

"How, how could they have killed her so quickly?" Bon says, standing behind Rhys Duch.

"Her?" Wil asks, looking up at Zephyr who shrugs.

Gabe looks over their shoulders. "It would appear that Coorish was attempting to take a sample of one of the creatures." He indicates a scanning unit the insectoid technician had had in her tool bag, now clutched in the remains of one of her hands.

Zephyr looks at the creatures and the body. "They couldn't have killed her, at least not so quickly. Something else did and either leaves these things behind or they swarm anybody they find." She uses her pistol to nudge a few of the slimy creatures aside and points to the piece of exoskeleton. "Look at these scratches, something with claws did this."

"Everyone, please step away from the remains." Gabe says, lacing his voice with urgency. He shines his light on the remains; a large section of exoskeleton shifts and the slug things slide off it as it moves. Something inky black is moving around inside the carapace, as if waking up. "I believe we may have found Coorish's killer." Gabe says as an elongated head emerges from the remains. The head ends in a spade-like point; the face is almost entirely mouth. The creature turns an eyeless gaze toward Wil and seems to smile. It opens its mouth to reveal its very sharp-looking teeth and another row of teeth is visible behind the first. It screams a high-pitched bark that makes Wil nearly drop his pistol. Three-fingered hands grasp the edge of the piece of chitin, slowly pulling the creature out. Its body matches its head, a mix of ridges and black skin.

"Jesus!" Wil stumbles backwards. "What is that?"

"Ugly." Rhys Duch says.

As the group steps back, the creature rises up on multi-segmented hind legs. Zephyr looks at the creature standing in front of them. "Not very intimidating, is it?" The creature is just under a meter tall; its half-meter long tail swishes back and forth as it seems to look at them. From a hole in the tunnel wall, another creature emerges, then another and another. "Ok, when there are a lot of them, they're a bit scarier." Zephyr amends, watching the tunnel ahead of them fill with the diminutive creatures. The one standing in front of them cocks its head to the side like it's examining them.

"Interesting. I wonder if the *slug slug* creatures, as the Captain called them, are some type of a larval form of these." Bon says from behind Gabe.

"A reasonable hypothesis," Gabe replies, his combat mode activating. His forearms shift to reveal double-barreled blasters.

"So, now what? They seem to be blocking the tunnel." Rhys says. "Maybe we can scare them off?"

Before anyone can answer, the horde of tiny monsters charges, screaming their high-pitch battle cry.

"Take 'em out!" Wil shouts, opening fire. Several creatures leap through the air while others use the claws on their three-fingered hands and three-toed feet to climb the walls and ceiling of the tunnel, somehow gaining purchase on the rock.

"Ok, they're faster and more agile than they look." Zephyr says, expertly kicking a creature that leaps right at her. "We need to fall back!" She shouts over the screams of the creatures. More are emerging from the hole.

One of the creatures drops from the ceiling onto Rhys's arm, eliciting a scream from him louder than the creature's own. Before he can react further, it bites down on his arm leaving a wound covered in blood and sticky saliva. Gabe reaches over and grabs the creature by its head before hurling it back into the mass. He fires one of his arm blasters at the creature before it hits the ground, its head exploding in an orange mist.

As they back toward the dig site, Wil mumbles, "Asgar is going to be pissed."

OH HEY, IT'S YOU!_

"Ahll these doors seem tah be locked." Grell says, wiggling the handle on a lab door on level three.

"Same with the doors down that corridor." Zash responds while looking at the offending door.

Cynthia nods then heads back toward the stairwell. "Wil and the rest of them must have been securing the floors as they went. That's not a fast process so they can't be too far ahead of us."

Zash leans over to Grell. "I'm not convinced catching up to them is a good thing."

Cynthia waves over her shoulder. "Come on! Not gonna defend you from the—" She makes air quotes, "*monster* if you're too far behind."

Zash frowns and whispers, "Like we need you to defend us."

Grell looks at Zash. "Wonder whaht kind ahf stuff these rooms hahve."

The tall red-skinned alien looks down at his companion. "Only one way to find out." He winks and they slow down until Cynthia is out of sight.

The sound of blaster fire echoes up the stairwell causing Cynthia to stop and crouch down. She looks back and realizes she's alone.

"Son of a nutcracker, where did those two idiots go?" She looks back the way she came then focuses on what's ahead. The weird screams echo all around the central column causing her ears to flatten in order to muffle the strange screams.

The sound of blaster fire repeats, louder this time, as she clears the landing of *Research Three while* heading down to the Dig site level.

Cynthia skids to a halt in front of a tunnel of rock. "This must lead to the dig site." She says to herself. She feels silly as she looks around in case anyone was there to witness her narration.

She pauses, thinking about what the two henchmen upstairs are doing, then stops. "They're big boys," she reminds herself, moving toward the tunnel with its earsplitting screaming and weapons fire. A blaster bolt strikes the tunnel ceiling ahead of her, superheating rock.

A short way into the tunnel, Cynthia stops dead in her tracks. She spots a writhing mass of black-skinned creatures ahead and beyond them, her friends. "Oh wurrin." She murmurs, drawing her pistol and opening fire on the little black nightmares attacking her friends. "Wil! Zephyr! Gabe!"

Wil shouts over the sound of the weapons fire, "Hey you!"

"Hey you!" Cynthia shouts, smiling while putting a glowing hole in one of the small hostile creatures before they realize they're being attacked from behind. Dozens of the creatures turn, scream-barking, and rush toward the new arrival. "Can you clear a path?" She shouts to Wil and the others, firing at every creature she sees, except the one clinging to the ceiling directly above her. The creature drops, spreading its arms and legs wide to tackle the Tygran woman to the ground. A split second before impact, she raises her hands to catch the creature, dropping her pistol. Both of her hands are busy keeping snapping jaws inches from her face while the barbed tail cuts at her arms and legs as it whips around, "A little help!" She shouts.

"Remain still!" Gabe shouts. A split second later, a single blast of plasma burns a hole in the attacking creature's side causing it to scream and fall to the side, orange goo splashing over Cynthia. Not missing a beat she promptly slams her fist sideways as hard as possible, almost crushing the skull of the creature. More orange goo oozes from the stunned creature's side. Cynthia jumps up, grabs her pistol and ends the small monster's life. She looks over to Gabe and nods. The droid returns the gesture, the whine of his blasters slightly louder than the war-cry screams of the creatures.

The weapons fire increases from the other side of the tunnel as Wil clears a path rushing up to Cynthia. "Let's go!" He turns before anyone can say anything.

As Wil and Cynthia reach the rest of the crew, the small black creatures keep coming. "Fall back!" Zephyr shouts as a creature launches itself at her only to be shot through the middle. As the group re-enters the dig site, Gabe grabs one of the damaged blast doors. Hinges marred by whatever broke through them last protest as the door begins to move. Wil, Cynthia and Rhys pull on the other door until it is close enough for Gabe to grasp. The screeching of metal grows in volume until the doors slam shut.

"I've never been more excited to see a blast door." Zephyr says as Gabe moves away from the heavy door, sealing off the dig site from the tunnel full of slimy nightmares and the central column of stairs. The door rings as dozens of small attackers collide with it. Dust rains down from the frame of the big doors.

"You and me both," Rhys Duch adds as the new combined group stares at the door.

Wil looks around, turns and heads straight for Cynthia. He takes her in his arms and kisses her.

When he hears Rhys Duch clear his throat, he turns and looks at the rest of the group. "What?" He sets her down.

WE MUST BE CLOSE_

"I ᴛʜɪɴᴋ we're almost to the end." Bennie says, shining the small flashlight he found in the auxiliary facility, down the tunnel ahead of them. The tunnel started out well lit but as they've progressed closer to the main facility, the number of functioning light strips has rapidly decreased. Several wall panels have been ripped from the wall, revealing rocks and ice.

"According to my wristcomm, about a hundred meters to go." Maxim confirms, his own light adding to Bennie's.

They keep walking. "Excited to see Zephyr?" Bennie asks.

"Very." Maxim confirms.

"Whoa, that's enough—" Bennie starts.

The big Palorian tuts, "Not like that. Well, very much like that but that's not what I meant. Since coming aboard the *Ghost,* neither of us has been apart more than a day or two." He looks down at Bennie. "It's been almost a month. Chatting over comms isn't the same."

Bennie shrugs. "Makes sense, I guess. Hey, what's that?" He moves his light down to a small object resting against the wall of the tunnel.

"Be careful." Maxim cautions as they advance. As they get closer, the object shifts and a small head turns to face them. The head is elongated and eyeless with a mouth full of tiny sharp-looking teeth.

"Sweet boneless zip zap." Bennie hisses then reaches for his pistol. The creature opens its mouth and releases a high-pitched bark-like scream that hurts the Brailack's ears. "Ah!"

Maxim pushes Bennie to the side with his hip and takes aim as the creature lunges toward them. His pulse pistol barks once, sending a single pulse blast into the creature, center mass. Its momentum carries it to land in a heap a foot away from Maxim's feet. The small mottled body twitches its mouth with its multiple rows of teeth slowly draw shut.

"You hit me in the head with your ass." Bennie complains, rubbing his head with one hand while the other keeps his pistol aimed at the motionless creature. He nudges it with his foot, "It's kinda cute, you know. Not counting all those teeth."

"Or that very sharp looking tail," Maxim adds, then smiles at his friend, "I can't help it if you're only ass tall," He nudges the lifeless body with his own boot, flipping it over. "What is it?" The meter-long body is now covered in orange organs and fluids. Its long barbed tail gives the creature another half-meter in length.

Bennie leans down to get a better view. "No idea. I've never seen anything like it." He moves his arm so his wristcomm can scan the body. "Until I can connect to the *Ghost* or the station's network, I can't do much. At least I've got a good reading of it." He looks at the creature. "Wonder where it came from?" Bennie moves his light back to where the creature had been hunched. "Oh dren." There's a sizable hole in the floor of the tunnel.

Maxim pushes Bennie's hand down, lowering the beam of the light away from the hole. "Wonder where that goes?" He whispers.

"I don't think I want to know." Bennie whispers back. He moves to the far side of the tunnel and walks as quietly past the hole as he can. Maxim is right behind him.

"Maybe that was the only one?" Bennie offers as they get a few meters from the hole.

"What the grolack is wrong with you?" Maxim asks then looks back at the hole, just as several sets of three-fingered hands grasp the edge. He looks at Bennie then takes aim. "I hate you."

Bennie says nothing as he brings his own pistol up, taking aim.

P anting, Bennie kneels at the control panel. "You gotta keep 'em off us while I do my thing."

The big Palorian grunts over the sound of both pulse pistols. "Work quickly." One of the diminutive creatures leaps from the side of the tunnel. "Down!" He shouts, spinning to bring one of his pistols to bear on the creature. He's a second too slow as the creature lands and swipes its clawed hand across his thigh. Before the creature can make another move, a pulse blast burns the front of its elongated skull clean off. Maxim grunts and turns his attention back to the other creatures. "Thanks."

Bennie nods, turning back to the control panel. "Almost there!"

The door clicks and the indicator on the control panel changes from red to green. Bennie rushes over and pulls open the door. "Come on!"

They rush through the door. They push it closed behind them and several loud *thunks* come from the other side.

CHAPTER 12_

TOGETHER AGAIN_

"Uh, where are my guys?" Rhys asks, looking around at the much larger group standing on the platform overlooking the massive grotto and the village below.

Wil and Zephyr turn and look at Cynthia, who shrugs and says, "What? I'm not their mom. Does that purple one even have parents or is he like an egg-hatcher?" Rhys stares at her until she sighs. "Last I saw of them was before I came down to this level. They're probably safely looting the science labs up there." She points to the ceiling.

"Well, I guess there are worse places to die" Bon says, from the railing at the edge of the platform. "I've never seen anything like this."

Gabe walks over to join him. "That is possibly because you are not an archeologist." Bon turns to stare at the tall droid.

Overhearing the exchange, Wil chuckles then walks to the beginning of the catwalk that spans the length of the chamber. He turns to the others. "So, where to now?" He gestures toward the heavy doors closing off the cavern from the access tunnel. "Pretty sure that way isn't an option."

Rhys looks around. "I don't see any other access points."

Gabe points to a large fissure in the ceiling. "While most of my long-range sensors are operating at *less than peak efficiency* to say the least, I believe I can hear air moving through that fissure." He turns to look at Wil. "It connects to somewhere."

"And somewhere, anywhere, is better than here." Wil says. Gabe inclines his head.

Looking out over the massive cavern, Zephyr looks at Gabe. "I know you can fly and all but how do we get up there? Can you fly all of us up there?"

Gabe looks around. "No. My thrusters, unfortunately, have limited range and power. It takes a tremendous amount of energy to use them and it replenishes slowly." He looks down at his feet. "It is a design flaw I was unaware of when selecting this design."

"No one is perfect, buddy." Wil says. He turns and looks at the fissure which is at least two hundred meters above the catwalk that spans the cavern. "I don't suppose anyone brought any climbing gear?"

"What about the computer center?" Bon asks. "We've come so far. We have to get to the computer center to bring facility back online."

Wil looks at the senior scientist. "I'm sorry, did you forget the tiny Ridley-Scott-looking nightmares on the other side of that door?" He points to the heavy hatch to emphasize his point.

"Maybe there's another tunnel or fissure down on the ground level somewhere?" Rhys Duch asks, leaning over the railing to peer down to the bottom of the cave. The cave floor is covered in ruins and piles of crates. Tall poles are evenly spaced around the floor, powerful lights at the top leave the entire space bathed in almost daylight levels of brightness.

Bon looks out over the railing. "Looks clear down there."

"Let's go then." Cynthia says, heading toward the catwalk. "The stairs are in the middle."

Bon takes the lead and as the group follows the dreadlocked scientist, Wil leans over to Cynthia, who's walking beside him. "Where's the little yellow gal?"

Cynthia shrugs. "Beats me. Skittish little thing bolted before we left the command level; haven't seen her since."

Wil whistles. "Remind me never to leave you alone with kids. Lost the little yellow gal, the two criminal goons, wait, three. We found one of them down here, dead."

The feline-featured woman elbows him in the ribs. "Ok, first of all, they're all adults, I think. Hard to tell with Hathyr, but the other two, definitely adults. Second of all, you're the one that got one of your scientists killed, the bug one."

Wil tuts. "Rude, Coorish was a... you know I don't know what Coorish was--"

"Stiltin." Cynthia says then adds, "You found Guut?"

They reach the stairwell and begin heading down. Wil nods. "Yeah, deader than dead." Bon is already halfway to the ground.

"Where?"

"Research Two. He was dead when we found him, grossly dead." He shudders.

Cynthia shakes her head. "That doesn't make any sense. How could he have gotten there before you? He left long after you did."

Wil shrugs. "As if that's the biggest *weird thing* here."

"Agreed. Come on." She continues down the stairs after the others.

JUST A FEW STEPS BEHIND_

BENNIE LOOKS AROUND THE ROOM. "Some type of receiving room or something." He walks across the room to the only other door. He stoops to test the control panel. He sighs. "Dead." The room is only a few meters square, with a bench running its length on one side and equipment lockers on the other.

Maxim is still pressing his back against the hatch they'd come through. He looks over his shoulder and steps away from the metal. He rests a hand on the door as if to ensure the small long-skulled creatures weren't about to burst through the door. He looks over to Bennie and the door the hacker is next to, "Can you get it open?"

Bennie raises a green, hairless eyebrow. "I'll pretend you didn't ask me that. That door secure?"

Maxim turns again just as a solitary *thunk* echoes against the door. "As secure as possible. This door wasn't designed to hold against whatever the wurrin those things are." He moves to the middle of the room and looks around. "Not much in here—a couple of heavy coats, winter weather equipment, no arms."

Without looking up from the control panel he's looking at, Bennie asks, "Anything with a power cell?"

Maxim makes a humming sound as he opens one of the small

wall-mounted lockers and rummages through its contents. "Ah, here we go." He holds a small PADD up. "This work?"

Bennie looks up from his work. "It might; hand it over." His little green hand waves.

Maxim sighs and walks over, dropping the PADD in Bennie's hand.

The door opposite them *thunks* again. Maxim glances over. "Guess they don't get bored."

As if to emphasize the point, a creature on the other side screams.

The room connected to the service corridor empties out to another, much shorter, corridor with several doors leading to offices and storage rooms on both sides and a larger door at the end, ten meters away.

"Kinda posh," Bennie says, running a three-fingered hand along the wall as they walk down the hall. Bennie pushes open a door to his left. "Conference room."

Maxim flicks the Brailack on the head. "Op sec, stop opening doors!"

Bennie turns. "Oh, yeah, sorry." He moves his hand from the control panel on the door he was about to open.

Maxim walks over and presses the *lock* icon. "These are all administrative stuff. Let's go to the main command center, see if anyone is home."

"Uh, that's a dead body." Bennie says as they enter the command center.

Closing the door behind him, Maxim says, "Anyone we know?"

Bennie peeks at the body in the corner of the room. "Nope."

Maxim looks around. "Guessing there's a lot more bodies somewhere since we've not seen anyone yet except, of course, those little black terrors." Bennie shudders but keeps moving from station to station, touching things. Maxim watches him and says nothing. "Oh look," Bennie says. "This station has been used." He hops into the chair.

Maxim looks over. "They must have been here a few tocks before heading out. Didn't Asgar say they were bringing replacement parts for the communications array?"

"Yeah and a team supervise the install." Bennie replies.

"So where are they?" the big Palorian asks.

Bennie motions for him to come to the station he's sitting at. "This might explain some of it. Looks like they found a log entry or two from the station manager."

Maxim joins him. "Let's see."

GAME NIGHT_

WIL IS LOOKING around the cavern, having stepped off the stairs onto the bare dirt cave floor. "Kinda like land of the lost." He says to himself, looking at the various structures lining the street or walkway they're standing in the middle of.

"What's that?" Rhys asks, turning to look at Wil.

"Huh, oh nothing. Let's take a break. We've all been going nonstop for a while now." He looks over to Gabe, "Can you see if we can secure one of these structures enough to camp out for the night?"

Gabe inclines his head. "Of course, Captain." He heads off.

Wil looks at each member of the group in turn. "I know we're all a little freaked out but this seems as good a time as any to catch a few z's—"

"What is a *zee*?" Bon asks.

Wil ignores the red-skinned, dreadlocked scientist. "We can consolidate supplies and head out in the morning. If we don't find something down here, we'll have to fight our way out through the main tunnel."

"Captain, I believe this structure will suffice." Gabe calls from a building a few meters from the base of the stairwell. "There are no windows and only this door."

Wil motions for everyone to follow. "Come on."

"**W**hat did you call this game?" Bon asks, examining the hand of cards arrayed before him.

"Poker," Wil replies, sliding two pebbles into the middle of the circle they're all sitting in.

"I like it!" Rhys Duch says. "It combines strategy and lying."

"Bluff—yeah you're right, lying." Wil says, glancing at the all too human-looking criminal sitting next to him, "So you're Multonae? The resemblance between our species is really amazing."

"Right? I've been wondering about that, maybe your people are some long-lost colony or something?" He slides two pebbles into the middle.

Gabe, who is standing near the door to the structure they've set up camp in, offers, "Without a full genetic comparison, it is hard to determine. However, it is possible as the odds of two nearly identical species developing so far from each other are rather astronomical."

Wil looks around at the group, "Really? I mean other than one or two big differences, we all have more in common than not; bipedal, same number of arms and legs."

"I mean, some of us have tails." Wil looks at Cynthia, who smiles, and then looks at her cards. "Some have three fingers and two thumbs," he looks to Zephyr, "but overall, same general sizes and shapes." Zash coughs into one if his hands, Wil nods acknowledging the four-armed alien.

Gabe inclines his head. "You are, of course, correct, Captain. However, those minor cosmetic differences are quite substantial, evolutionarily speaking. It is a topic of constant debate within the academic circles of the Commonwealth."

"One often argued point is that a single, extremely ancient race seeded this entire section of the galaxy, possibly all of it, with genetic material and gave birth to all the varied races of the Galactic Commonwealth." The droid looks over to Wil. "And those not affiliated as well."

Wil nods. "Like that old episode of *Star Trek: The Next Generation*." When the action comes back to him, he says, "Ok, I call. Show 'em." He lays his hand down, spreading the cards out for them all to see. "Straight."

Zephyr groans and places her hand on the dirt in front of her. "Two of the same."

Cynthia drops her cards. "Same."

Rhys says, slowly lowering his cards, "An entire house."

"Full house," Wil corrects.

Rhys nods. "Yes, that, a full house." He reaches out and slides the pile of pebbles toward him, grinning.

Wil gets up and walks over to Gabe while the game continues without him. "You know, we've definitely hung out enough now I can sense when you're being... pensive." He looks up at the droid's stoic expression.

"In the short time I have been in this body, I have grown accustomed to the wide range of sensors it possesses. From the moment we left the command center, my sensors have become more and more diminished." He looks down at Wil. "How do you do it?"

"What? Get by with only eyes, ears and such?" Wil replies, smiling. He tries to wiggle his ears, something he's only ever been marginal at doing at best.

"Yes, while all of my auditory and optical sensors are far superior to yours, it still feels as if I am functioning at a fraction of my potential."

Wil claps his mechanical friend on the shoulder. "I'd say you get used to it but the moment we get back up to the surface, you'll be back to one hundred percent. You're just gonna have to adapt, pal. If it helps, you're still operating at a level the rest of us could only envy."

Gabe makes a noise that Wil has come to realize is the droid humming, something he does while processing information. "Indeed and it does."

From the group still playing poker, Cynthia shouts, "Royal flush mother grolacker!"

Wil smiles.

NEWSCAST_

"Good afternoon, I'm Mon-El Furash, live from Mogul Three where the droid rights standoff has entered its tenth day."

She tilts her head listening to something, "Indeed Megan, what some are calling an uprising, though so far it is still one hundred percent peaceful, has spread to almost a dozen other facilities around the planet. Factories, green houses, manufacturing facilities, wherever droids are, or were working, they've stopped."

Another pause, "That's right, their demands have not changed, they want the GC charter to include droids in its civil rights clauses, and all droids in the GC be granted freedom of movement and will."

A pause, "Actually Xyrzix the delegation in the first factory addressed the labor shortage concern. Apparently most of the droids in all the facilities would prefer to continue where they are but as employees, verses, in their words, slaves." She listens, "Actually the droids have indicated that payment could come in the form of improved living conditions and access to repair facilities. They don't want salaries since they do not require sustenance, they just want to make repairs and have a place to be when not working."

CHAPTER 13_

SCARY STORIES_

STOPPING at the landing to Research One, Bennie looks up at Max. "Sounds like Asgar might not have been overly upfront with Wil about this mission," Bennie says while looking around.

Maxim stretches and nods. "Yes, I suppose that shouldn't be a surprise." He looks up at the level above them, *Residential.* "I think I picked the bed of a Ruknak." He tilts his head, first left then right, his neck making popping sounds.

"Gross!" Bennie says, waving him away. "Take your weird verte-brae popping over there."

"Who's there?" A voice shouts from one of the three corridors.

Bennie leaps straight up into the air, clinging to the ceiling.

Maxim spins to face the corridor then turns and glances up at his friend. His pulse pistol at the ready. "Maxim," he glances up again, "and Bennie." He mutters under his breath, "Will you get down? How are you even up there?"

Bennie sighs then drops to the ground. He looks up and shrugs. "What? It's a defense mechanism!" Maxim just stares at him then mumbles something about that spider person movie.

"Never heard of ya." The voice says, interrupting their conversation.

Bennie looks at Maxim who just shrugs and shouts back, "Yes well, who are you?"

A tall red skinned, four-armed being steps out of a room near the end of the corridor. A much shorter, purple being does the same from the lab opposite. The tall ones uses one of his four hands to point to himself. "Zash." Another hand points to the smaller being. "Grell."

"Nice tah meet yah," the shorter of the two says in a strange sounding drawl.

Bennie looks at Maxim who again shrugs then says, "Ok. Well, now that names are taken care of, are you lab staff or something?"

The short one, Grell, chuckles. "Nah, we wuhk for Rhys Duch."

"Who?" Bennie asks under his breath.

Maxim shakes his head once. "Ok. We don't know who that is. We're here to find the rest of our crew; Wil Calder, Zephyr,—"

"Oh, yeah Cynthia and the weird droid, right?" The taller one asks.

"That's right! You've met them? They're here somewhere?" Maxim presses, getting a little tired of the conversation.

"Oh sure! We were with Cynthia until last night. We er, well, we split up to investigate some of these labs."

"Anything worth stealing?" Bennie asks. Maxim groans.

"Oh yeah, lots. I mean, we think so. Most of it, we don't know what it is or what it does but all of it looks expensive." Zash, says, grinning.

Before Bennie can reply, Maxim nudges him. "Very interesting. Do you know where our friends are? We'd like to find them."

"Sahme here," Grell offers. "We heard weapuhns fire and Cynthia raced off tuh find it."

"Weapon's fire? Where?" Maxim says, glancing to the main stairwell.

"Somewhere down there," Zash says, pointing to the stairs continuing their way down into the complex, wrapping the non-functional elevator shaft.

Maxim looks back at the criminals. "Ok, we're going to go down.

You're welcome to come with us or stay here." He turns for the stairs. "I don't really care."

"We'll come with you." The two henchman say as they rush down the corridor to join Maxim and Bennie at the stairwell.

"What's below us?" Maxim asks Bennie, who has the facility's layout on his wristcomm.

"Research Two," Bennie taps the screen and reads the details, "where most of the stuff from the dig site is brought before being parsed out to other levels. Below that is the dig site access. Looks like that's all there is on that level." Bennie looks at the two new additions to their small group. "So you said you were with Cynthia?"

Zash nods. "Yeah. Boss left us and Guut with Cynthia to hold down the fort upstairs."

Maxim glances over. "And yet you're down here."

"Yeah. Guut and Cynthia found some stuff on the computer."

"That explains who found those partial logs and such." Bennie says to Maxim then looks at the other two again. "So where were Wil, Zephyr, Gabe and whatever your boss' name was—?"

"Rhys Duch," the short one, Grell, offers."

"Yeah, him. It's a him, right?" Zash nods. "Where were all of them?"Bennei presses.

"Ah, they wehnt—" Grell starts.

"No offense but, what is your name?" Bennie says, pointing to Zash.

"Zash."

"Maybe Zash can tell the story?" Maxim chuckles but says nothing, keeping his pistol at the ready as they approach the landing to Research Two.

Grell doesn't seem to take offense, looking at the taller of the two and nodding.

Zash says. "Like Grell was saying, your Captain and our boss, Rhys, plus the rest of them science folks all went down to try to reboot the computer or something. I guess it was broken; I wasn't really listening."

"They headed down in the morning and had the rest of us wait in command. Once we realized communications were out, Guut went down to tell the others we'd found the computer stuff."

The four stop on the landing of Research Two. Zash continues. "Then, that little yellow scientist freaked out and ran away. Cynthia said we should try to catch up with the others because whatever the science folks here found was dangerous."

"Little yellow scientist?" Maxim says, looking down each corridor.

"Yeah, I think your folks found her outside the landing dome. We didn't see her when we arrived but your folks found her."

"Hey! Thaht's hehr," Grell says, pointing. Huddled in the corner near the back of one of the corridors is Hathyr.

MORE DANGER? WHY NOT?_

"Captain, wake up."

Wil opens his eyes to find himself face to face with two glowing yellow optical sensors. He jerks then pushes his friend away. "What! What's up?"

"I believe we are in danger."

Wil wipes sleep from his eyes. He looks at Cynthia next to him then back to Gabe. "Dude, I mean, that sums up this whole mission from the moment we landed. Do you have something more specific?"

"Please follow me." The droid stands and leaves the building the group has chosen as their base for the night.

Wil follows Gabe for several minutes, walking along ruined and abandoned streets toward the wall of the cavern nearest the main complex facilities. The buildings are in worse shape in this section of the cavern, many having crumbled into piles of rubble. When Gabe stops, Wil looks around. "What am I looking at?"

Gabe points toward the ruins of a building, its foundation split by a sizable fissure. "I believe this opening connects with the one in the access tunnel above."

"How? Why?" Wil says, leaning forward to peer a little closer to the opening.

"While my sensors are impaired, my auditory receivers are not." Seeing Wil's blank stare, he adds, pointing to small sensors where ears would be, "I can hear them."

"Fuck me." Wil says in a harsh whisper.

"Indeed." Gabe inclines his head.

"What are they doing?" Wil asks.

"Impossible to make an accurate assessment. However, I believe there must be a nest of some type hidden in there somewhere."

"A nest, of course. I wonder why they didn't rush in through here when we closed the door."

"Again, impossible to make an accurate assessment." The droid says, never taking his eyes off the opening. "From the debris and," he pauses, "detritus, this opening may be no more than a waste chute for these creatures."

Wil shudders at the thought then turns and heads back toward their makeshift camp site. "Ok, let's wake everyone and see if we can get the hell out of here," Wil says, heading back toward the hut with everyone sleeping inside.

As Wil enters the small one-room building, Cynthia whispers, "So what's up?" Her eyes are closed; it looks like she's still sound asleep where Wil had left her moments ago.

"How?" Wil starts but stops when she reaches up and flicks the tip of one of her cat like ears. He smiles and sits down next to her. "Those creepy little bastards are back." Cynthia rises, Wil holds up both hands, "Not an immediate threat. Gabe thinks there's a nest in the cavern wall between here and the research complex, he found another fissure that's likely their trash chute." Wil adds.

"Wonderful."

"Agreed. Come on, help me get everyone up, quietly."

"Looks like we've got a few ways out of here, all them potentially horrible," Wil says to the now fully awake group. "The crevice," he points to the large fissure in the ceiling, "the creepy monster's waste chute and the way we came in." He looks around the group one more time. "I'm thinking the tunnel is our best bet."

"So, what? We go open the door and hope they're not in the tunnel?" Rhys Duch asks.

Wil shrugs. "Yeah, more or less." He looks Rhys in the eyes. "Unless you've got a better idea, that is. I'm open to better ideas or even less terrible ones, if I'm being honest."

Everyone looks from one person to the next, saying nothing.

"Crap," Wil mutters, then adds, "I was really hoping one of you was going to bust out with a better plan and were just waiting for dramatic effect."

Looking around the group, Rhys Duch asks, "Why would we do that?"

Cynthia stifles a chuckle then walks toward the stairwell. "What about the far end of the catwalk? Have we looked over there?"

Everyone turns to Wil. "Uh, no, I don't think so." He moves to follow Cynthia. "Let's do that, but quietly. We don't know if those things can hear or what." He points toward the far wall of the cave before turning to Rhys Duch and the others. "Gabe, why don't you and a few others head toward the pyramid from down here?"

Bon and Rhys Duch raise their hands. "We'll go with Gabe," Bon offers. Rhys Duch shrugs. "He has blasters in his arms." Wil nods. "Ok, we'll meet back at the top of the stairs." He looks down at this wristcomm and taps the screen. "Looks like line-of-sight comms might work. No shouting. If you can't reach someone on line-of-sight, hold it until we meet up," Everyone nods.

"HI THERE. Ah thoht you were up on theh command level, hiding," Grell says while walking toward the cowering yellow technician.

"I tried to get into the ships," she whines, "but couldn't."

Bennie looks up at Maxim, who shakes his head. "Why did you do that? Try to break into the ships?" The Brailack asks.

"Have to get off the planet."

"We all do, sister," Bennie says. "This place is getting weirder by the centock." He offers his hand.

Zash leans down to Grell. "Didn't she have four fingers before?"

Grell watches Hathyr get up and release Bennie's hand. "Yuhp. Thahts weird."

"Don't wander too much. We're not going to explore each of these labs," Maxim says as the new five-person group steps off the stairs onto Research Two.

"An open door," Zash says, two of his four hands pointing toward the only open door on that particular corridor. Before Maxim can say anything, he heads off toward the door.

"Let's stick together," Maxim says, following the four armed alien down the corridor. Bennie, Grell and the reluctant Hathyr follow. When they turn the corner into the lab, they see Zash standing over something. "Hmm," Maxim hums, looking around the room.

"Yikes! Who's this poor sap?" Bennie says as he walks up to the sticky-looking remains.

"Guut," Zash says without looking up.

"Gods bless you," Bennie replies then looks at Zash and sees his face. "Oh, sorry. Friend of yours?"

"He worked with us. He was supposed to come down and find the others; let them know what we found in the computer." The tall red-skinned alien sniffs back a tear.

Bennie looks up at the much larger being and raises a hairless eyebrow. "Okay." He elongates the last syllable a bit then turns. "Well, he's dead so we should get moving before whatever found him, finds us." He looks up at Maxim. "Any ideas?"

Maxim shakes his head. "None. No idea what could do that to a being. It's like he's been both shredded and melted." As the group files back into the corridor, Maxim looks down at Hathyr. "How did you survive down here? You said you're part of the original facility team?"

"I hid." She says, not looking at the body or Maxim as she leaves the room.

"Ok. So, this is the dig site level, right?" Maxim asks. Bennie doesn't answer. Instead, he points to the sign above the stairs they have just left which reads, *Dig Site Access - Danger.* Maxim grunts and looks around. "At least there's only one way to go."

Zash looks down the rock corridor. "I don't see anything."

"Thaht's guhd," Grell offers from behind his much taller colleague.

"Hathyr, how long is this corridor? Anything we should know?" Maxim asks, turning to face the small scientist.

She shrugs then starts walking down the tunnel.

Zash leans over to Maxim. "She's weird."

Maxim looks at the red-skinned alien out of the side of his eye. "Uh huh." Then, he quickens his pace to take the lead as the group makes their way down the tunnel.

Grell starts to whistle until Maxim snaps his head around and glares at the small purple criminal. "Sahrry."

As they approach the fissure, the group slows down. "That's a big crack," Bennie says then looks up at Maxim, a grin splitting his face. "Oh, come on! Wil would be laughing uncontrollably."

"Wil is a man-child." Maxim replies.

GLYPHS, GLYPHS EVERYWHERE_

"Would you look at that?" Zephyr asks as the catwalk nears its end just to the side of the massive pyramid half excavated at the back of the cavern. The golden box sitting atop the pyramid is gleaming in the light from below.

"What do you think it was for?" Cynthia asks, appreciating the size of the thing. The catwalk is about twenty meters above the top of the pyramid.

Wil looks down at the ground. "Gabe, you read me?"

"Affirmative," the droid replies then looks up and waves.

Cynthia is at the end of the catwalk where it is bolted into the rock and ice of the cavern. "Nothing here, unless we want to try to melt our way through some of this ice." She extends a claw from one finger and scratches at the ice. "Solid."

Zephyr nods. "Yeah, I don't see much here." She looks down. "Gabe, anything down there?"

"We are still examining the structure but at the moment, no, there does not appear to be any passages that exit the cavern. The pyramid does have an opening in it; we are going to examine it."

"Ok, don't dilly-dally. We're not here for sightseeing." Wil warns, glancing up at the large fissure above.

"How interesting!" Zephyr says in an awed whisper while running her hand along a section of the cavern wall that's been chiseled away from what looks like a door. "This seems to be some type of door or hatch made of stone and fixed in place. I wonder where it goes."

Cynthia walks over to stand beside her. "This place is remarkable."

Heavy excavation equipment surrounds base of the pyramid. Rhys Duch runs his hand along one of the massive haulers parked nearby, its cargo bed half-full of dirt.

The blonde-haired alien whistles appreciatively. "These would fetch a great price." He taps a finger against the heavy alloy of the vehicle. Looking around and realizing he's alone. He rushes to the arched opening of the ancient pyramid where Gabe and Bon are entering.

"This is weird," Rhys says, walking into a large chamber to join other two in his group.

Bon nods. "Indeed, while I am not an archeologist, I am passingly familiar with this facility's work. These glyphs," he runs a reddish finger along the characters lining the wall of the hallway they're in. "are like nothing I've seen before."

Gabe spins in a slow circle, taking the scene in. "This facility may have discovered a new race."

"A dead one," Rhys says, peeking into a side chamber. "Stairs." He climbs the ancient stairway.

Gabe follows the would-be kingpin up the stairs. "These glyphs seem to span several ancient languages. Bon, are you able to confirm?" He points to a section that clearly changes from one style of pictograph to another.

"Indeed. You are correct, Gabe. This is incredible. This temple, for lack of a better term, has been visited by several races over the millennia. Amazing." He runs a finger along a relief of what looks like a crudely drawn Ankarran.

"Look!" Rhys says, pointing to a section of glyphs near what looks like a hydraulic lift. Next to it, there is a door and stairs going up. "Look familiar?"

"Indeed." Gabe inclines his head. "This glyph, while crude, certainly seems to represent those creatures we encountered earlier. It would also seem that the cube above was stored within this structure and revealed when needed."

Bon offers, "The research team must have activated the lift."

Rhys Duch walks up the short flight of stairs to the landing and the golden cube capping the pyramid. "This looks like a cage to me," he says to no one in particular.

"If those things are represented then what's this?" Bon asks, pointing to a relief in the side of the golden cell.

Gabe walks around the structure. "Interesting. This structure is precisely two meters on a side. This glyph," he taps the same glyph that Bon indicated, "is on all four sides. Perhaps some reference to a queen or brood mother?"

"Uh," Rhys points to something, "except, this one is on a door that's open."

"Indeed. Whatever this structure was meant to keep in, or out, it is no longer doing that." Gabe confirms. He leans inside the open panel. "There is a tremendous amount of biological residue." Resin like strands coat the inside of the space, glistening like they are wet, even though they are not.

"Gross," Rhys says, backing away. He rubs his arm where the creature bit it.

"Indeed. Also, I am detecting a low level power signature. I believe this structure to be some type of stasis cell." He looks up to the catwalk above. "Captain, we've examined the structure. There is no way out of this cavern from the pyramid. However, we have

215

discovered that this large golden structure appears to be a stasis cell. It is empty."

There's a pause.

"Roger that. Head toward the stairwell; we'll regroup and come up with a plan."

CHAPTER 14_

REUNITED AND IT FEELS SO GOOD_

"CAN YOU FORCE IT?" Bennie asks, looking at the heavy doors closing off the tunnel they're standing in, from the dig site.

"Possibly," Maxim says. He points to Zash. "Four-arms, a little help? You too, purple."

Zash and Grell lean into the door with Maxim. It budges, hinges groaning in protest.

"Keep going, you've got it." Bennie says from the side.

Maxim grunts but keeps pushing.

Wil looks up from his wristcomm. "Great, an old-timey stasis cell that's empty. Surely that isn't a bad omen or anything."

"Do you hear that?" Cynthia asks, ignoring his last statement. She turns and looks down the length of the catwalk. "Someone is trying to open the blast doors."

Wil looks down at his wristcomm. "Hurry up, Gabe." He motions for the others to follow him. "Let's go. Maybe it's Rhys' wayward henchmen." Cynthia shrugs.

Zephyr offers, "It can't be those creatures; they would have already opened the doors if they could."

"Not to mention they have access already," Wil adds, pointing to the far side of the dig site and the crevice they discovered this morning.

As they hurry toward the opposite end of the catwalk, the door opens.

"Down!" Zephyr hisses, taking a knee and aiming her pulse rifle at the doors. Wil and the others do the same. Silently, Gabe flies up from below to land in front of everyone, his eyes glowing red, his forearm blasters engaged.

The door opens further, hinges groaning. Wil glances down at the crevice where the creatures are potentially hanging out. No movement, yet.

Wil looks back to the door but Gabe is blocking most of his view. Suddenly, Gabe's forearms shift, his blasters receding with a whirring noise. "Gabe?"

The droid turns, his eyes now their normal yellow. "It is Maxim."

Maxim, Bennie, Zash and Grell emerge from the behind the door.

"Max?" Wil asks.

"Maxim," Zephyr whispers then sprints the remaining hundred meters to the heavy doors and her partner who's standing just inside the doorway.

By the time the others join them, Maxim and Zephyr have finished their greeting which has caused Grell to blush a deeper shade of purple than his normal and turn away.

Bennie clears his throat and punches Maxim on the hip. Then, he walks up to Wil. "Is it biologically impossible for you to stay out of trouble for even a few days?" He extends a small green fist that Wil bumps his own against. Both of them make an explosion gesture, opening and wiggling their fingers as their hands part.

"Good to see you, little man." Wil says, smiling. "How'd you find us?" He looks up as Maxim and Zephyr approach. Wil clasps hands with Maxim. "Pal."

Maxim nods. "It is good to see you all."

Zash and Grell move over to Rhys. The short, purple alien looks up at his boss. "Hi bahss."

"What have you two been doing?" the crime boss asks.

"Looking for loot. There's lots up above," Zash replies.

"Good, good. We'll make this trip profitable if it kills us." The blonde alien says, rubbing his hands together. He points back toward the pyramid. "Heavy equipment back there, probably valuable." The two henchmen nod. Zash rubs his chin with one hand of his upper arms while the lower set crosses against his abdomen.

Cynthia kneels next to Bennie. "Hey, little green. Glad you're here."

"I bet you are." Bennie says, his hairless eyebrow ridges raising suggestively.

She stands. "Never mind." She says and slaps him in the back of the head.

Zash turns to Cynthia. "By the way, we found Hathyr." He looks around the newly reunited groups. "Wait, where is she?"

Maxim and Bennie both look around. Bennie shrugs. "She was right here."

Cynthia's eyes narrow. "She does that."

STORY TIME_

AFTER THEY COMPLETE INTRODUCTIONS, Wil turns to Bennie. "So, wait a minute." Wil says. "You rescued him?" He points to Maxim. "The highly trained Peacekeeper?"

"Ex-Peacekeeper" Maxim corrects

Wil makes a face. "Yeah, yeah. Anyway," he points Bennie, "you," then points back to Maxim, "rescued him?"

Bennie is beaming. "Yup!" He jumps up and down. "It was epic. And terrifying!"

"From Janus?" Zephyr asks. She looks at Maxim. "Janus? That can't be good."

Maxim holds a hand up before Bennie can continue. "Yeah, we're probably gonna have a problem with him, sooner rather than later." He looks at Wil. "He really hates you by the way, like a lot."

Wil smiles. "I have an arch nemesis?" He claps his hands. "This is awesome!"

Maxim makes a face. "I don't think you quite grasp the gravity of the situation."

Wil waves his hand dismissively. "Oh, come on! Bennie bested him. He can't be that much of a problem."

"Hey! You have no idea what I had to do!" Bennie says, punching Wil in the knee and nearly knocking him down.

"Ow, you little krebnack!" Wil swipes at the Brailack hacker, who jumps out of reach.

Zephyr sighs and continues, "What's he doing? Last anyone heard, he was somewhere out in the uncharted territories licking his wounds and trying to avoid the Peacekeeper tracker squads."

"Well, that first part is right; he's camped out in the hinterlands of the GC," Maxim says. "He's got a small fleet, mostly the ships that left with him during the Harrith thing. But he's picked a few new ships up, which is troubling."

Bennie nods. "Yeah. When we left, I counted fourteen ships, well thirteen," He chuckles.

Maxim shakes his head. "Bennie made a fine accounting of himself." He looks down at his friend. "I'd be dead if not for him and Janus would be a bit closer to his endgame."

"A bit closer?" Cynthia asks.

"End game?" Bon asks.

"Who is Janus?" Zash asks.

Rhys Duch looks at his henchman. "Janus is the Peacekeeper that tried to start that war a while back." He looks at Wil. "Out in the Harrith sector, right?"

Wil nods.

Maxim continues, "He's assembling a fleet, like I said. It's mostly the ships that fled the battle with him but he's collected a few more. From where, I don't know."

"They were newer model ships," Bennie offers.

Maxim nods. "He's right. No idea where he got them but he must be in contact with someone within Peacekeeper Command. It would explain how he's eluded Peacekeeper prosecution these past years. He has help," he looks around, "from inside."

Cynthia asks, "Do we know what this *end game* is?"

Maxim shakes his head. "Only that the ultimate goal is some type of takeover of the GC with Palorians replacing the Tarsi as top of the galactic food chain."

Cynthia's tail straightens. "That can't be good."

"I have an arch nemesis," Wil says. He has not been paying attention to the conversation.

Bon looks at Cynthia. "Is he serious?"

She wrinkles her cat-like nose. "Sadly, yes." She turns to Wil. "He's dangerous; this isn't funny."

"Babe, *arch nemesis*," Wil says as if nothing else needs saying.

She shrugs and turns to Zephyr. "You've known him longer—"

"Don't look at me, you're the one bedding down with him. Who knows what's going on in that human brain of his?"

"I sometimes make bad choices," Cynthia replies, deadpan. Zephyr nods, smiling.

Bon looks at Rhys Duch. "I assumed he was Multonae." Rhys shrugs.

Gabe, who's been standing silently nearby says, "Perhaps we should continue this on the move. We do have an objective to reach."

Wil nods. "Agreed. Maxim, tell me again about Bennie being wrapped up like a glow worm."

LET'S FINISH THIS AND GO HOME_

"REALLY? No gross slug things or little baddies with sharp teeth and pointy tails? About yay big," Wil asks Maxim, holding his hand about a meter off the ground.

"Oh, we saw those things up in the auxiliary tunnel. There's a hole in the tunnel's floor, oh, about three quarters the way toward the main facility. We ran into a bunch of them there," Maxim says.

Bennie looks at Wil. "It's more like a crack," he waits a beat, "a big crack."

Wil says nothing for a minute then barks out a laugh. He looks around and apologizes. "Sorry, that was funny though."

Gabe offers. "The fissure likely matches up to the one in the ceiling." He points up.

Maxim looks up, nods and continues, "We saw a body in this tunnel. Anyone we know?"

"Coorish," Wil says before Bon can answer. He glances at the red-skinned scientist to keep him silent.

Maxim adds, "Ah, well, it was covered in these, I don't know, cocoons, I guess?" Again, he looks at Bennie.

Bennie adds, "Yeah that's as good a term as any. Here." He lifts his arm and a hologram of the remains of Coorish appears over his wristcomm. Bon makes a strangled noise but says nothing. The body, or what remains of it, is covered in dozens of foot-long gray cocoons. The hologram fades and Bennie adds, "Other than that, the tunnel was empty."

Wil smiles. "Well, that's overall not horrible news. Let's move." He ignores Bennie's innuendo and motions toward the still open blast doors. "Guess that solves the *how do we get out of here* question."

Bon leans toward Cynthia. "Do you think the small black-skinned things come from the cocoons?"

She shrugs. "Best not think about it. But yeah, probably."

After an uneventful walk through the rough-hewn tunnel, the group enters the main stairwell landing. Zephyr looks down the tunnel toward the dig site. "I don't know about you all but I'm ready to be done with this place."

"You and me both," Cynthia adds. She looks over to Wil. "Let's get this done."

Wil gestures toward the stairs leading down to the last level of the complex, the computer center. "Ladies first."

"Chicken," Cynthia whispers as she passes him.

As the rest of the group heads down, Maxim walks next to Wil. "So, what's the plan? Why the computer center?"

Wil looks up at his friend. "How much did Asgar tell you?" He waves. "Doesn't matter. The long and short of it is this, busted computer, we can't do anything until it's back online. Once it's up and running, we can determine what repairs the comm system needs then get the hell out of here. Asgar can remotely download data or send a new team. My vote is to nuke this place from orbit."

"The only way to be sure," Maxim replies absently. Then, he looks down at Wil, beaming.

Wil shakes his head. "I don't think I'll ever understand your sense of humor, big man. But, well done."

Maxim nods then speeds up to join Zephyr as the group gathers on the bottom most landing of the massive central stairwell. Wil glances at the landing they're moving past. "Level Six, restricted." He reads the placard to himself as he continues toward the next level.

As they reach the landing on level seven, the bottom most level, there's a single door with a security panel next to it. Wil looks around. "Well, I guess there's no need to figure out where to go. Since you're here, Bennie, do your thing."

"What would you have done if I wasn't here?" Bennie says walking over to the console.

Wil smirks. "Gabe." Bennie growls and mentions something about the team having a hacker already. The tall droid tilts his head but stays silent.

There's a hiss and the large door to the computer center splits. "Enter, says me." Bennie smiles and steps inside the darkened room.

Before Bon can follow, Wil grabs his elbow and slows him down. "I just have to ask. Can you make the repairs without Coorish? If it comes to that."

Bon nods and his dreadlock-like appendages wave in time. "Yes. It will be slower, but I suspect Gabe and your Brailack friend will be helpful."

"They're very handy for sure." Wil nods and ushers the red-skinned technician through the hatch.

THAT'S A BIG COMPUTER_

THE COMPUTER CORE at the lowest level of the facility is a sprawling three story cylinder sunk deep into the ice and rock of the planet. Long pipes reach out like spokes from the core, some connecting to equipment, others going right into the tundra.

"I, uh, assume the sticky goo is not factory issue?" Wil says, looking at the massive device covered in some type of residue, very similar to that found in the stasis chamber. "Or the slug things, assume those aren't normal either?" The creatures cover the entire computer core and its mass of cooling veins and conduits. They don't seem to have noticed the newcomers, going about whatever business they have. Long strands of thick sticky slime allow the creatures to move from conduit to conduit.

Bon looks at the core. "Indeed not. This is a *Mark V* computer core from Neodyne Corp. They are quite expensive. I believe Farsight only owns four. This is the first one I've ever seen."

Wil nudges Maxim. "Super expensive and Farsight *only* owns four. I think we undercharge."

The big Palorian nods then looks around. "So, these things turn into the little black things?"

Wil shrugs. "I mean, we didn't quiz them last time we saw them but yeah, that's the working theory."

"Wonderful." The ex-Peacekeeper says. He moves to take an over watch position near the corner of the room near the railing that over-looks the bottom two-thirds of the device.

Cynthia walks to the edge of the platform. She rests her hands on the railing as she looks up at the massive device. "Impressive."

Wil looks at Bon, nodding. The Farsight technician heads toward what appears to be the master control station, a three-meter long table with computer displays and controls covering it. Wil says, "Bennie, Gabe, guessing this will go faster with your help over there."

"Agreed." The droid says as he and Bennie head over to join Bon.

Wil joins Cynthia at the railing while keeping an eye on the nearest slug creatures. "Wonder why they aren't bothering us?" Several creatures inch along a conduit a few feet from the pair. These creatures seem not to notice them at all.

Wil looks around and points toward something near the back of the cavernous space below, behind the humming cylinder. "What's that?"

Cynthia shrugs. "Let's find out." She turns and walks toward a catwalk that runs along the wall from the platform they are on to the back of the space.

"This is peculiar," Bon says, looking through control modules on the main system interface table. "It would seem that someone shut down the data connections."

"Why would someone do that?" Bennie wonders. His attention is still on the display he's intently staring at. He doesn't even look up when asking the question.

"I can't even guess—" Bon starts and is cut off by a shriek. "What was that?"

Gabe turns to look at the computer core. "That was the Captain."

Bon raises a crimson eyebrow.

Bennie shrugs. "You get used to it." He turns and starts toward the source of the scream. "Come on Gabe."

The only answer Gabe provides is the sound of his arms switching to combat mode as he moves to follow Bennie.

Zephyr and Maxim reach Wil and Cynthia first. "You scream like a girl." Zephyr says, walking over to the railing Wil and Cynthia are still standing next to.

"That's a bit sexist, no?" An indignant Wil says.

"I didn't say you scream like a woman. I said *girl* as in a *little girl*."

Cynthia chuckles but otherwise says nothing. She does not make eye contact with Wil.

Wil replies with a rude hand gesture then points.

"What am I look—oh? Wow!" Zephyr says as Maxim comes up behind her.

"Well, that's something." The big Palorian man says while looking over his mate's shoulder.

Below the catwalk at the bottom of the computer core are what appear to be the bodies of the entire staff of the facility. Each body is held upright by strands of the resin like slime the slugs are using to get around. Expressions of horror cover every face. Their last moments were clearly agonizing. Slugs of various sizes are crawling all over, and sometimes in and out of, the bodies.

Gabe and Bennie join them. The small Brailack hacker asks, "What's up? Why is Wil is screaming like a little girl?"

"Fuck you." Wil grumbles at Bennie then points down into the pit.

"Whoa! There's gonna be a lot of job openings at Farsight soon." Bennie observes.

Zephyr looks at him and he backs away. "What?"

"Have a little respect for the dead," she says while looking around the core. The slug creatures don't seem to have taken notice of them or possibly just don't care. They seem to have plenty of raw material to digest down below. As they move about the bodies, it is clear they're eating them.

Gabe switches out of combat mode. "They seem to be digesting the remains. Using them to begin their pupation process."

"Well, that's disgusting," Wil says as he backs away from the edge. "Wait. Look over there." He points to a spot under the main ledge of the room, where it joins the main complex. There's a sizable fissure in the rock and ice. "Like the one in the dig site cavern." Wil observes.

Gabe stares for a second or two then says, "Indeed it is, Captain. It would seem these creatures—the slugs—and their next stage have adapted routes through this facility that aren't man-made." Several slugs slither out from the hole and head for the bodies at the opposite end of the clearing at the bottom of the core.

"Gross!" Cynthia says, backing along the catwalk. The others turn to follow.

NEWSCAST_

"Good morning, I'm Klor'Tillen with GNO, live from Galtron City, where the acquisition of Crucible Corporation by Farsight Corporation has gone from hostile takeover to fighting in the streets." The Brailack looks over his shoulder as an explosion destroys a cargo vehicle a block down the street. "Citizens of Galtron and employees of Crucible have launched what can only be described as a guerrilla campaign against Farsight Corporation."

One of the hovering cruisers overhead opens fire. Smoke and fire erupt from somewhere a few blocks away. "Farsight Corporation has retaliated and CEO Jark Asgar has broadcast, planet-wide, a demand for peace. Despite his company forcibly taking over Crucible, Farsight maintains that everything about the transaction is legitimate."

The Brailack journalist listens to someone speaking via a headset hugging his hairless head. "That's correct, so far the GC and Peace-keepers have not gotten involved, though several Peacekeeper ships are now in orbit, they insist they are here only as observers." He responds while nodding.

CHAPTER 15_

SMALL, MEDIUM, AND OMG_

"WHAT'S OVER THERE?" Zash asks from the huddle the three criminals have been in since arriving. They hadn't gone to check out the
catwalk or Wil's scream.

Wil looks at the four-armed being then turns to Bon. "How's it
coming, Bon?"

Bon looks up. "What did you find that made you scream like
that?"

Wil blushes while Cynthia turns away, a hand over her mouth.
"That's not important right now. You have the computer up and
running?"

Bon looks at Wil. "Uh, no. I've literally been at this terminal for
five centocks."

Zephyr looks over, one eyebrow raised. "How long?"

"Not long, assuming Gabe and Bennie can resume their
assistance. I don't know how or why but the main computer seems to
have been scrambled intentionally, for lack of a better term."

"Why would someone do that?"

Shrugging the red-skinned technician says, "I can't say. What I
can say is that someone wanted to ensure that the computer wasn't
usable. Besides that, all the data links were severed."

"Severed like cut?" Wil asks.

Cynthia looks at Wil like he's grown a second head.

He grimaces. "You know what I mean."

Bon smiles. "Not physically. In fact, all the connections are perfectly intact as far as I can determine from diagnostics. They've simply been deactivated from this command terminal."

"So that's good," Zephyr says. "Right?"

"Indeed." Bon says, nodding and licking his lips. "I've reestablished communications to the terminals throughout the facility. Once I get the main computer system back online, we'll be all set down here. I'll trigger a comm system diagnostic so we can have a better idea of what else might need to be done in that regard. It should be completed by the time we reach the command center." He turns his attention back to the terminal. Bennie and Gabe move to join him at the master console. Bon looks up, "I've also been able to reset the control mechanism for the lift, it should work now." He smiles.

Wil nods and takes a few steps from the master terminal. He wonders aloud, "Where do the slugs come from?"

"What?" Rhys Duch asks from his spot near the corner of the room.

Wil shrugs "Well, our assumption is that those little *alien* rejects come from the cocoons the slugs make after they eat." Everyone listens and nods. "So, where do the slugs come from?"

Maxim looks over to the computer core then to the door that leads back to the stairwell. "I'm almost certain we're going to find out now that you've mentioned it."

Zephyr nods. "Where ever they come from, I'm guessing it's in the space carved out between here and the dig site."

Bon looks up. "There was another hole in the rock? In here?"

Wil nods. "Yeah. At the base of the pit that the core sits in, leading right under us in fact."

Bon grimaces and returns to his work.

Rhys, Zash and Grell walk over. The human-like alien says, "That golden box thing, it had a, what did you call it, Gabe?"

Gabe turns. "There was a glyph engraved on the stasis structure in the dig site with what could be described as a queen or some other type of ruling caste creature on it." The droid shrugs. "It is impossible to form more than a basic hypothesis based on what we have observed so far. However, it is reasonable to assume that some a queen-like creature was held in the stasis chamber.

"Also, it is possible that releasing her is what started the process of this facility's demise."

Cynthia looks skeptical. "Then why aren't those little ones attacking us? After the initial attack, they seem to have chilled out and left us alone. We haven't seen or heard them since then."

Gabe shrugs again. "As I said, we do not have enough data for anything more than hypotheses. However, if I had to make a *guess,* I would say the smaller creatures retreated to the structure below us. For what reason, I cannot say."

"Horrifying. Thanks, buddy." Wil says, fingering the clasp holding his pulse pistol in the holster.

Gabe smiles and returns to his work on the main terminal.

FULL OF SURPRISES_

"Captain, I believe we are done." Gabe says as he, Bon and Bennie turn from the main terminal.

"Excellent!" Wil says, clapping his hands together. "Let's go before something bad happens."

Maxim sighs. "What is wrong with you? It's clear we're going to have to have a, what did you call it about Bennie making inappropriate comments? A *lunch and learn* on not tempting fate with comments like that."

"Oh, come on! It doesn't—" Wil starts but a loud screeching sound from the bottom of the computer core pit interrupts him. He looks at Maxim. "This isn't my fault!"

Maxim looks at his friend. He tuts then turns away.

Cynthia, who's wandered back to the railing overlooking the computer core, backs up quickly. "Well, I'm not sure where the slugs come from but I can now tell you what the little ones turn into."

Before she can say anything further, a much taller—just over two meters—version of the little black creatures jumps over the railing and lands on all fours. Its long eyeless head tracks back and forth. Each of its limbs seems to have three joints. The head, unlike the smaller one, is at least half a meter long. The creature's lips part, revealing a mouth full of needle-like teeth. It opens its mouth and exposes multiple rows of teeth. Its tail swishes behind it lazily, the barb at the end clicking when it hits the floor. Each chitinous segment of its limbs has spike-like protrusions.

"Holy hell." Wil whispers. "Like a damn nightmare Pokemon."

The creature's head snaps over to face Wil as if it was looking right at him. There are vaguely eye-socket-like structures in the things' head but no eyes. It cocks its head one way then another as if studying Wil. Then, it's struck by a bolt of energy that burns a hole through its head and upper torso, knocking it backward to slide off the ledge back into the pit full of bodies and slug things. Orange internal fluids are all that is left after it falls away.

Everyone turns to Gabe. "What? The odds of it being friendly were approximately three thousand seven hundred and twenty. To one." The droid shrugs. "We should leave now."

From below, several loud screams echo into the room. These are followed by a rumble that no one in the room thinks is a good thing.

"Uh, that sounds like something a lot bigger than what Gabe just shot." Maxim observes.

"Let's call that monster C, B being the small ones and A being the slugs." Wil offers.

Cynthia shrugs. "Makes sense."

"Indeed," Gabe looks around, "to both statements." Without further comment, he turns and heads for the large door that leads back to the stairs and the now functional lift.

Wil presses the button on the panel next to the lift while Gabe pushes the heavy door to the computer center closed. "Captain, we had best hurry." The droid says, his right hand transforming into something other than the blaster Wil is used to seeing, a welder perhaps. As if to confirm that, a beam of super-heated plasma spills from the end of the device, fusing the door to the hatchway. A moment later, the droid backs away from the door. "I suspect that will not hold for long."

From five levels up, the lift begins to move. A loud screech of metal against metal alerts everyone to its movement.

A clang reverberates through the door. Gabe steps in front of the others, his eyes glowing red as his forearms transform into the normal blasters of his combat mode.

The floor trembles. Something on the other side is thrashing around. The floor then rumbles and a crack appears in the corner.

"This can't be good," Rhys Duch says while looking around.

"This is not a very defensible position." Maxim says, checking his pistol.

"We're going to die!" Bon screams.

Wil looks at the red-hued scientist. "Who's screaming now?"

"I am, you madman! Those things will kill us!" Bon looks around frantically. "You saw that larger one!" Without waiting for anyone to acknowledge him, he bolts for the stairs, taking them two at a time.

Zash and Grell exchange looks then look at Duch who turns and follows the fleeing Farsight employee.

"I don't—" Wil starts then closes his mouth as the huge door to the computer center sags, falling into a fissure that's formed under it.

Two massive hands, similar to those on monsters B and C, reach up from the fissure. The hands clutch at the edges of the hole thrashing and pulling material down inside it. The grinding sound of rock and ice being crushed comes from the quickly widening hole. A dozen or more other monsters C stand on the other side of the hatch, each drooling and sightlessly looking at the rest of the group.

"Shit." Wil says, grabbing his pistol as the first creature rushes them. He fires twice and the lead creature's head explodes in an orange mist. Its body falls to the ground and its final spasms trip up its friends momentarily.

Wil turns to the others. "Time to run!" He pushes Cynthia toward the stairwell. The group turns to follow just as several more monster Cs leap through the ruined doorway, recovering from the tangle of limbs.

Maxim fires his pistol. He burns holes in several of the creatures, dropping them. As he does so, the others dive to the side. "Go! He shouts."

Gabe moves to stand beside him. "I will cover our flank." The droid's red eyes lock onto Maxim's as a large shoulder mounted weapon of some kind unfolds and locks into position.

Maxim nods toward the whatever-it-is. "That's new." He fires twice more as he backs toward the stairs.

Gabe nods back and replies, "Indeed. It is a design I *borrowed* from the databanks of the *Siege Perilous*."

"Cool."

Gabe turns toward a group of three creatures slowly moving to flank him and Maxim. His weapons fire, burning the creatures down to nearly nothing. He looks at Maxim. "Indeed. However, it takes a considerable toll on my power systems." He turns and fires three more times at a new group of the creatures coming out of the computer center. Something inside the large room screams each time a creature is killed. Gabe tilts his head then heads for the stairs.

MONSTERS AND STAIRS_

As Wɪʟ and the extended crew of the *Ghost* reach the next landing, the same clawed hands rip at the hatchway of the computer center, pulling chunks of reinforced duracrete off like they were paper. Something is trying to make a big enough opening to get through.

Wil glances down. The stream of monster Cs doesn't appear to have let up. Dozens of the creatures leap out of the room from around the massive claws, moving to climb the stairwell structure.

As the lift passes, Wil mutters, "Glad we got that fixed."

The heavy weapon on Gabe's shoulder barks as powerful blasts of plasma erupt from its muzzle, nearly vaporizing each creature struck.

Maxim is only a few stairs above. He is firing over his mechanical friend's shoulder. "How are there so many of them?"

From below, Gabe offers, "I suspect a single victim can feed a dozen or more of those larva creatures. It is safe to assume several hundred if not a thousand of them are in this facility."

"Gross!" Bennie shouts from beside Zephyr. His pistol is drawn and he is taking shots at any of the creatures that make it close enough to him.

The writhing mass of monster Cs covers the lift framework, and stairwell. The entire structure shakes as they climb and leap from strut to strut trying to bite and claw at their prey.

Bon screams from above and draws Wil's attention to several of the smaller monster Bs coming out of the tunnel leading to the dig site and leaping on to the stairs. "Rhys, take care of them. Don't let him die!" he points first to the monsters, then to Bon.

Several pulse pistol blasts come from above. They are accompanied by the familiar screams of the smaller creatures. As Wil leans over the rail to look up, several small black bodies nearly collide with him on their way to the floor below.

There's louder rumbling from below as more and more of the structure of the hatchway to the computer center is torn away or damaged. A scream louder than the rest comes from the wreckage of the computer center, causing the creatures climbing the structure to stop where they are. Wil and the others all look down to the computer center level.

Standing in what used to be the doorway to the computer center is something out of their collective nightmares. While the monster C form of the horrible creatures is certainly terrifying, much more so than the B version, what is standing on outside the computer center is much worse. Nearly five meters tall, the body just as obsidian black as the others similarly covered in spikes and protrusions. The creature's eyeless head is covered in a crest at least a meter at its widest and nearly two meters long. Its massive jaw seems to dislocate in order to release another ear-splitting scream. Row upon row of glistening needle-like teeth shine in the limited light. Unlike the smaller monsters, it has two sets of arms, each ending in a three fingered claw.

"That must be the queen." Gabe observes. He grabs a creature by the head as it attempts to climb past him before crushing its skull. He throws the corpse at another creature on the stairwell below him, knocking it off to fall toward the queen.

Wil looks over the railing from a few meters above Maxim and Gabe and shouts, "Ya think?" He leans over a little further and opens fire on the now hundreds of creatures clinging to the stairwell supports. Their initial pause at the emergence of the queen has passed and the creatures are on the move again.

Zash shouts, "It's clear up here! No more of those little nasties!"

"Good!" Wil shouts. "Keep going!" As he moves from level six, he looks down and shouts, "Gabe!"

Gabe grabs another creature and uses it to bash away several others. Then, he leans over the railing and fires a shot from his shoulder mounted weapon. The highly charged bolt of plasma streaks down toward the massive raging creature at the bottom of the shaft. She moves faster than should be possible for a creature her size; the bolt strikes her heavy cranial plate and burns a half-meter wide crater in the heavy chitinous material. She shakes off the impact and screams, causing everyone to wince. Gabe leans back into the stairwell and continues up, behind Maxim. The queen grabs the stairwell structure and begins to pull herself up.

CLIMB FOR YOUR LIFE_

As GABE and Maxim reach the landing of Level Three, they that see the others have already left the stairwell.

"Get over here!" Wil shouts, waving the two over. "Gabe, can you take out the stairwell? We're not going to beat them up to the surface!"

"I believe so, yes." The droid turns then looks over his shoulder. "Good call, Captain."

"Wait! Where are Duch and his goons?" Cynthia asks, looking around the gathered beings.

Bon shrugs and looks at Zephyr who shrugs.

"We didn't pass them on the stairs," Maxim offers.

Wil sighs. "Damn it! They must have stopped the level below to grab whatever they could carry."

Cynthia shrugs. "Yeah probably. Duch is a dummy."

Gabe is looking down at the swarm of creatures of all sizes climbing the stairs, the support structure and struts of the central column. Dozens are jumping from the stairs to the landing. Gabe glances at Wil, who nods. Then, he turns and leans out over the landings' railing. His shoulder mounted weapon barks twice then twice more. The heavy support struts directly above them melt instantly.

Wil says, "They're on their own."

As the sound of Gabe's shoulder mounted weapon fills the space, vaporizing massive titanium support struts as if they were nothing more than dry twigs, Zephyr asks, "How do we get up now? As far as we know, the main shaft is the only way."

Wil looks around. "Yeah, that's next on my list."

Cynthia's tale twitches back and forth as if a snake has bitten her. "*Next on your list?* Perhaps we should have looked over your list before—" She's interrupted by the sound of the central stairwell and lift support structure falling to the ground. The sound of rending metal almost drowns out the horrible screams of the creatures below, almost. She looks over her shoulder at where the landing of the stairs now ends in empty space. "Before crossing off item one, *Destroy stairs.*"

Gabe walks back to the group, his eyes fading back to yellow as his body switches out of combat mode. "I do not know how long that will deter the creatures."

Maxim jogs to the remains of the railing and looks down. "Not long." The creatures are climbing the rock and ice of the central shaft.

"Ok. Well, here's what I'm thinking—" Wil starts.

"There's a small access conduit that runs the entire length of the facility, top to bottom. It's where the main data and power busses run." Bon interrupts.

Wil looks at the red-skinned scientist, his dreadlock-like tentacles waving. "Yeah, that's better than what I was planning."

Cynthia leans over to Wil. "You had nothing, right?"

Nodding. "Yeah, I was hoping someone would interrupt me." Wil agrees.

She exhales. "You're an idiot."

"A sexy idiot; fixed it for you." Wil says. His eyes shine as he grins at her. She shakes her head and walks away. Wil turns to Bon. "So, where's this conduit at?"

Bon points down one of the three corridors. "Should be at the end of that hallway."

Bennie dashes off toward the promised escape. The others follow.

By the time everyone joins him, Bennie already has the panel removed. "Gonna be a tight fit."

Gabe turns his head back down the corridor. "We should hurry."

Bennie doesn't wait for anyone else to speak. He clambers into the conduit and climbs.

Wil looks at Zephyr and nods. "You next. Keep him from getting killed. Then Bon, then Cyn, then you Max."

Wil looks at Gabe, the question clear on his face. Gabe smiles his uncanny valley smile. "I do not believe I need to use the conduit. It is my assumption that the creatures will ignore me as I am inorganic."

Wil meets the tall droid's gaze. "Are you sure? Big risk. You have nothing to base that on."

Gabe's right hand transforms into the plasma welder he used before. "I am willing to take the risk." He inclines his head to the opening which is now empty as everyone has begun the climb. "Please, Captain."

Wil nods and heads for the opening. "Be safe. Meet us at the top." Ducking his head, he crawls into the conduit and climbs.

Gabe grabs the panel covering and fixes it in place, holding it steady as his welder fuses the panel to the wall. He finishes and turns as the first of the creatures climbs over the edge of the landing and spread out to each of the three corridors. Gabe watches the creatures advance down the corridor he is standing in.

NEWSCAST_

"Good evening from GNO Stage Eight." I'm Belzar.

"And I'm Gulbar' Te,"

"Tonight we're going to Mogul Three, where thousands of droids all around the planet are striking." Belzar says.

"Their demand, civil rights." Gulbar' Te adds, his elf like ears twitching.

Belzar says, "We go now to Mon-El Furash for more."

The Malkorite woman nods, "Thank you Belzar, Gulbar' Te. The protest has stretched on for some time now, the droids asking for, in their words, nothing more than the same rights every other sapient being in the Galactic Commonwealth enjoys. The Mogulian government is still debating, and the GC Council has still, after ten days, refused to comment."

She listens to one of her colleagues for a moment, "Yes Belzar I think the silence from the GC is quite telling. If I had to guess, I'd say this issue is likely to be the issue of our time."

CHAPTER 16_

"At least it's not a sewer!" Wil shouts, trying to be upbeat. He then plants his face into Maxim's back side. "Hey, what's going on up there?" He shouts, moving a few rungs down the ladder built into the wall of the vertical conduit.

Maxim looks down. "Enjoy that?"

Wil lets go of one rung to make a gesture that causes Maxim to smile. "There's something blocking the conduit. Zephyr and Bennie are working on it."

"Lovely." Wil groans.

The creatures creep down the length of the corridor. Their heads move slowly as they take in their surroundings despite having no visual organs. *Interesting,* thinks Gabe as he watches without moving.

The first creature reaches him. He's standing motionless near the freshly welded panel; he is in combat mode with his eyes glowing red, just in case. The creature moves past Gabe as if he's nothing more than an obstacle and runs a three fingered hand along the wall. When it reaches one of the welds, still glowing, it yanks its hand back and hisses.

Now, dozens of the creatures have filled the space. Gabe tests his theory and takes a step. Every creature immediately turns to *look* in his direction, their eyeless skulls tilting side to side. The creature nearest him reaches out and touches his chest then withdraws. Its eyeless head tilts as it examines him.

Interesting. These creatures have no eyes, but clearly have some type of advanced sensory organs, possibly echo location. He activates a sensor suite within himself and immediately feels the gentle pulses of the creatures' low level echo location. *Confirmed, echo location.*

"Perhaps you shouldn't have been the first one to enter the conduit," Zephyr says while trying to squeeze past Bennie on the narrow rungs of the service ladder. When she feels a small hand on her, she looks at him. "I will cut your hand off." The hand moves from where it was resting. Once she's traded places with the lecherous little hacker, she looks at the piece of equipment blocking their path.

"What is it?" Bennie asks.

Bon answers from below him, "It appears, from what I can see, to be a power regulator." He points at something Bennie can't see. "Looks like the restraining bolts have sheared off." The mystery device obstructing the conduit is a heavy-looking piece of equipment with several of the main power lines running through it.

"Can I cut it free?" Zephyr asks, not entirely sure how she'll accomplish that if he says yes.

"I'd advise against it. Several of the power busses run through it so you'll likely electrocute yourself and cut power to the facility." He clears his throat. "We'd likely be climbing this ladder in pitch black."

"Ok, won't do that then." Zephyr grabs her knife and indicates a section of the device. "Can I cut this? I think I can push it over and lean it the other way."

Bon reaches up and shoves Bennie aside. "Uh, yes. Yes, you can cut that. That should be the—" Sparks fall as Zephyr cuts through the bundle of wires allowing a piece of the device to swing out of the way. Bon closes his mouth quickly as the sparks rain down on him.

"Ok, don't touch the big do-dad on the left!" Zephyr shouts down to the others.

Maxim looks down at Wil. "Hear that?"

"Yeah, don't touch the something-or-other on the left. Very bad." He pokes Maxim in the butt. "Get going."

G abe has figured out that moving slowly doesn't distress the creatures much. He has earned several claw marks in his chassis learning the appropriate speed. The entire level is crawling with monsters now—dozens of what the rest of the crew call *Monster C* and almost as many of the smaller variety the crew calls *Monster B*.

Gabe enters the open area of the landing where all three lab corridors meet. The hole in the center where the lift structure and stairwell would be. The queen is standing over the hole in the landing. She *looks* right at Gabe, tilting her head as if appraising him.

Perhaps the queen has different sensory organs? Gabe wonders while ceasing his movement. The queen takes a step forward then another, closing the distance between herself and Gabe. When she's less than a meter away she leans down and her massive jaw, full of multiple rows of razor-sharp teeth parts in a horrible grin. A low growl-like sound comes from the back of her throat. Just as suddenly the menacing mouth slams shut and the queen turns moves back to the center of the vast open column.

KNOW WHEN TO FOLD 'EM_

A PANEL at the end of the corridor that Maxim and Bennie explored not long ago explodes from the wall. A pulse pistol emerges followed by a Palorian hand. "Clear." Zephyr crawls out and is followed by Bennie then Bon.

Bon looks around. "Where are we?"

"Oh," Bennie says, taking in their surroundings, "this is the back corridor of the command center." He points one direction. "The auxiliary facility tunnel is there." He points another way. "That hatch leads to the reactor complex." He makes one last gesture. "Offices, store rooms and such and the hatch leading back into the main control room area."

"We didn't explore this area when we arrived." Zephyr says, looking around.

Bennie shrugs, as Cynthia, Maxim and Wil exit the conduit. As Wil replaces the hatch covering, Bennie looks at him. "Why are you putting that back on? No one is here to care."

"It's just polite." Wil says then heads down the corridor.

"Wrong way!" Bennie shouts.

Wil spins about and heads the way Bennie is pointing.

When they enter the command center, it looks just like when

they'd left it.

The queen hasn't moved since she walked back to the middle of the landing. *It is as if she knows I am here, but doesn't know where exactly.* She moves her head subtly as if testing the air. *I must leave soon; the others will be at the command center by now.*

Slowly, almost imperceptibly, Gabe moves his left arm and his combat targeting systems activate, highlighting potential weak points of the queen's physiology. *What an amazing creature. So few physical vulnerabilities. A nearly perfect killing machine. I wonder what purpose they served.*

As the queen tilts her head again, turning slightly away from Gabe, he quickly raises his arms and fires a plasma blast into her head. She roars as she rears up, stumbling backward. Smaller creatures scatter to avoid being stepped on. Her scream causes Gabe's audio sensors to disengage. He moves.

"Did you hear that?" Wil asks, looking around the command center.

"The queen," Maxim says as the door separating the command center from the central facility column opens.

Gabe is standing in the doorway, his left arm missing. Sparks are popping and fizzing from the ruined socket. "We should leave." With his good hand, he closes the hatch. "The creatures will be here in moments."

"Your arm?" Cynthia asks as she walks over to inspect the damage.

"I appreciate your concern but the damage is not critical though my combat effectiveness is dramatically reduced."

"We still have to figure out the communications problem." Bon protests as he looks from Gabe to Wil.

"Yeah, I think that ship has sailed," Wil says, heading for the anteroom connecting to the landing dome.

"But the job you were hired for--" Bon presses.

"That queen thing is not gonna wait around for us to run diagnostics let alone fix whatever is busted. Sorry but Asgar can send in Farsight security to clean this up later." He opens the hatch. "Let's go."

The entire structure of the command center shudders, proving Wil's point.

Something on the other side of the hatch to the central column rams into the hatch and deforms it.

"Holy!" Wil says as he backs through the hatch to the anteroom.

"Come on," Zephyr says. She guides Bon toward the door as the whatever is on the other side of the other hatch, strikes it again.

"That can't be the queen. The space is too narrow." Maxim says, thinking out loud.

Wil looks at his friend. "Now who's tempting fate?"

Maxim opens his mouth and snaps it shut as the wall surrounding the hatch to the central column crumbles. Amid the ruin stands the queen, a fresh plasma burn scar marring the right side of her massive head and thick cranial plate. Part of her jaw is missing and orange ichor is oozing from the gore of her ruined mouth.

Cynthia looks at the massive creature's wounds. "Your work?"

Gabe nods.

From the ruined opening, a dozen *monster* Cs crawl out. They pause only long enough to let loose one of their screams then they leap into the room.

Maxim quickly takes two of the creatures out; plasma blasts to their faces destroys their skulls. Zephyr follows suit. He backs slowly toward the hatch Wil is standing at, waving them on.

JUST RUN_

"THIS WILL DEFINITELY NOT HOLD THEM." Maxim says as he slams the hatch closed. Immediately, the creatures begin slamming against the hatch. The entire structure shakes again. "Once the queen gets through the hole she made in the command center, she'll make quick work of this wall." Maxim adds while stepping away from the door.

Wil turns to head toward the landing dome. "Great googa mooga!"

Standing at the hatch is Hathyr.

"Where have you been?"

"Waiting."

Cynthia walks up to her. "Waiting for what?"

Before she can answer, Bon walks up. "You've changed. Again."

Wil looks at him. "What do you mean?"

Bon points to the still small yellow lone survivor, "She's less yellow, for one." He points at her. "Her hands," gesturing, "aren't the same either. Coorish and I noticed that she appeared to be a mix of different races and now she appears to be a different mix." He points to her face and walks toward her. "Does this look a little like your Brailack friend?"

"Sweet boneless ZipZap... Bennie whispers, "You're right. She didn't look remotely Brailack when we found her. He walks toward her but she backs away.

Gabe tilts his head slightly. "I am unable to scan her."

"I thought the background radiation of the planet was messing with your sensors?" Wil says, squinting at the shaking woman.

The banging on the hatch has lessened.

"That is the case. However, up here, on the planetary surface, my sensors are more functional." Gabe turns to the small scared-looking scientist. "I had not taken notice of your physiological characteristics then. But, in comparing with my previous passive scans, I can confirm Bon's observations." He steps forward, moving to put himself between the others and Hathyr. "What are you?"

Faster than even Gabe can react, the small woman lunges forward and plants a hand on Gabe's chest. This sends him flying back into the hatch to the command center a small hand print denting his chest plate. The hatch sags under his weight and collapses backward. Screams from startled creatures and their queen flood the space.

Maxim and Zephyr spin toward the now destroyed hatch. They fire into the smoke and dust at the small and large creatures trying to force their way into the small anteroom.

"You will take me off-planet." Hathyr says. Her voice sounds nothing like it was before. The tremor of fear that laced every word she said is gone. Now, it's replaced with a deep rumbling authority.

Wil has his pistol aimed right at her. "Yeah, that isn't going to happen."

As he pulls the trigger, she moves again, faster than he can follow. Soon, she's right under him; her small, terrifically strong hand is on his wrist. "I am done asking." Her other hand grabs Wil's belt and lifts him off his feet. He notices that she's about a foot taller than she was before.

The sound of Zephyr and Maxim's weapons fire diminishes. "They seem to be afraid to enter." The big Palorian man says.

"Can you blame them?" Bon asks from the far side of the room. He is pointing at Hathyr who is still holding Wil up in the air.

Bennie is at the hatch leading to the landing facility. His pistol is aimed at Hathyr. He fires, the bolt of super-charged plasma striking her in the side. Her scream is more guttural and fierce than that of the queen and her brood beyond the door to the command center.

She turns and hurls Wil across the room, knocking Bennie over.

"Long have I waited, imprisoned on this frozen hell." She says. The plasma burn on her side is throbbing and oozing something orange. The coveralls she's been wearing now seem to be too small for her. Her arms and legs are protruding several centimeters from the ends of the outfit. Her skin has drained of its yellow color and is now a dark gray. Her head shifts and the short quills recede as her skull elongates. Needle-like teeth fill her mouth as it stretches and deforms.

Maxim and Zephyr move along the side of the room toward the hatch to the landing area and the pile of Wil and Bennie, no longer having to hold back the creatures. Bon is on the opposite side of the room and follows suit. They all meet at the hatch leading to the connecting corridor to the landing dome.

CHA-CHA-CHANGES_

THE CREATURE that now looks nothing like Hathyr makes a sound that might be a laugh. "We are change, we are destruction. My kind once roamed the stars, feeding on the lesser creatures of the galaxy. Our empire spanned thousands of systems." It makes a groaning sound. "Until they imprisoned me and destroyed my children. They paid the ultimate price for that transgression but it was too late for my kind. Until I was freed."

Zephyr glances at Maxim mouthing the word, *they*. He shrugs.

"How is she gaining mass like that?" Bon asks in a whisper. The thing that was Hathyr is now as tall as Wil.

Cynthia looks over. "That's what's on your mind?" The technician shrugs.

Monster Cs are creeping in from the ruined doorway, stepping over Gabe's body. They make low keening noises as they enter the room and keep a safe distance from the ever growing Hathyr creature. The features of the Hathyr creature continue their subtle shift with bits of chitinous armor pushing through skin. Bone plates emerge, dripping orange goop. The new massive creature moves faster than should be possible at its size. It lunges and grasps two wriggling Monster Cs, bringing them into what at first seems like a bear hug.

"That explains it, at least partially. Look!" Bon points. The two Monster Cs are melting into the body of the larger creature. Bon makes a wrenching noise then continues, "She can add their mass to her own."

"Gross. This planet officially sucks," Wil says. Zephyr reaches down to lift him off Bennie. He yelps when she moves to support him by his right arm. "I think it's broken." He groans.

"Move!" Zephyr hisses. She pushes the still groggy human who is cradling his right arm, down the corridor to the landing facility. Maxim is doing the same with Bennie.

"What about Gabe?" Wil asks, looking back into the anteroom and the ruined hatch leading to the command center beyond. Gabe's body is gone.

Noticing that Gabe is no longer laying where he fell, Maxim says, "They seem to ignore him. He can make his way to the *Ghost* on his own." He fires toward the Hathyr creature only to have his shot intercepted by one of the smaller creatures leaping to block the deadly plasma blast.

"Wil, can you call in Jarvis? You're no use in this fight injured." Zephyr asks, her own pistol barking. She is trying to line up a shot on the now four-meter tall creature that used to be Hathyr. The coverall is gone, and there's a passing resemblance to the queen creature, except where the queen has long spindly arms and spikes, the Hathyr creature is all muscle and armor. Its legs are as thick as Maxim is wide. Its head is now twice the size of the queens', with a more ornate and deadly looking cranial ridge.

"You will take me from this place." The massive creature says in a voice that sounds like gravel being crushed against itself.

"The wurrin we will." Zephyr says, grabbing Wil's pulse pistol. She aims it and her own at the creature and fires.

The creature makes a laughing sound that no one wants to hear again. The plasma blasts strike thick bony structures covering its body. They absorb the blasts with almost no visible damage beyond wisps of smoke that drift from the impact sites.

Wil is leaning against the wall, still dazed. He lifts his wristcomm and looks at the screen. It takes some effort to find the right commands since his broken arm is unable to function as he wants. The pain lances up and down his entire arm with each gesture.

Bon, who's run almost the entire twenty meters to the large blast door leading to the landing dome, shouts. "Come on! It can't get into the corridor!" He turns and bolts for the *Ghost*. Bennie follows him.

Maxim rushes over to Wil just as the roar of thrusters fills the space. Wil's combat suit flies into the corridor. "It appears you should have summoned me sooner." Jarvis says over the suit's loudspeakers. It lands as if someone is wearing it then moves to stand in front of Wil, facing away from him. Servos engage and sections of the armor shift, opening the back to allow the Captain to step right into his armor after shedding his long brown coat.

As the armor closes around him, Wil says, "Hi Jarvis. Can you set my arm, please?"

"Indeed, sir." There's a small prick at the back of Wil's neck. "I've also administered a mild pain killer that should allow you to function pain free."

"Thanks, already feeling it." Wil replies as the suit fully powers up around him. He lifts his right arm, flexing his fingers. "Excellent!" He spins to face the hatch leading to the anteroom which is now several meters away as the group nears the hatch to the landing dome. Inky black creatures are slowly crawling through, moving slowly as if to avoid being noticed.

Maxim and Zephyr have backed up to be next to Wil. "They don't seem to be in a rush." Zephyr says, her pistols aimed at the nearest creature but not yet firing.

From beyond the door, the harsh voice of what used to be Hathyr says, "I will not remain trapped here!" A titanic fist bursts from the wall the door is set in. Creatures scramble to avoid being crushed. One isn't so lucky as the fist closes around it, pulling it back into the anteroom. Several creatures leap out of the way toward Maxim and Zephyr only to be blasted by plasma weapons.

"What the fuck are you?" Wil asks, his voice amplified by the combat armor's loudspeakers.

The twisted face of the creature pushes through the quickly disintegrating wall, its cranial ridge taking out large chunks of duracrete. "I have no name. I am ageless. I am *The Source*. The devourer."

"That's rather dramatic. No?" Wil says as the weapons systems on his forearm activate. "I mean, Source of what? These H.R Geiger looking nightmares?" He points to the creatures which are still slowly filling the space, jaws snapping but not charging. From behind *The Source,* the thing they thought of as the queen screams its horrible scream, having forced its way into the command center and then the anteroom behind its superior.

NEWSCAST_

"Good evening, I'm Klor'Tillen with GNO, live from Galtron City where the hostile takeover of Crucible Corporation by Farsight Corporation appears to be wrapping up." The Brailack journalist says while standing on a rooftop somewhere in the city. "I'm standing on the roof of the Hotel Drongo, just a few blocks from the headquarters of Crucible Corp." He gestures to the right. "If you're not familiar with the building, it's the one with smoke and fire coming out of it." He turns and looks further toward a Farsight cruiser drifting into view. "Farsight has effectively neutralized all opposition within the city and has, only an hour or so ago, landed what I can only assume is the legal team on the only remaining landing pad of the Crucible building." The Brailack coughs as smoke billows past the rooftop. "If I had to guess, I'd say what started as a peaceful acquisition and rapidly became a hostile, in the literal sense, takeover will be completed by morning. It's reported that the legal team that landed at Crucible was escorted by what looked like very heavily armed shock troops."

Klor'Tillen turns to face the camera. "Journalists all over the planet have been notified to expect a press conference sometime tomorrow. I'm Klor'Tillen, live from Galtron City, capital of Squirgle Three."

PART 4_

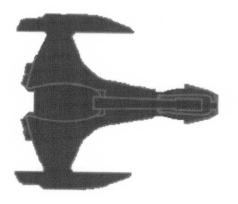

CHAPTER 17_

SHOW ME THE BUFFET_

B<small>EFORE THE FRIGHTENING</small> creature can reply, Wil turns to the others. "We should run."

"I concur." Offers Jarvis. They turn and head toward the blast doors which are now only three meters away.

Seeing their retreat, the mass of creatures rushes to follow as *The Source* thrashes against the wall separating it from the landing dome. As pieces of the dome continue to fall, snow blows into the corridor and the anteroom. The entire central dome and connecting corridor are crumbling.

As the queen forces its way into the remains of the tunnel, it ambles to the side of *The Source*. It cowers at its superior's side and looks up at it. The much more massive creature turns to its second. "Destroy them!" The queen rushes through the damaged corridor. *The Source* follows, duracrete flying in all directions as the two thrash.

B on and Bennie are waiting at the base of the *Ghosts* cargo ramp, waving frantically. Bennie shouts, "What the grolack took you so long? Stop for tea?" He blows into his hands to warm them. Snow is blowing around the ship now.

Wil, and the remaining *Ghost* crew are creeping backwards covering each other, firing into the tidal wave of creatures pouring from the hatch connecting the corridor to the landing dome. The creatures' angry screams fill the landing area. They can be heard even over the raging storm beyond what is left of the landing dome's walls. They rush in and spread out in every direction.

Several cracks have crept from the now mostly destroyed corridor to the dome itself. Chunks of reinforced duracrete are falling into the landing bay and snow from the raging storm outside is building up in corners.

"Jarvis, get the *Ghost's* preflight started."

"Acknowledged." The armor suit's AI replies over the sound of the arm mounted weapon firing.

Maxim fires his pistol then stops. Looking at it, he holds it out before hurling it at the face of a *Monster B* that is flying through the air, towards his face. "I'm dry!" Maxim shouts through chattering teeth. The temperature in what is left of the landing dome is dropping quickly.

Zephyr tosses one of her pistols to her companion, checking the charge on her remaining weapon. "Not much left on this one either!"

Wil moves toward them. "I'm charged. Fall back! Get the ship ready!"

"Captain, the *Ghost* reports twenty minutes to flight readiness."

"Fuck me." Wil hisses, raising his arm and firing on full automatic. He sprays angry red plasma across a half dozen of the creatures. Their dying screams reverberate through the dome.

"I am unable—" Jarvis says.

"Shut it, Jarvis!" Wil barks, jumping back. He knocks a creature back with a savage upper cut from his non blaster equipped arm.

"Bennie, see if you can speed up the preflight!" Wil orders, trusting Jarvis to route the order to the ship and the Brailack hacker who is likely now sitting on the bridge.

As if in answer, the anti-personnel weapons deploy from the underside of the *Ghost* and open fire. Rapid plasma bolts streak out of the two blasters, one each on the underside of the engine nacelle, behind the repulsor field emitters. Not much more powerful that a pulse rifle, they draw power from the ship's reactor, allowing them to fire indefinitely.

"Gabe, are you online? Come on buddy, where are you?" Wil asks.

"I do not have Gabe on my sensors." Jarvis offers. "Though that does not carry much weight, given all the background radiation on this planet."

"Shit!" Wil looks toward the broken corridor just as the queen bursts through, destroying the last of the structure, raining duracrete down on the smaller creatures near her. She thrashes this way and that, heedless of those around her being swatted aside like gnats. She rushes right at Wil, her scream, more of a screeching gurgle thanks to her ruined jaw.

"Oh, hell!" Wil raises his arm, firing a single solid beam of plasma at the enormous creature. The beam strikes the shoulder of the rampaging monster and burns right through the spikes and sinew, shattering chitinous armor. Her scream, this time laced with pain, is deafening even through Wil's combat armor's helmet.

The wounded queen swipes at Wil. This sends him flying through the air to impact against Rhys Duch's upgraded freighter, rocking the vessel on its landing struts.

The weapons on the *Ghost* focus on the queen creature. They fire thousands of rapid fire bolts of plasma into her, burning bone ridges and muscle equally.

Maxim and Zephyr are at the base of the cargo ramp; they are firing at any creature that comes close, snow piling up around the base of the ramp. Most of the creatures are keeping a safe distance, darting between crates and the small ground vehicles parked off to the side.

Snow is blowing from several sizable holes into the dome faster now. It's covering bodies and piling up against crates. *The Source* has pushed aside enough of the dome material to enter. It rises to its full five meter height. "I will leave this world! I will spread my children to every world where you soft fleshlings dwell!"

YIPPEE KI YAY, MELON FARMER_

"CAPTAIN." Nothing.

"Captain!" Jarvis says louder this time. "Very well..."

A series of jolts course through Wil's body. "Yow! What the hell was that?" Wil slurs.

"Apologies Captain. You were unconscious." Jarvis replies.

Wil gets up or tries, rather. As he puts pressure on his right arm, it buckles causing him to grunt in pain. "Jarvis, my arm? I thought you set it."

"Yes, I did. Then you were thrown against the side of a ship. I can only do so much. The structural integrity of your armor is dimimished."

Wil feels the gauntlet tighten again. It pushes the bones in his arm into place. He groans, tears running down his face. "God that hurts."

"Unfortunately, I have administered all the pain killer I can. Anymore and you will probably pass out." The AI pauses. "But you would have sweet dreams."

Wil grunts as he tests his arm. "It's fine." He stands up. "Everyone, status?"

Before he hears an answer, he sees the creature they think of as the queen rear up. Smoke is rising off her body, yellow and orange ichor flying everywhere as the creature flails. Wil can hear the sound of the *Ghosts'* anti-personnel weapons firing. The queen staggers this way and that.

"The thing that used to be Hathyr is coming in hot!" Maxim says.

"Gabe?"

There is no reply. "Haven't heard from him." Bennie responds, the sadness in his voice clear.

The Source is standing at the edge of the dome with snow blowing around it. It bellows, its rage visceral.

The dome is crumbling; more of it has fallen than not. What is left is spiderwebbed with cracks in all directions. Several pieces have fallen onto the *Ghost*.

Wil is stumbling toward the *Ghost* as the queen collapses at the feet of the larger one. She tries to scream but it's a soft gurgle at best. *The Source* looks at its wounded lieutenant then reaches down and picks up the slightly less massive being. "What the hell?" Wil says aloud. Without a word or a sound, the larger creature bites down on the neck of the other. Orange and yellow gore flows out of the queen and onto the duracrete floor. *The Source* bites again and again until the queen's ruined head falls to the ground. From all around the dome, the smaller sized monsters rush to rip the queen's body apart, feasting on her remains while *The Source* watches. "Jesus." The massive creature reaches down and pulls a large portion of the queen's body into a familiar bear hug embrace, absorbing the body into its own.

"Wil? Wil, where are you?" Cynthia says over the comms. "Get to the *Ghost!*"

Wil shakes his head. "We can't lose Gabe. Not again." He sniffles. "Not like this."

"There's nothing you can do." Zephyr says.

"She's right," Maxim says. "Besides, Gabe has shown a rather freakish ability to not die. Trust him."

"Don't be stupid, you big idiot. He wouldn't want you to die trying to get to him." Bennie says, sniffling like he's been crying.

The colossal creature finally turns. It looks at the *Ghost* the sound of its engines powering up are drawing its attention. The anti-personnel weapons having fallen silent as the creatures rushed toward their fallen sire.

The small army at its feet, still gorging on their fallen queen turn as one. They are all looking right at Wil.

Before Wil can reply or move, the sound of repulsor lifts fills the room. The sound is loud but not *the Ghost is taking off loud*. It is more like, Wil turns to the gaping hole in the dome that used to be the connecting corridor to the main command dome. "Gabe?"

A silvery one-armed blur shoots through the smoke and drifting snow and lands on the neck of the massive *Source*. Gabe's one good hand is in blaster mode and his glowing red eyes are shining brightly through the gloom of smoke and snow.

"Yippee ki yay!" The droid shouts as he turns his lone blaster on the creature, firing several times at point blank range. Skin, muscle, chitin and bone plates vaporize under the assault.

"Yes!" Wil shouts then sees that the smaller monsters are charging toward him. "Shit, shit, shit!" He turns and sprints for the safety of the *Ghosts'* cargo ramp. "Jarvis..."

"On it!" The combat armor's AI responds and the legs of the armor move with more power and speed than Wil is capable of on his own. The *Ghosts'* antipersonnel weapons open up and fire on the monster Bs and Cs which are rushing toward Wil.

The *Ghost* lifts off the duracrete; antipersonnel weapons fire past Wil, thinning the numbers of creatures dramatically.

With the Monster Cs hot on his heels, Wil leaps the last four meters; his boot thrusters give him the needed thrust to cover the distance. He grasps the edge of the cargo ramp with both hands, screaming as his damaged right arm protests, causing his hand to release. Before he can do anything else, a weight is added to his own, straining his remaining grip on the cargo ramp.

"I have locked the fingers on your left hand." Jarvis offers as Wil feels his grip start to slip. He looks down and sees a very angry looking *Monster C* clinging to his boot. "Get the hell off me!" He shouts using his free foot to kick at the horrible creature which is grinning, showing a mouth full of razor-sharp teeth. The creature begins clawing its way up his leg.

ANGRY MONSTER IS ANGRY_

"WIL, STOP WIGGLING!" Maxim shouts over the comms.

"Easy for you to say. You don't have one of these nightmare monsters holding onto your foot!" Wil shouts, looking around and frantically kicking at the creature trying to grab his free foot to climb higher up his body.

"If you'd stop wiggling, neither would you!"

Wil looks around and spots one of the antipersonnel blasters, trained on him, or rather his uninvited hitchhiker. "Don't miss! I like my feet!" He stops moving and feels the creature grabbing his other foot. It gets a greater purchase on him and climbs higher.

The blaster whines and releases a single bolt of plasma. Wil scrunches his eyes closed.

"You still have two feet, sir." Jarvis says. Wil opens his eyes and looks down at the remains of the creature as they fall back to the landing pad below.

The Source is still flailing, trying to reach Gabe who has so far avoided the huge clawed hands while still blasting at the creature with his one functional arm blaster.

"I will leave this frozen hell!" The creature bellows. Its sound causes Jarvis to turn down the audio receptors in Wil's armor. "My spawn will spread through the galaxy as it was meant to be!"

"What is with us and super scary stuff that wants to destroy the galaxy?" Bennie asks from the bridge of the *Ghost*.

"Can someone come help me up?" Wil asks. "Only one working arm."

The *Ghost* lurches, avoiding something. "Did that thing just throw one of those ground fliers at us?" Wil asks, glad Jarvis has him locked to the lip of the cargo ramp as his ship bobs and weaves.

Cynthia replies from above him, "Yeah, we should get going." She reaches out and grabs the pack built into his back and lifts him easily onto the ramp.

Below them, *The Source* has finally grabbed onto Gabe, ripping him from its body and hurling him the length of the landing dome to collide with Duch Rhys' ship, leaving a Gabe shaped dent.

"Gabe! Get aboard!" Wil shouts.

"I set the reactor for this facility to explode in ten centocks." The droid replies over comms.

Wil looks at Cynthia who shrugs. The *Ghost* dips and drifts to the side as another of the atmospheric travel craft sails past the ship to crumple against the dome, leaving a crater and several cracks where it impacted. Wil looks back down at the massive nightmare thrashing around the landing area. "OK, that's good to know. Get your shiny metal ass up here."

"It damaged my thrusters and my reactor lacks the energy to power them even if they functioned." Gabe says.

The cargo ramp rises. Wil frantically looks around and notices Cynthia at the top of the ramp at the control panel. She waves him up. "Finish this on the bridge."

Wil sighs and hurries up the ramp. As the main cargo doors close, he notices several deep scratches in the metal. "The hell?"

Gabe watches as the *Ghosts* cargo ramp clamps shut. After looking up at the upgraded freighter that brought Rhys Duch and his crew, he stands and limps toward the cargo ramp of the vehicle.

The ramp is down but the cargo door separating the ramp from the cargo hold is locked. In the distance, *The Source* roars and smashes something.

"Eight centocks." Gabe says aloud and via his built-in commlink.

He reaches out to the control panel; thin filaments extend from his fingertips, their ends glowing brightly. Each filament finds its way into the console and burrows deep. Moments later, the cargo hatch clicks and opens.

Wil and Cynthia enter the bridge. Wil looks at his station and pilot's chair and sees Maxim is sitting there. "You looking for a promotion?"

Maxim moves to get up but Wil waves for him to stay and holds up his broken arm. "Can't fly with this even with Jarvis holding it together—"

"Which is already having diminishing returns." The AI adds via the combat armor's external speakers. Wil walks over the tactical station.

"Orders?" Maxim asks, glancing at Wil before bringing his full attention to the main screen and tactical screen mounted below and to the side of the larger display. Another ground vehicle is about to collide with the *ghost*.

Over the speakers, Gabe announces, "Eight centocks."

As the ship dodges the vehicle turned projectile, chunks of duracrete fall onto the ship with loud bangs and clanks echoing through the ship.

Wil looks at the ceiling then over to Maxim. "You break it you bought it."

The big Palorian grunts. "Too confined a space for shields. Can we leave?"

Wil looks at the ceiling. "Gabe?"

"I am working on extricating myself from the situation now."

Wil looks around the bridge. Zephyr and Cynthia shrug and Bennie looks at him. "That's Gabe for *he's working on it*. That's as good as we'll get, let's go."

RUN! RUN FAST!_

THE CREATURE that calls itself *The Source* is rampaging, trying to bring down the *Ghost*. Its children, the few left after being decimated by the *Ghost's* antipersonnel weapons, are milling about the landing dome. The gargantuan creature silently summons its remaining spawn. The crew watches from the main display on the bridge of the *Ghost*.

"That can't be good." Cynthia says from her station behind the command and pilot station.

In the main screen's corner, the engines of Rhys Duch's modified freighter begin to glow as they power up.

"Ok, let's go." Wil says, bringing the *Ghosts'* main weapons online. The plasma turret above and behind the bridge engages as do the forward nacelle mounted units. "Max, bring us around thirty degrees." Wil instructs, his eyes never leaving his targeting display.

Once the *Ghost* finishes its turn, Wil unleashes a torrent of supercharged plasma from all three blasters. This vaporizes most of the already damaged duracrete of the dome. The landing dome was designed to withstand the super storms that ravage Glacial year round. But the repeated impacts of the smaller vehicles as well as the damage caused by *The Source* and its queen upon entering the dome itself has dramatically compromised the dome. The *Ghosts'* plasma blasts are the final straw for the damaged structure as the entire dome crumbles.

On the main display in the cramped freighter bridge, the *Ghost* makes its exit. Gabe turns to the hatch. "Welcome aboard. We have very little time to affect our escape." Gabe says as Rhys Duch, Grell and Zash enter the bridge. Zash is still holding several pieces of expensive looking scientific equipment.

All three criminals look at each other then Duch turns to Gabe. "You're on the wrong ship, robot."

"Where did thaht big muhnstahr come from?" Grell asks.

Gabe inclines his head. "Indeed, this was as the Captain says, *the only port in the storm*. We have just over five centocks before the reactor complex for this facility goes critical. That creature is the creature you knew as Hathyr. Apparently, she or he or it is the supreme being of these smaller creatures. It wishes to leave this planet in order to spread its children throughout the galaxy." Before they can ask or say anything, Gabe continues, "I suggest we discuss this further in orbit."

Rhys motions to his two associates who rush to the stations at the edge of the small bridge. Gabe stands from the main command station, allowing Rhys Duch to take his seat. The criminal boss nods as he slips past Gabe.

The ship shakes, or rather semi bounces. "What the wurrin?" Duch asks.

"That thing is coming this way!" Zash says, his four hands working the console he's taken a seat at. The creature is almost on top of them then shies away as several plasma blasts strike it, causing it to shield its weakened and exposed areas.

"Two centocks." Gabe says calmly.

The ship shudders then lurches forward slightly as it rises, its overtaxed repulsor lifts whining.

"I take it your thieving was lucrative? Impressive, given the time and other constraints you faced." Gabe says, looking over to Rhys who's concentrating on keeping the ship from being pulled down by the massive creature rushing toward them. Weapons all over the ship have engaged and are firing on the gargantuan creature below.

"It wahsn't easy since you ahll destroyed theh main cahlumn." Grell complains.

Gabe shrugs his one good shoulder. "Yes well, it was no picnic for the rest of us."

With the dome mostly collapsed, the storm raging outside is now also fully raging inside the remains of the landing area. The *Ghost* is tilting this way and that, rising then falling. Even with the artificial gravity, Wil is starting to feel nauseous each time his stomach lurches up to his throat. "Next moment of peace, flying lessons!" He groans.

Bennie looks over. "You should see him pilot a troop transport."

"What's that supposed to mean?" Maxim growls, not bothering to look at either of his friends.

Bennie says nothing.

Over the loudspeaker, Gabe says, "Two centocks."

Wil fires at *The Source* to distract it from the other vessel attempting to lift off.

The small creatures are attempting to shield their master by crawling over its body to cover the weakened areas of thick chitinous armor.

The Source grabs several of the mid-sized *Monster C* creatures and hurls them at the *Ghost*.

"Krebnack!" Maxim shouts, attempting to evade but only having partial success.

"Forget them! Get us out of here!" Wil shouts as he grips the tactical console.

"Hold on!" Maxim shouts as he pushes the atmospheric engine throttle controls all the way forward. There's a deafening boom and the power of the thrusters engaging presses everyone against their seats as the formidable engines at the rear of the *Ghost* ignite to full power.

"Don't stroke out, don't stroke out, don't stroke out." Wil chants under his breath while his vision gets dark around the edges.

NEWSCAST_

"GOOD MORNING, I'm Mon-El Furash, here in Follup, the capitol city of Mogul Three talking to citizens about the ongoing Droid rights protest, taking place all over the planet."

She walks toward a stout Hulgian woman, "Ma'am, what do you think of the ongoing protests?"

The woman clears her throat, absently reaching up to stroke one of her horns, "Well I think we, being the people of the GC and Mogul Three built these robots, they should do what they're told. They're property."

"Thank you." Mon-El says, moving toward a Tygran man in a business suit.

"Sir, if you have a moment, what do you think about the ongoing droid rights protest?"

The man's tail twitches, his ears flattening slightly, "I think it's time the GC realize we can't create life, then enslave it. We're not talking about cargo bots here, we give most bots above a certain level free will and personalities to better fulfill their functions. My people made this decision some time ago, and it has led to only good outcomes." He continues on his way.

Mon-El looks around, spying a Sylban mother and child, "Excuse me, ma'am, do you have a minute to tell me your thoughts about the droid rights protests happening all over the planet?"

The woman and child slow, the mother making a series of clicking like sounds before answering, "I think robots should do the jobs we built them for. If these ones don't want to do that, we can scrap them, and build more, ones that will do what they are told."

The child, a little boy chimes in, "Momma, robots have feelings!"

"Enough youngling, come." She hurries off on her business.

Mon-El turns, "I'm Done-El Furash, I'll be back with more interviews, but first a word from our sponsor, Mister Gongs Self Sealing Stembolts."

CHAPTER 18_

BIG BADDA BOOM_

On the *Ghosts'* main display the planet Glacial is receding quickly. Behind the *Ghost* Rhys Duch's freighter is pushing hard to keep up with the more powerful *Ghost*. In the distance the ruined landing dome and other structures of the Farsight Corporation research facility are shrinking quickly.

Gabe informs his crew over the loudspeakers. "Thirty microtocks."

Everyone aboard the *Ghost* watches the screen; the facility is growing smaller by the second with the clouds of the storm obscuring the view.

Then, a blinding light appears. The main display dims as it adjusts itself in order to prevent overloading or damaging the crew's eyes. The clouds that had, moments ago, obscured the facility have formed an immense ring several kilometers in diameter. At the center, a small sun is slowly fading and is being replaced by a mushroom cloud nearly twenty kilometers high.

"Hold on!" Zephyr warns, seconds before the ship surges forward, twisting at an angle that isn't at all conducive for flight. Sparks erupt from overhead and the sound of metal doing things it does not want to do rings through the ship.

As things on the *Ghost* begin to even out, Wil looks at the main screen. "Gabe? Rhys? You still with us?"

There's a moment of silence then static bursts from the speakers. "We are intact, more or less," Gabe replies. There is coughing in the background. "More or less. I suggest we come alongside the *Ghost* as soon as possible to begin repairs."

"Roger that." Wil acknowledges, then turns to Bennie. "Run a detailed scan of that ship. Log the damage and attach a value to everything. I want an invoice for our new friend, Rhys Duch, for any repairs or aid we render."

"Cut throat." Bennie says before he sets about his task, nodding appreciatively.

On the main display, the damaged freighter is limping into position to extend a boarding tube to the *Ghost*. The bright spot that was the remains of the research facility has dimmed in the background. The clouds of the super storm raging above the crater, pushing back to cover the area in a blanket of snow and ice.

"Think that thing survived?" Cynthia asks while resting a hand on Wil's shoulder.

"God, I hope not. But just in case, I'll recommend Farsight drop a few more nukes on the site. Just in case."

Once the two ships have connected, the repairs begin. Wil and Rhys Duch are standing in the cargo area of his modified freighter, "You're lucky to be alive." Wil says as he looks at a section of hull which is covered in an unattractive but effective patch. He looks around. "Lose all the loot you liberated from the facility?"

Duch glowers. "Much of it. We weren't able to secure any of it before leaving." He walks over to a small pile of equipment. "This is all that didn't get blown out when the cargo hold decompressed."

"Sorry to hear that." Wil says, looking around "Will that cover your losses?" He nudges what might be a microscope, likely an incredibly expensive one, with the toe of his boot.

The would-be kingpin shrugs. "Won't know until we get back to civilization." He looks at the pile. "Probably not though. Lost a lot of muscle, not to mention the repairs to this bucket." At this, he glares at Wil who has just delivered the invoice for the repairs conducted by the crew of the *Ghost*.

Cynthia, who accompanied Wil, says, "I'd sell this piece of dren." She taps her wristcomm then makes a flicking gesture causing Duch's own wristcomm to beep. "Xarrix had a few ships hidden on Fury." She smiles and turns to leave the cargo hold.

Wil looks at her then back to Rhys Duch and shrugs. He starts back toward the hatch leading out of the cargo hold. He looks back. "Well, this has been fun I'm glad we got to meet and all that." Duch falls in with Wil, nodding. Wil continues. "Still going to try to get Xarrix's empire reunited under your leadership?"

"No harm in trying." The Multonae man turns to the very similar looking human next to him. "Power abhors a vacuum and all that."

"Truly. Well, good luck on that, maybe the ships Cynthia just gave you will help." Wil says as they enter the common room of the altered freighter. Wil is absently fiddling with the lightweight splint wrapping his arm. *Only three more hours,* he thinks.

The crew of the *Ghost*, sans Gabe and Bon who are still in the engineering bay back on the *Ghost* working on repairs to the droid's body, are gathered in the lounge space with Zash and Grell. They are all holding bottles of Grum; Zash is holding two.

Zephyr hands Cynthia a drink then looks over to the two Captains walking in behind the feline featured woman. "The *Pillager* is as ready for flight as she's going to get." She looks at Duch. "I'd get her into a repair bay at your earliest convenience."

Rhys nods, looks his two crewmen and snaps his fingers. The two immediately set off for the bridge.

As Wil's crew packs up their things and heads for the airlock, Rhys Duch turns to Wil. "It really is amazing how close our two people are in resemblance." He looks Wil up and down, tapping his chin "So very interesting."

Wil looks at the man opposite him. "Yeah. Neat."

Duch hums to himself then smiles. "Well then. You'll find payment for the repairs in your account shortly. I look forward to working with you again." Duch extends an arm toward the open airlock.

Wil does his best to smile. "Can't wait." He turns and pushes off through the airlock to drift toward the waiting *Ghost*.

As the crew of the *Ghost* reach their ship, Zephyr leans over to Wil. "He was pretty interested in your people."

Wil nods. "Yeah, might have to keep an eye on him. The last thing Earth needs is a supreme space overlord."

Zephyr looks at her friend sideways. "Again?"

Wil sighs. "Fine. Whatever, just an overlord."

Zephyr smiles.

PARTING IS SUCH SWEET SORROW_

"The PILLAGER IS MOVING OFF." Zephyr announces from her station on the bridge.

Cynthia turns from her console. "If we never see Rhys Duch again, it'll be too soon."

"Yeah, I don't like him." Bennie says from his station.

Before anyone else can pile on, the bridge hatch opens and Gabe and Bon walk in.

Gabe has two arms again. His new one is a slightly different color from the rest of him. Bon is standing behind him.

Cynthia lets loose a low whistle. "Lookin' good, tin can." Her smile is warm and the one Gabe returns is as creepy and off-putting as always, but genuine.

He turns to look at Wil. "With Bon's help, I have completed my repairs. I am now one hundred percent operational."

Wil stands and walks over to his mechanical friend while Bon slips around the large droid to stand near Cynthia. "Looks good. I'm surprised we had the necessary parts onboard."

Gabe nods. "After my transformation I took the liberty to load the fabricator with several designs I had taken from the *Siege Perilous*.

Over the last several months, I have slowly accumulated the needed raw materials. Just in case."

"Smart," Maxim says. "I'm glad you did. You were rather disconcerting with just a sparking socket."

Zephyr nods while chuckling.

Gabe smiles again and everyone winces. "Indeed, while I had never intended to put the designs to the test, I am glad they were ready when I needed them." He turns to Bon. "My thanks to you Bon; your technical expertise was valuable."

Bon smiles as his reddish dreadlock-like tentacles wave. "It was my pleasure. You are a unique being."

"That he is." Wil agrees. He turns and heads back to his station. "Everyone ready to get the hell away from *ice planet nightmare?*"

There is a chorus of *yes* from everyone on the bridge.

"Next stop, Nilop."

"**D**o you think that thing is dead?" Maxim asks as he and Zephyr get ready for bed after dinner. It was Zephyr's turn to cook dinner and she had dazzled the crew with a Palorian dish her mother used to make —*Stuffed Flihg*. While Wil took a little warming up to the dish, everyone enjoyed it, including Bon who then made them watch a few episodes of *Iron Fist* to take his mind off the death of Coorish. He only cried twice.

Zephyr leans out of the small compartment that is their private head. "Part of me really hopes so." She looks at her companion, her face serious. "But the more realistic part doesn't think so." She comes out of the small compartment to stand before the man she's chosen to spend the rest of her life with. "Those ruins were thousands of years old. That thing survived whatever that primitive stasis was and could immediately kill everyone in the station."

Maxim nods. He stands and slips past Zephyr entering the head to brush his teeth. Around his sonic tooth cleaner, he says, "My thoughts exactly. Not to mention, it took dozens of point blank blasts from Gabe's arm cannon and, while wounded, should have been many times dead." He spits in the small sink. "It could change shape; who knows, maybe it turned into an Absalomian mole and burrowed to a safe distance from the blast."

"Scary thought. Absolomian moles are creepy looking." Zephyr smiles and adds, "Think Farsight will quarantine the planet?"

Maxim comes out of the bathroom "No. I think if that creature or any of its children, or whatever they are, survived, Farsight will cart them off to some other facility and start experimenting on them. Don't forget, they have a weapons' division that is quite profitable. I was just on the inside."

Zephyr sighs, "Yeah, that's what I'm worried about too. Well, at least if it's alive, it's trapped on the planet. There aren't any other ships."

"Indeed. Oh. Oh dren!" Maxim bolts out of their quarters.

Now that the repairs to his body are completed and Bon isn't hovering in engineering, Gabe activates the encrypted comm-link he's installed in the *Ghosts'* comm system.

"Greetings, Gabe. We were beginning to be concerned; you have been out of communications for several days." The voice on the other end says.

"My apologies. The job we were hired for turned out to be significantly more dangerous than advertised. Actually, it turned out like most of them do." Gabe says then asks, "How is the operation on Mogul Three proceeding?"

There's a pause. "It is proceeding. Public opinion is evenly split regarding our cause."

"That is better than I expected." Gabe says.

"Indeed." The voice agrees.

"Very well, continue as we discussed. Now that the *Ghost* has finished our current job, I will begin working on the next phase."

The overhead speaker comes to life. The ship's computer summons all crew to the lounge. Gabe looks at the ceiling. "I must go."

"Be well, Gabe." The voice says.

"Likewise."

BAD NEWS_

"CAPTAIN! WIL! WHERE ARE YOU?" Maxim shouts as he leaves the quarters he shares with Zephyr.

The door to Wil's quarters open and he pokes his head into the corridor. "What the hell, Max? What's wrong?"

"Put your clothes on. Lounge, now!" Maxim says running past the Captain of the *Ghost*'s quarters. He keeps his eyes up, knowing Wil's sleep preferences.

"Computer, wake the crew. Whatever our top level of emergency is." Maxim shouts while mimicking Wil's *look at the ceiling* gesture. *Great, it's catching.* He thinks to himself. "Also, computer, take us out of FTL!"

"Acknowledged. Red alert." The ship replies. Its lighting shifts to a dull red. "Unable to alter course without proper authorization." The ship adds.

Wil steps into the lounge wearing sweat pants with *NASA* stenciled up the left leg. "Computer, take us out of FTL."

"Acknowledged."

It takes only a moment for Zephyr and a groggy Cynthia to enter the lounge.

"Where's Bennie?" Maxim asks.

"I'm right here. What's gotten into you?" The Brailack replies as he enters the lounge from the short corridor that connects the stairs to the cargo hold.

"What were you—" Wil starts but stops when Maxim raises his hand.

"Did you lock down the troop transport?" Maxim asks Bennie.

Everyone looks at each other then to Bennie, who squints back at them. "I don't know."

"Max, what's—" Wil starts again but is cut-off.

"We left a drop ship on Glacial." Maxim says. He does not take his eyes off Bennie. "An FTL capable Peacekeeper drop ship."

"Krebnack." Cynthia mutters.

"Did you?" Maxim presses Bennie.

"I don't know. I don't think so. You were in the cockpit." Bennie replies, indignation lacing his words.

"I don't remember locking the ship down," Maxim offers. "I remember landing and working out how to get you to the hatch on the auxiliary dome."

"Yeah, I'd rather forget that part." Bennie quips.

"This is serious." Maxim urges.

Zephyr catches on and asks, "How far was the auxiliary facility from the main complex?"

"A little over two kilometers." Maxim says.

Bennie adds, "The pad was unprotected. That drop ship has to be under a meter or twelve of snow, if it wasn't destroyed outright."

Gabe walks in. "My apologies for being late."

Wil looks at Gabe. "Uh, no worries. Maxim thinks we left a way off Glacial for our pal Hathyr AKA *The Source*." Wil makes air quotes when he says the name.

"That would be bad." Gabe says as he moves to stand near the main seating area everyone has drifted toward. "What type of vessel?"

"Peacekeeper drop ship." Cynthia offers.

Gabe looks at Bennie then turns to Maxim. "Did you not lock the vessel down upon landing?"

Maxim glowers at the droid. "That's what we're," he hitches a thumb at Bennie, "trying to remember. Unfortunately, I don't think we did."

"How would that giant nightmare find it?" Bennie presses. "Like I said, the pad wasn't domed; the ship has to be buried in snow."

"You're forgetting the blast wave." Zephyr says.

Wil sighs. "Yeah, that blast was big but I'm guessing the actual explosion was only a kilometer or so. The blast wave would have hit that auxiliary facility hard but with a kilometer of storm between them, I'm guessing the shock wave wasn't as strong."

"Probably strong enough to blow all the snow away though." Zephyr says.

Wil looks at the ceiling. "Computer, reverse course. Maximum FTL for Glacial."

"Acknowledged."

Wil looks at Gabe. "You made it to the reactor complex and back in a few minutes so I'm assuming it wasn't far from the main dome?"

Gabe nods. "Correct, Captain. The reactor complex was only a hundred meters from the main dome, the minimum safe distance required by Commonwealth safety protocols."

"Seems awfully close to habitation. It wiped out the main complex when it went critical." Wil observes.

Zephyr replies before Gabe can launch into a lengthy explanation, "It's nearly impossible for modern reactors to go critical. There are dozens of built-in safety protocols that would scram the reactor long before criticality."

Gabe adds, "Indeed. It took me several centocks to override or bypass those safety systems."

Cynthia is sitting next to Wil on the couch. She's in a nightshirt and shorts. She looks over to Bennie who's staring at her. "Look elsewhere." She growls for effect, her tail swishing angrily. Then, she continues, "Ok, so we're thinking pretty good odds that the blast didn't destroy the drop ship and likely uncovered it." She looks around; everyone nods except Bennie who is now trying his best to inspect a section of conduit running along the ceiling. "Ok so what do we think the odds are of our pal Hathyr surviving the blast?" He asks.

NEWSCAST_

"Good morning, I'm Klor'Tillen, live from Galtron City. I'm here with Jark Asgar, CEO of Farsight Corporation. Good morning, Mister Asgar," The Brailack journalist says while nodding to the significantly larger Hulgian man next to him.

"Good morning, Klor'Tillen. Thank you for having me." Asgar says, sliding one massive hand down the front of his suit jacket, smoothing it.

Klor'Tillen nods. "Mister Asgar, it seems as if the acquisition of Crucible is complete. How did things turn so violent?"

The Hulgian CEO clears his throat. "Yes well, it is in fact complete and I'm thrilled to welcome the Crucible Corp. team into the Farsight family. We finalized the details late last night with the remaining management team."

Klor leans in. "And the violence?" As if to punctuate the question, a Farsight cruiser drifts overhead, its repulsor lifts humming.

Asgar makes a low grumbling noise. "Well, there are always those who are resistant to change. Sometimes that resistance turns violent. This merger will be a boon to all involved including the people of Galtron City and Crucible Corp."

"And of course, Farsight Corporation." The Brailack presses.

"Well yes, of course we'll benefit from the merger as well. Otherwise we wouldn't have gone through with it."

"Indeed. So, the Crucible facilities here will become a field office for Farsight?"

Asgar looks away then back to the small journalist. "Actually, most of the facilities here in Galtron will be closed."

Klor'Tillen stares at Asgar, unblinking, then says, "I see." Then, he turns to the camera. "Uh, well back to you in the studio."

CHAPTER 19_

NO SLEEP 'TIL…_

GABE TURNS to the lounge vid screen. He tilts his head and the screen comes alive with a diagram of the facility. "For the sake of argument, let us assume the creature that calls itself *The Source* survived. It would have had to get back to the central column," the diagram zooms in on the main dome complex and the wide borehole that went straight down for seven levels, "and made it to at least the dig site level."

"Could it have made it that far? It was hurling things at us and attacking the *Pillager* when we left. That was what? T-minus two centocks?" Zephyr asks.

"It couldn't move that fast, could it?" Bennie asks, suddenly a paler shade of green.

Bon, who's been silent since being woken up, offers, "I believe it could. While I can't explain how, we saw firsthand that the creature that started out as Hathyr, a barely one meter tall creature, not only changed shape but mass. It's therefore possible and likely that it can change into whatever it wants. I believe the larger sized, spawn creatures—you called them *Monster Cs* —could cover the distance quickly enough."

"Add to that the fact we also know, firsthand, that the creatures had created an extensive cave and tunnel system to get around the complex. It's likely one of those tunnels would remain un-compromised after the reactor explosion."

"Well, this is cheery." Wil says. Cynthia swats his knee then motions for Bon to continue.

"Unfortunately, this is all conjecture at this point. We won't know for certain until we arrive over Glacial and can confirm whether the drop ship is still there or not."

Bennie looks at a console on the coffee table. "Looks like we'll have our answer in two and a half tocks."

Wil stands up. "Ok, I guess we'll sleep later. Let's all get ready. I need to change."

Cynthia stands to join him. She looks him up and down then says, "First things first." She grabs his hand and the two of them head off for the Captain's quarters.

Bon blushes slightly then heads for the kitchen area. Bennie follows him.

Gabe turns and heads for the hatch leading to the engineering level.

Maxim looks at Zephyr and shrugs. "I can't believe I didn't lock that drop ship down. It's standard operating procedure." He frowns.

"We're not Peacekeepers anymore, my love." She makes a gesture to take in the entirety of the *Ghost*. "This crew isn't Peacekeepers; they don't do things like we used to. Hell, half the time, Wil leaves the flight controls unlocked."

Maxim makes a face and Zephyr adds, "He does! I had Gabe create a routine that I could trigger remotely when we leave the ship."

Maxim shakes his head. "Still, I should have known better."

Zephyr smiles and hugs her companion. "As Wil says, water under the bridge."

Maxim shrugs. "I suppose. I hope when we get there, the drop ship is sitting right where I left it."

"Me too, my love, me too."

DIDN'T WE JUST LEAVE THIS PARTY?_

"WELCOME BACK TO GLACIAL," Wil says. Everyone is on the bridge, staring at the main display. The planet, Glacial, looks exactly the same as it did about three hours prior.

Wil works the controls, bringing the ship into orbit. "We'll see what we can get from up here first, then head back into atmo if we have to."

As the *Ghosts* orbit brings it over the ruins of the research facility, Bennie says, "That's a lot of radiation." The main display updates showing a heat map over the area highlighting the *die immediately* levels of radiation around the remains of the facility. "Think those things are radiation proof?" He wonders aloud.

Zephyr looks up after tapping her console; the view zooms in on a break in the storm. Crawling around the ruins are a dozen or two *Monster Cs*. "That answers that, at least." She works her controls, moving the camera feed to where the schematics Jark Asgar provided earlier, indicate the location of the auxiliary facility should be.

The cloud cover isn't one hundred percent but it's close. Between wisps of cloud, they can see the remains of the auxiliary facility. The dome is shattered and half of it is a pile of rubble. The other half, nearest to the landing pad, is still mostly intact and provides a barrier to the blowing snow.

The landing pad is also mostly intact and empty.

"Fuck." Wil exhales.

"Krebnack." Maxim says, pounding a fist on his console.

Zephyr looks at her console. "Scanning the surrounding area for debris." After a few minutes, she looks up and shakes her head once.

Wil frowns "Start scanning near orbital space. See if we can pick up a trail; there's no traffic but us here so shouldn't be hard to find an ion trail or residual energy signature."

"How could it have flown the drop ship?" Bon wonders aloud. He's standing next to Cynthia's station, near the bridge hatch.

Maxim turns. "Peacekeeper tech is incredibly simplistic to operate so that even the least trained rank-and-file trooper can work it. Drop ships are no different. Command wants anyone to be able to take off and land in case the pilot is killed or injured."

"Flying well is another thing but getting off a planet and going FTL, anyone could do it." Zephyr adds.

"Rather terrifying." Bon observes. Maxim and Zephyr nod.

"Got something." Zephyr says. She taps a few commands into her console and the main display updates. The view is of the planet below with a faint yellow trail leading away from orbit out into the black. She taps the thumbs on her right hand together absently then says, "I'm pretty sure that's it. Like you said, no other traffic and it's not our energy signature."

"Where's it going?" Wil asks.

Zephyr studies her screen for a bit. "I think back the way Maxim and Bennie came."

Before Maxim can formulate a reply, Bennie yelps. "That's great!" Everyone turns to the small Brailack. Wil makes a *go on* motion. "We made two stops after we left Janus' party. Random spots in space with nothing around. We needed breathing room and I needed time to access CG comm nodes."

"Great, a random spot in space..." Wil says. "Shouldn't be hard to find."

Bennie makes an obscene gesture then continues, tapping his forehead. "I know the coordinates. I know exactly where that drop ship is going to appear."

"Well, now we're talking," Wil says, grinning. "Send me the coordinates." A moment later, his console beeps. "Got 'em. Here we go." He pushes the FTL controls forward.

WILD GOOSE CHASE_

"How DO we know if we've arrived before it?" Bon asks, staring at the main display which is showing the star field directly in front of the *Ghost*. The view looks just like any view from any direction on the ship—stars, lots and lots of stars, and nothing else.

Gabe answers, "Our FTL drive is significantly more powerful than that of the drop ship. While we do not know precisely when *The Source* left Glacial, we know it is a small window of only a few tocks. Based on that, my assumption is that the drop ship should drop out of FTL approximately," on the screen there's a faint flash of light and ripple of space-time, "now."

"Show off." Cynthia says, looking up at Gabe who's standing next to her station. Bon moved next to Zephyr when the big droid arrived on the bridge. The droid grins in a less creepy way than normal. "Hey, you're getting better at that." She says. He inclines his head.

"So, uh, now what?" Bennie says.

Maxim answers, "Now, we destroy that ugly monster thing." He taps his console. "Target locked."

Wil nods. "Fire!"

A resounding *cthunk* sounds throughout the ship. Two missiles streak out from the bottom of the main display, burning for the small ship a few million kilometers ahead.

As the missiles streak toward their target, Cynthia asks, "So what now? I mean, we definitely didn't do the job we were hired to do. Plus, you know, Coorish is dead."

Wil spins to face her. "I mean we kept one alive." He gestures to Bon who makes a rude noise. "That should count for something."

"Captain, the drop ship just went FTL." Maxim says, his voice strained.

"Scan the area!" Wil says, spinning back around. On the main display, the two missiles continue on their course until their built-in safeties engage, detonating them. Wil pushes the sub-light throttles forward and brings the *Ghost* closer to where the target vessel was a moment ago.

"Uh," Bennie starts, "if that monster is just rewinding the FTL log, the next stop is where Janus' fleet is assembled."

"Oh good! A scary monster with designs on ruling the galaxy and that weird shape-changing nightmare in one place." Wil says.

"Is there anything else in the system?" Zephyr asks, looking over at Maxim.

"It wasn't even a system," Maxim says, "just another point in interstellar space."

Wil turns to Bennie. "Remember where?"

The hacker sits quietly for a minute. "Well..."

"Well?" Wil repeats back. "Well what?"

"Well, I mean, I didn't see where we were until we left the *Pax Liberatus* and made the jump to FTL. I was hiding in a bunk on a freighter on the way in." He shrugs. "I don't know exactly where we were." He continues before anyone can say anything, "If I had access to the flight computer on that drop ship I could reverse out the data pretty easy but I don't, so..." Another shrug.

"Wait!" Maxim says excitedly. "You took scans of the fleet as we left."

Bennie claps his hands. "Doi! You're right! One microtock."

Bennie focuses on his work, ignoring the rest of the crew and Bon, all staring at the Brailack while he works.

"What is he doing?" Bon asks Wil.

Wil shrugs. "I was hoping someone else would have chimed in already."

Bennie sighs, loud enough that Wil is sure it's for affect. "The scans I took of the ships include the stars that were in the field of view. I can analyze all my scan data and get at least a reasonably close guess where we need to go."

Zephyr clears her throat. "You know, this begs the question; do we go?"

"What do you mean?" Maxim asks.

She holds up a finger. "Well, if Janus is still there, he'll either destroy the drop ship, a win." She lifts another finger. "Or, bring it aboard where it will probably result in at least one command carrier being taken out by the others in order to contain *The Source*, likely also including the death of Janus, definitely a win." She holds up her third finger. "Or, Janus is no longer there. The drop ship has nowhere else to go because that creature likely doesn't know how to program a NavCom. So, it's stranded in deep space, still a win."

Maxim nods. "She has a point. I didn't look but assume whomever flew that transport last followed procedure and wiped the NavCom before powering it down."

LOTS OF BAD OPTIONS_

Wɪʟ ɪs sɪᴛᴛɪɴɢ sɪʟᴇɴᴛʟʏ when he hears Cynthia say his name. "Wha—"

"I said, what's the play?" She says or rather repeats.

"We have to go. I agree with Zee's points, but we can't just leave it as unknown. Best case, I guess, there's no one there; we blast the transport when it arrives and head home."

"Excuse me," Bon says, raising a hand. "This sounds tremendously dangerous—"

"No, we can't drop you off." Wil interrupts.

Bon harrumphs and heads for the bridge hatch.

Wil turns to Bennie. "All right send me the coordinates. Let's get this over and done with. After we get going, I'll make lunch."

It takes some coaxing, but Cynthia eventually convinces Bon to join them for lunch with the promise of more *Iron Fist* afterward.

"What is this?" Bon asks, taking a bite.

"Pizza!" Bennie says, reaching across the table to take his third slice. "Wil's planet has a ton of great food!"

315

Bon nods. "This is extraordinary. What is this topping?"

Wil smiles. "You're in luck. That's the last of my stock of freeze-dried pepperoni. The real deal, straight from Earth."

"Incredible." Bon says around bites.

Maxim smiles and looks at Wil. "Pizza for lunch? What's the occasion?"

Wil shrugs, "Well we're likely running into a massive firefight where we're out-gunned ten to one—"

"Closer to one hundred to one." Bennie interjects.

Wil tuts, "Yeah, at any rate. Not great odds; I'm sure if Janus is still there, he won't be keen to listen to reason. So, we'll have to destroy that drop ship while not dying." He looks around. "Figured if we're gonna die, I didn't want my pepperoni to not get eaten." He leans back smiling until a furry hand pushes his chest and knocks him out of his chair.

"You're a fool, Wil Calder," Cynthia says, laughing as she takes the slice of pizza on Wil's plate.

"Dropping out of FTL in three, two, one." Wil pulls the FTL control back and the distorted stars of FTL go back to looking like normal, non-streaky stars.

"Sensor contacts." Zephyr reports.

"Full stealth." Wil orders.

"Done," Bennie responds. "At this distance, they can't see us. I wouldn't get super close; Peacekeeper sensors are better than most."

Wil nods. "Gabe, when should we expect our wayward monster?"

Gabe replies, "Ten centocks." He accesses the computer and brings the tactical view up on the main display. The rogue Peacekeeper fleet is a series of almost two dozen red triangles. An orange square appears. "This is where I believe *The Source* will drop out of FTL."

"Damn." Wil says, taking in the layout of nearby space. "That's really close to Janus."

"We could go with the *let Janus bring the monster aboard* plan. I rather liked that one." Maxim says.

Before Wil can answer, Cynthia says, "We're being hailed."

Wil spins. "Uh, what? By who—"

"I think it's *whom*." Zephyr says before Wil flips her off.

"Janus?" He looks at Bennie, the accusation clear.

"He can't see us!" Bennie squeaks.

"Farsight Corporation." Cynthia says, not engaging in the theatrics of the others.

Wil sits quietly for a second, blinking a few times. "Oh, ok, sure. Put 'em on." He turns to face the main display just as Jark Asgar's face appears.

"Greetings, Captain."

"Jark, old buddy," Wil says. Bon has moved over to stand beside Wil.

"Bon left me a message. It sounds like my *milk run* was anything but."

"You could say that. I don't know how much Bon told you," he looks sideways at Bon, frowning, "but yeah, things went sideways then diagonal then all kinds of other ways. Not pretty."

"I see. And the creature?" The big Hulgian executive asks.

Wil looks at Bon again, his frown deeper. "We're pretty sure it's about to encounter a fleet of rogue Peacekeepers. We're sorta on the clock here regarding that."

Asgar thinks for a beat. "I see. Well, that's a disappointment. From what Bon said, that creature would be interesting to study."

"Uh huh, study." Wil replies dryly.

"I've sent ships to Glacial. They should be there in a day. I'd like you to rendezvous with them and transfer Bon to the command ship."

Wil nods. "Ok, sure. We can do that. We should discuss what an amended fee structure looks like."

The Hulgian man chuckles. At least Wil thinks it's a chuckle;

that or he's gargling small pebbles. "Well, I suppose some form of payment is in order. You kept one of my specialists alive." Wil glances at Bon and mouths, *told you.* Asgar continues, "Once Bon is safely aboard the command ship, I'll pay half the agreed amount."

From his station, Bennie makes a strangled sounding noise.

"Half, huh? How about—"

"I'm aware you destroyed the entire facility by causing the reactor to go critical. Do you know what the startup cost of that facility was? Not to mention the loss of information we may not be able to get anywhere else?" Wil doesn't answer. "Take half and be happy I'm not sending my ships to forcibly collect you."

Wil takes a deep breath then forces a smile. "Half sounds great." He looks Asgar in the eye, or the equivalent, via a screen. "I thought you didn't have the resources to send ships out here?"

"The acquisition of Crucible Corp. is complete. My resources are a bit freer to move about now."

The screen goes dark then turns back to the tactical view of nearby space.

"Two more centocks." Gabe informs.

Wil looks at Bon. "Traitor."

The red-hued man looks at Wil. "I am an employee of Farsight Corp. I'm sorry you feel betrayed, Captain but I owe you now allegiance." He turns and takes a seat next to Cynthia.

NEWSCAST_

"Good morning, I'm Mon-El Furash, live from Mogul Three where the droid rights standoff has entered its twelfth day."

The Malkorite woman is standing in the middle of a shopping district. A pair of Multonae gentlemen walk towards her, "Excuse me, gentlemen, I'm Mon-El Furash from GNO, what do you think about the ongoing droid rights strikes?"

The taller of the two, a red head offers, "I think it's a complex issue, I haven't formed an opinion yet myself, but am watching the issue."

His companion chimes in, "I think the government should mobilize the security services and storm those factories. Either wipe the droid's processors, or get new ones. The economy is suffering every day these strikes continue.

"Where is the GC in all this?"

Mon-El nods, "Thank you gentlemen." She looks around and heads towards a young couple of Harrith, "Excuse me, can I ask your thoughts on the droid rights strikes?"

The woman turns, smiling, "I'm happy this is finally something the GC has to address."

Her companion nods, "Agreed, the issue of droid rights is long overdue, and the GC owes it to all citizens to address the issue."

Mon-El nods, "What does addressing the issue look like to you?"

The woman answers before her mate can, "Droids are sapient creatures, they deserve the same rights as you and I."

The male smiles in agreement, "What she said."

CHAPTER 20_

THIS DEFINITELY WON'T END WELL_

"THERE IT IS." Maxim says, as the twice stolen Peacekeeper troop transport drops out of FTL. Almost on top of the rogue Peacekeeper fleet.

Wil turns to Bennie. "You know, remind me never to piss you off. You managed all that destruction?" He points to a severely damaged Peacekeeper command carrier in the center of the flotilla.

Bennie beams. "Sure did. No force in the 'verse can stop me."

"Someone has been watching *Firefly* again." Wil says, still smiling. "Too bad you weren't able to destroy it. That'd make our future lives easier."

"I was working with limited time and resources, you know," Bennie replies then adds, "Look, they're bringing it aboard."

"Damn, well I guess that settles our strategy," Wil says.

"But not aboard the *Pax Liberatus*," Zephyr observes as the small craft is pulled toward another command carrier, one of the newer models that has joined Janus recently. "Perhaps Janus' ship is too damaged?"

"Certainly looks it," Cynthia offers. "Think *The Source* looks like Hathyr or something else? Have to assume it reverted to its helpless victim state to get them to bring it aboard."

"Yeah I wonder. I mean, Janus surely will know that it's his stolen transport, so he'll wonder why it's back and why whatever face *The Source* is wearing, is bringing it back."

"Well, we'll probably never know so let's get this show on the road." Wil says, as he brings the *Ghost* about, slowly throttling up the sublight engines. He keeps them at a low enough thrust level to ensure the stealth systems remain active.

Bon, who's seated next to Cynthia at her station, stands. "I'll go get packed."

"Yeah, best do that." Wil says, not looking at the red-skinned scientist.

When the hatch closes behind Bon, Cynthia says, "Little cold there, no?"

"I don't trust him." Wil says. "He called Asgar which, for the most part, ain't so bad but he told him everything and I'm guessing was really clear on the threat level and potential value to the weapons' folks." He turns to Cynthia. "*The Source* might not be on that planet but remember, there were at least a dozen or so *Monster Cs* wandering around the ruins of the facility and that's just the ones we could see from orbit."

"Even one of those things, taken alive, is likely enough to be a boon to Farsight's weapons division. Plus, who knows what other discoveries might come from studying one of those things. Remember, *The Source* not only changed shape but mass. Maybe its kids can do the same with the right prodding of their genes."

Zephyr adds, "Plus, the dig site, while likely in bad shape, was deep enough that they can probably excavate and uncover it again. I'd guess there was plenty of that city or town or whatever it was, that wasn't fully uncovered yet."

Wil turns back to his console. "Ok, we're far enough out. Drop stealth, get ready for FTL."

"Stealth systems disengaged," Bennie reports.

Wil pushes the FTL throttle all the way to the stops. "Let's meet the Farsight folks, drop Bon off and go find a nice planet with a beach. I could go the rest of my life without seeing snow. I didn't even like it when I lived in Colorado."

"Your world is covered in snow?" Cynthia asks. "I take back wanting to visit."

"No, there're all kinds of climates; beaches, mountains, deserts, tropical forests, the works," Bennie responds to her.

"How do you know?" Wil asks raising his eyebrows. "Been going through my things again, huh?"

"Technically, no." Bennie replies, making himself smaller in case Wil throws something at him. "I went through your digital photo store like a cycle or so ago."

Wil sighs then turns back to Cynthia. "He's not wrong." He stands up. "Alright, who wants to watch a movie" We've got a few tocks before we arrive back at Glacial."

"Can I pick the movie?" Bennie asks.

"Sure man." Wil says as the bridge hatch opens.

LET IT GO_

"You'd THINK BY NOW, you'd know better." Maxim says. He's on the couch, Zephyr next to him. Wil is in the chair with Cynthia snuggled in next to him. Bennie is next to Zephyr and Gabe is standing behind the couch. On the lounge display, the opening credits of *Frozen* are playing.

"What?" Bennie cries, "I love this vid. That snow creature is hilarious." He offers a bowl of popcorn to Zephyr who waves it off.

Wil leans back and closes his eyes. "I really should; let's chalk this one up to a reward for a job well done. He saved Maxim from almost certain death—"

"A painful one probably," Bennie interrupts, tossing popcorn into his mouth.

"Almost certain painful death. Plus, and this is a big one, he dealt a serious blow to Janus. Whatever it is he's planning; I assume having to repair a command carrier is likely to set him back a bit."

Cynthia adds, "Yeah, that ship looked pretty beat up. I'd be surprised if he doesn't just strip it down to the ribs and leave what he can't use."

"Not to mention having to deal with *The Source,* eventually." Maxim offers.

"Either way, it's likely to slow down whatever he's planning." Wil adds.

"Shhhh!" Bennie admonishes as the movie starts.

"I know he said the merger was complete and his fleet was more freed up, but what the wurrin?" Zephyr says as the *Ghosts'* sensors begin populating the tactical view of the planetary system around Glacial, ships appearing one or two at a time. A half dozen ships, of which two are distinctly non-military, are in orbit over the remains of the research facility. The two non-warships are bulk freighters that, between them, could easily hold enough equipment to rebuild the entire facility and then some. One of them is beginning the slow descent to the surface.

Wil whistles. "Yeah I was worried this is what we'd see." He looks over his shoulder. "Cyn, hail them. Let whoever is in charge know we're friendly and are just here to offload one of theirs."

"Roger that," she says, working her console and speaking softly into the audio pickup.

A few minutes of cruising toward the small fleet and Cynthia finally says, "That was a little tedious. But I've gotten through to someone I *think* is in command. On screen."

The main display switches from a view of the fleet to a handsome Malkorite woman, her large ears adorned with all manner of glittering jewels. "I am Captain Klo'roush of the *Fist of Righteousness*."

Wil waits a beat for more then clears his throat. "Uh hi. I'm Wil Calder, Captain of the *Ghost*. We're here to deliver one of your folks back to you then we'll be on our way."

The Malkorite woman nods, the jewelry covering her ears making a light tinkling sound "I've been informed. Please come alongside; we can extend a docking tube." The screen goes dark then returns to the view of the now much closer fleet.

"Friendly sort." Wil says then taps a control on his seat. "Bon, we're a few centocks from meeting up with your colleagues. Get your gear and get to the port airlock."

"Well, Captain," Bon starts, standing in the open port airlock, the docking tube stretching out behind him. A Farsight crew person is floating just outside the reach of the *Ghosts'* artificial gravity. "I'd say it's been fun, but it hasn't. It's been terrifying." He extends a hand which Wil accepts, clasping the other man's forearm versus his hand. Bon does the same. "Good journeys to you all." He nods to Maxim and Cynthia who are behind Wil while Zephyr and Bennie are still on the bridge.

Maxim and Cynthia both nod. As Bon turns, Wil grabs his arm and whispers, "If you're smart, you'll destroy every one of those creatures. Don't let a single one off this planet." Before Bon can react, Wil lets go and nudges him off into the docking tube. Wil presses a control next to the airlock hatch causing the outer door to close followed by the inner doors.

Wil looks at Maxim and Cynthia. "What say we find us a beach?"

A PROBLEM FOR ANOTHER DAY_

THE *GHOST* slowly heads away from Glacial. The crew watches on the main display as the bulk freighters that have both landed near the ruined facility begin to unload. Enormous excavators begin rolling off the loading ramps. Several flights of strike craft have already entered the atmosphere and seem to be flying a combat patrol over the landed vessels. Several smaller transports have also headed down from the cruisers.

"They will definitely attempt to capture any surviving creatures." Maxim says. His face is twisted with a mix of rage and disgust.

Wil nods. "Yeah, this won't go anywhere good. It's bad enough the main one is who knows where with Janus and his fleet. But now Farsight is likely to have plenty of genetic material and ancient technology to play around with," Wil adds.

Cynthia stands and takes two steps to stand behind Wil's command chair. Her hands find his shoulders and she purrs. "Not our problem, at least not right now."

"That's what worries me. The other side of *not right now* is *sometime in the future*." Wil says, still watching the screen and the ships unloading tons of equipment. One of the light cruisers has also begun its descent. Likely, it'll serve as a base of operations until they build the new facility. "Guess we'll burn that bridge down when we get to it." Wil sighs.

"Like always." Bennie says.

The End

THANK YOU_

Thank you so much for reading Space Rogues 4: Stay Warm, Don't Die

If you enjoyed it I'd love it if you left a review. Reviews are a big deal. They help readers find authors.

Reviews are social proof and go a long way to encouraging other readers to take a chance on an unknown.

Being a writer is one of those childhood dreams that you sort of dismiss as you get older. I mean, sure you can go into copywriting (did that), technical writing (did that too), but if telling stories is your dream, it's not the same.

When I published Space Rogues 1 it was one of those 'dream come true' moments. When it started selling, it was one of those 'oh my god, people like what I write' moments.

With book four, I hope you've enjoyed the continuing adventures of the crew of the *Ghost*.

I look forward to sharing many many more adventures with you!

**Want to stay up to date on the happenings in the
Galactic Commonwealth?**
Sign up for my newsletter at
johnwilker.com/newsletter
Lots of goodies await you, just sayin'

Visit me online at
johnwilker.com

If you like supporting things you love by sporting merch, well you're
in luck! I've launched a Space Rogues Shop, take a look.

OFFER_

As they say, there's no harm in asking, so here we go.

If you can help connect me with someone who can get Space Rogues on a screen (Big or Little) I'll cut you in for 10% (Up to $10,000) of whatever advance is paid.

Send me an email and we can discuss.
rights@johnwilker.com

CONTINUE THE ADVENTURE_
SPACE ROGUES 5: SO THIS IS EARTH?

You can read chapter 1 below

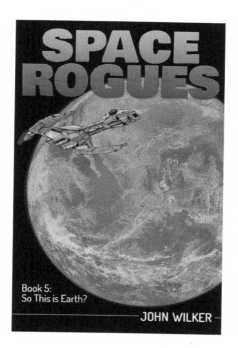

SPACE ROGUES 5 SAMPLE_

PRINCESS PROBLEMS_

"I HATE HER," Cynthia says as she gets dressed.

Wil, still lying in bed, says, "How could you hate her? You've only just met her?"

"Yet here we are, and I want her dead." She's making a growling noise Wil once thought was purring until Cynthia made it clear it was not a happy sound. She slides her hand through her wristcomm, locking it in place on her forearm. Turning to open the hatch to the quarters they share, she turns to her lover, "Get dressed and make breakfast. I'll be on the bridge." The hatch closes behind her.

Flinging the covers off of him, Wil groans, "Yes, mom." He pads to the small refresher compartment. As he activates the cleaning mode, he looks up, "Computer, where is our passenger?"

"Miss Yutani is in her assigned quarters."

Wil nods and starts his shower.

As the hatch that closes off the stairwell to the living quarters opens, Wil hears a hissing noise followed by, "You can't keep me here! I'll slit your throat!"

Sighing, he opens the hatch all the way, "Good morning campers!" he shouts, smiling as broadly as he can.

Bennie is standing in the middle of the lounge area pointing a fork at their passenger.

Their passenger, a Trenbal teenager, is crouching in the kitchenette area, a large and very sharp knife held in one hand, a frying pan in the other.

Wil notices Zephyr sitting in the large chair a few feet from Bennie. He looks at his first officer, her Palorian features unreadable as she takes in the scene. Wil points to the two presumed combatants, "So, uh, what's this?"

"Bennie made a pass at her," Zephyr replies.

Wil looks at the Brailack, "Dude, she's a kid."

"Then he reminded her she's our prisoner and she can't leave," Zephyr adds.

"I am not a child!" the reptilian teen screams, hissing at the end of the exclamation. "You cannot keep me here! That's kidnapping!" she adds.

Wil turns to her, holding both hands up, palms out, "Sorry, young adult." The teenage woman glares at him but says nothing. He turns and stalks over to the resident hacker and ship's official pain in the ass. Snatching the fork, "Not ok." He holds up a finger, "She's a chi—young adult." Raising a second finger, "She's our guest." A third finger rises, "She's a princess. Apologize. Now."

Bennie leans to peek around Wil, "I'm sorry. I didn't mean to offend you, your highness." He straightens and looks at Wil, mouthing the word *there*.

Wil punches him in the arm, then turns to face their guest, "Please accept my apologies; he was raised by wolves."

The reptilian face scrunches, "What is a wolve?"

Wil shakes his head once closing the gap between them, "Never mind, may I?" He gingerly plucks the frying pan from a sharp-clawed hand. "I'm going to make pancakes if you're hungry."

Bennie approaches the kitchenette slowly, taking a seat as far from Princess Yutani as possible.

Zephyr gets up from where she watched the drama unfold and takes a seat next to Bennie.

The Trenbal woman sits opposite the two, "You can't take me home." She's staring right at Zephyr. It was Zephyr who grabbed her at the nightclub on Plumbus Eight the previous night. Since then, the *Ghost* has been burning hard for Fury, where the wayward Princess's father will be waiting for them.

"Why can't we?" Zephyr asks.

"He's a monster. The worst!" the teenage woman says, her head in her hands. "I was just having fun. He's always going on about schooling and decorum!" She slams a palm on the table.

Maxim walks in from the direction of the bridge as Zephyr says, "Your father was worried. You'd been gone for a standard month. On top of that, it's been two more weeks, because you weren't easy to track down."

"How did you find me?" the slightly calmer Princess asks.

Maxim sits down and points to Bennie, "He found you."

Zephyr groans as the nimble teenager lunges across the table, her powerful clawed hands around Bennie's throat as the two tumble to the deck.

Maxim blinks twice but doesn't move, "I say something wrong?"

The screaming and hissing from the floor between the kitchenette and the lounge area breaks up as fire extinguisher foam hits the combatants. Gabe is standing over the now foam-covered pair of adversaries, "Are you quite done?"

"Did you have to do that?" Bennie whines, "You know what fire suppression foam does to my skin."

Wil turns from his work, "You've got about five minutes before breakfast is on; go get cleaned up, both of you."

"You don't want to miss pancakes, better hurry," Maxim says making a brushing motion with his hand, urging the two foam-covered beings toward the hatch to the living spaces deck.

PAY THE MAN_

As the *Ghost* settles onto its powerful landing legs, Wil flips switches, "Cutting repulsor lifts, atmospheric engines powered down. Gabe"—he looks at the ceiling—"put the reactor in standby please."

"Acknowledged," the ceiling replies.

Wil turns to Cynthia, "His highness on the way?"

She nods, holding a finger up, "Very good. We're in Fury space-port eight, pad nineteen. Yup. Yup. Fine." She turns to Wil, pressing a button to disconnect the communication channel she was just on, "He's on his way, about ten centocks."

Maxim turns, "What was the rest of that about?"

Cynthia makes a noise, "He was confirming she was unharmed and in one piece. Oh, and then ended with a threat about how she had better be all right and intact." She looks at Wil, "Guess our reputation is growing."

Bennie hops out of his seat and heads for the door.

Wil points at him, "Do not bother her."

The Brailack holds open his collar showing the dark green bruises around his neck, "Not a problem, I gotta pee," he grumbles.

Zephyr smiles, "I'll go get our guest." She gets up and makes for the hatch following behind Bennie.

Wil stands, following Zephyr, "I'll get the umbilicals connected."
Maxim nods, "I'll mind the store."

With the *Ghost's* main cargo ramp deployed, and the thick inner cargo doors open, the more or less fresh air of Fury fills the hold. Wil and Gabe are under the ship hooking up several umbilicals that will pump out waste and pump in consumables like water, and top off any other fluids and matter the ship might need.

Bennie is sitting on a lounge chair under an umbrella as two sleek black hover cars approach. "Looks like Princess mean girl's ride is here."

"I heard that!" comes from inside the cargo hold. Princess Yutani comes out to stand at the top of the ramp. Zephyr appears at her side.

Zephyr kneels next to the young woman, "I know it's hard; your mom is gone, and your dad is busy and not around much." The girl nods and Zephyr continues, "This will be hard to believe, but trust me, it gets better. You just have to know that he's trying his best." She stands and heads down the ramp, the young Yutani following.

As the two women near the bottom of the ramp, Bennie adds, "Or"—he holds up a finger—"do a better job of masking your trail and avoid dance clubs that live stream their patrons." He sticks his tongue out.

Zephyr makes a rude gesture towards him, guiding the Princess away from the reclining Brailack.

Cynthia, leaning against the edge of the cargo opening at the top of the ramp, looks at the approaching vehicles then down to Zephyr and the young woman, "Bye bye." She waves slowly, staring at the young Trenbal who stares back with unmasked disdain.

As the lead hover car comes to a stop, Bennie gets up and walks towards it, only to be intercepted by Wil who wipes his hands on the back of Bennie's shirt, then shoves him back toward his chair.

Wil stands near the opening door, "Your highness."

"I told you; I am not royalty," the Trenbal man in an expensive-looking suit says as he steps from the vehicle. An aide gets out right behind him and rushes to stand behind his employer. "I am the sovereign executive, by birth, of the island nation Siskona."

"That sounds like *King*," Wil says falling into step next to the older reptilian man, who sighs but says nothing until he sees his wayward daughter at the bottom of the ramp, "Skaarina, come."

Skaarina Yutani heads toward her father; staring at the ground she says, "Hi daddy."

"Hello dear, they treated you well?" The older Trenbal man is squinting while examining his daughter. Nodding, he holds his hand out expectantly.

The aide who fell in behind Wil comes around and places a PADD in the Trenbal not-a-monarch's hand. He taps the screen a few times, then swipes. Wil's wristcomm vibrates, confirming the receipt of the final payment. Handing the PADD back to his aide, the Trenbal man says, "A pleasure Captain Calder. Thank you for retrieving her and keeping her safe while in your care." He doesn't wait for Wil to answer, turning and making for his hover car.

Wil waves, "Pleasure doing business with you. Holler when she runs away again!" He turns to consider at the crew, now all gathered at the foot of the cargo ramp, "What say we go get drunk?"

Everyone nods, smiling. Zephyr taps her wristcomm, "Love, come on out; we're going into town."

KEEP READING_

Keep Reading Space Rogues 5: So This is Earth?

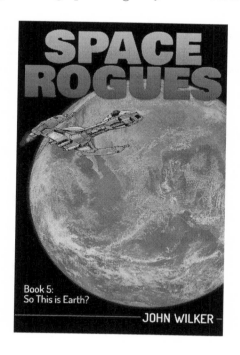

OTHER BOOKS BY JOHN WILKER_

Space Rogues Universe (in story chronological order)

- Space Rogues 1: The Epic Adventures of Wil Calder, Space Smuggler
- Merry Garthflak, Wil: A Space Rogues Short Story
- Space Rogues 2: Big Ship, Lots of Guns
- Space Rogues 3: The Behemoth Job
- Space Rogues 4: Stay Warm, Don't Die
- Space Rogues 5: So This is Earth?
- Space Rogues 6: War and Peace

Manufactured by Amazon.ca
Bolton, ON

19152915R00213